NIGHT'S
MISCHIEF

KENSINGTON BOOKS are published by

Kensington Publishing Corp.
119 West 40th Street
New York, NY 10018

All Kensington Titles, Imprints, and Distributed Lines are available at special quantity discounts for bulk purchases for sales promotions, premiums, fund-raising, and educational or institutional use. Special book excerpts or customized printings can also be created to fit specific needs. For details, write or phone the office of the Kensington special sales manager: Kensington Publishing Corp., 119 West 40th Street, New York, NY 10018, attn: Special Sales Department, Phone: 1-800-221-2647.

Kensington and the K logo Reg. U.S. Pat & TM Off.

ISBN-13: 978-1-4967-0492-4
ISBN-10: 1-4967-0492-4
First Kensington Mass Market Edition: August 2016

eISBN-13: 978-1-4967-0493-1
eISBN-10: 1-4967-0493-2
First Kensington Electronic Edition: August 2016

10 9 8 7 6 5 4 3 2 1

Printed in the United States of America

For Mom, who inspired my love of books and storytelling.
For Dad, who taught me I can do anything I set my mind to.
For Scott, who captured my heart.
And for Sage, who showed me that magic is real.

PROLOGUE

The intruder knew it was wrong to be there. It was not only illegal; it was indecent. The old woman was dead, for God's sake. She had passed away not even two days ago, hadn't even been laid to rest. *Yet here I am*, the intruder thought. *Sneaking around her home in the dark, like some kind of common criminal.*

I am not *a criminal.*

Sure, the intruder might exceed the speed limit more often than not. Who didn't? And, okay, maybe there was a slight deception or two come tax time. But the intruder had never stolen anything.

Well, nothing of real value, anyway.

Until now.

But this was different. These were extraordinary circumstances. Chances like this didn't come along every day.

One by one, the intruder searched all the rooms in the house, quickly but carefully. It wouldn't be tucked away in some obscure location. It had to be wherever the old woman had left it before she died. Still, the intruder took a cursory look in the bathroom, the bedrooms, and every closet along the way to the front of the house.

Creeping through the tidy living room, the intruder made sure the curtains were closed, then peeked under the coffee table, peered behind the potted ficus, opened the oversize sewing basket in the corner—all the while trying to avoid looking at the framed family photos lining the walls and standing watch on the mantel.

I am really not a bad person.

Opposite the living room was an old-fashioned home library. Standing on the threshold to this room, the intruder's heart started thudding uncontrollably. Maybe it was nerves. Time was running out. The longer this took, the bigger the risk of getting caught. Or maybe it was the intruder's conscience finally kicking in.

Or maybe it was the fact that the intruder had finally found it.

There it was, not ten feet away. A real, genuine four-hundred-year-old treasure. There for the taking.

The intruder's hands started sweating inside brown leather gloves. It was now or never. Noticing that the curtains were open in this room, the intruder dropped to the carpeted floor and crawled quickly over to the canvas messenger bag that lay open on a floral-print love seat. The bag was next to a stack of week-old newspapers and a crossword puzzle book, from which a pen stuck out to mark the last puzzle the old woman had been working on.

But thoughts of the old woman soon skittered to the dusty corners. The intruder was fixated on the prize now, which was poking out of the casually placed bag like in a game of peekaboo, just daring someone to grab it. Kneeling before the love seat, the intruder used both hands to remove the treasure.

For a moment, the intruder just stared at it, hardly believing it was real. Bound in faded leather, it was fragile yet whole. The stitching faded and delicate, yet intact. It was surprising how light it felt, especially for a nine-hundred-page work. Gingerly, the intruder opened the cover and read the amazing words *Mr. William Shakespeares Comedies, Histories, & Tragedies. Published according to the True Originall Copies.*

Beneath these words was a copper-engraved portrait of the immortal man himself. *What an odd-looking dude.* The "Bard." Looking positively Mona Lisa–ish, with that steady gaze and indecipherable expression. Did he know he was a genius? Did he realize the impact he would have on the world in the centuries to come?

Did he know this collection would fetch a cool million or two? Or three?

Exhaling softly, the intruder closed the book, then carefully wrapped it in a sweatshirt, placed it in a duffel bag, and surrounded it with another sweatshirt, sweatpants, shorts, and socks. Clean, of course. The canvas messenger bag was left behind, a little flatter but still in the same spot.

How could the old woman be so careless? She hadn't deserved to own this book, anyway. Maybe no one person should own it. But somebody would want it badly enough to pay big, big money. No doubt about it. And someone else would reap the mighty profit.

Someone like me.

At any rate, the intruder had as much claim to the treasure as the old woman had had. More importantly, she was gone, and the intruder was here.

But not for long.

After a quick look around to make sure no evidence was left behind, the intruder hurried to the kitchen and slipped out, quietly pulling the door shut.

Shielded by two overgrown lilac bushes on either side of the back stoop, the intruder paused for a moment to remove the gloves and stick them in the pockets of a hoodie. Glancing at the overcast sky and feeling grateful for the gloom that darkened the yard, the intruder breathed in the heavy, charged air.

I did it.

All that remained was to cash it in.

From somewhere in the shadows, an owl cried a single lonely call. And then it was quiet once more.

CHAPTER 1

Four days earlier

The soft breeze caressed my shoulders like a lover, and I slowed my steps to enjoy it. I had shed my blazer the minute I left the office, had tucked it over my purse strap, and had traded my heels for flat sandals. I was cutting through Fieldstone Park. The air was fresher there under the trees. The breeze carried the scent of roses mingled with the spicy-earth aroma of mature pines and flowering shrubs. I inhaled deeply. Summer had come early this year.

Just above the horizon, a vivid crescent moon, larger than life, began its nightly ascent. All around me, the first fireflies flickered in the dusky shadows, while hidden crickets chirped a timeless serenade.

As a matter of fact, the evening was so damn romantic, I couldn't take it anymore. I stopped in my tracks.

"Come on!" I said out loud. "What are you trying to do to me?"

A startled skateboarder skidded to a stop next to me, stamping one foot on the ground.

"Not you," I said. "Her! This!" I flicked my wrist, waving a hand at the trees, the sky, the beauty. "Oh, never mind," I muttered.

The skateboarder rolled his eyes and sped off. I sighed and continued down the path. I strolled past Memory Gardens and around Wedding Cake Fountain, breathing in the sultry fresh air. It was peaceful, for sure, but I felt restless. As I gazed around the park, I couldn't help feeling it was a setup. The Goddess was putting on a spectacular show tonight, and it was all for me.

My bag suddenly felt heavier, and I shifted it to my other shoulder. Why did I feel so irritated all of a sudden? The slender headband that earlier had reined my long locks into a sleek retro bouffant now felt like a vise on my temples. The flower-scented air, now humid and dense, was suddenly cloying. The whole world pressed in.

Despite this momentary unease, I still loved it here. Honestly, I loved it all: the big park, the small town, the perfect evening. After all, Edindale wasn't called the Eden of Southern Illinois for nothing. Yet, it was times like these that made me feel the most alone. That was it, I realized. The lovelier the night, the more deeply I felt my heart ache.

When I rounded a bend and caught sight of a dreamy-eyed couple heading my way, hand in hand, I decided I'd had about enough. I veered to my left, cut across a grassy stretch, stopped for a quick second to break off a purple stem from a riotously abundant bush clover, and then stepped onto the sidewalk toward home.

A few minutes later I climbed the steps to my cozy brick row house. Luckily, there was no sign of my neighbors, a happy older couple on my right and newlyweds on my left. Normally, I didn't mind chatting with them, but I wasn't in the mood just then. Even before my atmospheric walk home from work, I had been too painfully aware of my decided *singleness* today.

It had all started with the new client who walked into my office that morning. And it had ended when I flipped the page of my wall calendar and saw what I knew to be true but wanted to forget: My birthday was coming up in two weeks. I would be thirty.

Sigh.

I entered the row house and headed to the master bedroom. After shedding the suit and the headband, I pulled on yoga shorts and a soft old T-shirt and set about my usual evening chores. I seemed to have fallen into quite the domestic routine lately. First, I watered all my plants—the potted flowers on the front stoop, the hanging ferns in my front window, the herbs in my kitchen window boxes, the potted vegetables and palms and flowers on my back deck, and the houseplants throughout. Then I made myself a quick but tasty dinner consisting of granola cereal topped with fresh strawberries and organic almond milk—my go-to meal on nights I didn't feel like cooking—and sat down in front of the computer in the den to browse online dating profiles.

"Cute . . . nah. Nice . . . or not. Hot, but . . . nah."
I found a reason to reject each one. The whole
process seemed so shallow and hokey. These dating
services might be helpful for some people, but they
didn't feel right for me. They seemed to lack that
almost magical element of serendipity in meeting
people the old-fashioned way. This way felt too
contrived.

Speaking of old-fashioned, I found my mind
wandering back to the new client I had counseled
today. Her name was Eleanor, and she was about
the sweetest old lady I'd ever met. With her short
gray hair, polyester slacks, and embroidered top,
she was the picture of grandmotherly. In fact, what
with her twinkly blue eyes and soft plumpness, I
had had to resist the urge to hug her as we said
good-bye.

Eleanor was my favorite kind of client. I loved
helping nervous people navigate the legal intrica-
cies that went along with so many momentous life
events. Some such events were happy, like adop-
tions and real estate closings. Others, like divorces,
could be contentious or sad—or joyous, depending
on the client. My firm handled all sorts of family law
issues, but I'd come to specialize in trusts and estates.
Oftentimes, people put off preparing a will, not
liking to face the idea of their own mortality. And
sometimes they were distrustful of lawyers. Eleanor
was like that at first, but it didn't take me long to
put her at ease.

Plus, she was nearly bursting with excitement
about her secret. Besides her daughter, Darlene,
and the expert who had appraised her find, I was

the only one to know that comfortably middle-class Eleanor was about to become a very wealthy woman.

I had learned this morning that Eleanor's husband, Frank, had died four years earlier, with a simple will that left everything to his wife. She had avoided having a will herself, thinking, like a lot of people, that however her assets were distributed by law when she was gone would be just fine. Besides, she'd thought she didn't have much—certainly nothing worth fighting over. But that had all changed last week. Going through some of her late husband's things in the attic with her daughter, Eleanor had made an astonishing discovery: a rare book in excellent condition. And not just any book. She had found one of the most valuable books in all the world: a 1623 compendium of Shakespeare's plays. It was the first ever Shakespeare publication, called the First Folio.

Eleanor knew what it was. Still, she was stunned to find it in the attic. Frank had inherited the prize from his great-uncle, an antiques collector, decades ago. Family lore had it that the book had been lost under somewhat mysterious circumstances. Some said it had been destroyed in a fire; others claimed the book had been stolen or maybe lost in a bet. Nevertheless, here it was, tucked in the bottom of an army trunk, under some olive-drab wool blankets.

Eleanor didn't know if Frank had even known the book was there, and she'd probably never know. Regardless, she realized that her estate would be significantly bigger now than she had ever dreamed. It was her daughter who had got her thinking about bequests and had encouraged her to see a lawyer.

I smiled to myself as I remembered how excited Eleanor was at the prospect of leaving substantial gifts to causes near to her heart—her alma mater, her favorite museum, the local animal rescue shelter— not to mention individual gifts to her family members. Eleanor had two children and five grandchildren, plus an adorable new great-grandbaby, whose photo Eleanor had proudly showed me. She also had a brother who was still living and several nieces, nephews, and cousins. It was quite a big family.

A big, loving, supportive family.

I came from a pretty big family, too. I had a mom and dad, two older sisters, and an older brother. But they were all miles away and not really a part of my daily life anymore.

My house seemed exceptionally quiet.

I got up and took my bowl to the kitchen, washed it, and put it away. Then I threw in a load of laundry and generally puttered around, all the while feeling lower and lower. At one point I flipped on the radio and promptly shut it off. "What's the deal with the mood tonight? Is there something in the air?" Sometimes I spoke to the Goddess, like *Bewitched*'s Samantha Stephens called out to her mother in an empty room. Of course, on the TV show that was usually because Endora was up to some new high jinks to trouble Samantha's boringly mortal husband.

I laughed in spite of myself and shook off the gloom. There *was* something I could do, I knew. I didn't have to pine around, a victim of unalterable circumstances. I could take matters into my own hands. I had the means; I had the power.

But should I do it?

I felt a little sheepish, even though no one was around to know.

I went back to the kitchen and poured a glass of Merlot. Then I walked around the house, drawing the shades.

What I needed was a man. Strike that. I didn't *need* a man. Still, I longed for a partner. And not just any partner. I stopped, with my wineglass raised halfway to my lips, as the realization sank in. I was yearning for my soul mate.

I went back to the kitchen and pulled out containers of herbs and spices from the corner cabinet. Then I got out my mortar and pestle and started mixing in a bit of this and a dash of that: patchouli, rose hips, cinnamon and basil, rosemary, jasmine, and a touch of hot chili pepper. I wasn't following any particular recipe, but experience and intuition told me what to add.

Grinding the dried leaves and powders was like a meditation. As I breathed in the heady aroma, I thought about the idea of having a soul mate. Was there one person out there meant for each of us? Was I truly incomplete without my missing other half? The thought of *needing* another person, especially a man, made my fiercely independent self bristle. I could take care of myself, thank you very much.

Still, people needed people . . . obviously. Community and cooperation were pretty much the last, best hope for this calamitous world. Or so I'd heard.

Besides, even if there was not one *particular* person destined for another, I did believe in balance.

Like work and play, yin and yang, and the two broken parts of a heart-shaped locket, one without the other just wasn't right. Plus, you needed two to tango. I was looking for my perfect dance partner.

I spooned my herbal concoction onto a piece of cheesecloth, brought up the four corners, and tied it with a red thread. Then I poured another glass of wine and took it to my bedroom upstairs.

There's nothing wrong with what I'm doing, I told myself. Why was I so nervous?

I set the herb pouch on my antique console table, next to the sprig of bush clover I'd picked at Fieldstone Park. Then I gathered some candles and arranged them in a circle on the Persian rug before the console. I placed a large vanilla-scented pillar candle in the center, and on that candle I carved my name within the outline of a heart. I lit the candles.

Then I took off my clothes.

It was time for a serious love spell.

Afterward, I sat quietly on my deck, listening to the crickets and katydids and breathing in the night air. The slender moon was now completely overhead, and I basked in the soft glow while I came down from my psychic high. Spell casting could be a pretty intense experience. Even after sending the energy I raised back to the earth, I felt as if my cells were vibrating.

Not for the first time, I pondered what my friends and family would say if they could see me. What would they think if they knew I was a Wiccan?

Actually, I could imagine what they would think, which was why I couldn't tell them. Not that I was ashamed or anything. In fact, I was quite comfortable with who I was. I was secure in my identity and confident in my spiritual path. This particular pursuit of mine was probably the one area of my life where I harbored no dissatisfaction or misgivings whatsoever.

That is, as long as no one found out.

My Irish Catholic grandmother would blame my father and his whole side, and my Italian Catholic grandmother would blame my mother and her side. At worst, they'd all think I was mixed up in a cult of devil-worshipping crazies, worse even than my aunt Josephine, who ran off and joined a hippie commune back in the day. At best, they'd worry for my immortal soul. Or, more likely, they'd fear this would damage my chances of marrying a nice young Christian man.

As for my friends, they might just think I was a bit flaky, even weirder than they already knew. My current friends, anyway, already called me a hippie chick—not even knowing about Aunt Josephine— given my dietary leanings and other earth-friendly tendencies. But my old friends, from high school and earlier, would likely be surprised to learn I'd never actually grown up. It was with them, all those years ago, that I had first learned about Wicca and the exciting world of Goddess worship.

That was back when witchcraft was über-trendy. We watched *The Craft* and *Charmed* and read books like *Teen Witch*. We wore lots of black, painted our fingernails black, drew tattoos on our hands and ankles with permanent marker.

I smiled as I recalled our secret "coven meetings." We collected crystals and stones, wore pentagram jewelry, and read each other's palms. There were spells, of course, incantations read from books to curse our enemies and attract our crushes. Then again, there was also a good amount of high-minded antiestablishment, feminist rebellion. In spite of my affection for *Bewitched*, we were *not* the daughters of housewife Samantha Stephens.

But before long, hot-blooded vampire romance edged out witchy girl power, and my friends pretty much lost interest. Not me. The Goddess had taken hold and wasn't letting go. My teenage experiment had morphed into a real-life spiritual journey. And it was a spiritual path that suited me perfectly: there was no dogma, no fearmongering, no judgment. There were no authoritarian gatekeepers standing between me and the Divine—the Divine was already in me. And in the trees and the trails, the rivers and streams, the birds and the bees. It was a beautiful religion.

Unfortunately, Wicca was not exactly an accepted, let alone mainstream, religion.

Which was another reason I had to keep this part of me under wraps. If anyone at work were to find out—or anyone in the community—it could cost us clients. And that would cost me my job.

I started to feel chilly sitting on the deck, and my stomach began to growl, chastising me for the too-light dinner. I had just gotten up and gone into the kitchen to scrounge up a bedtime snack when my cell phone buzzed from the counter where I'd left it. I glanced at the caller ID and picked up at once.

"Hey, groovy chick!" I said brightly.

"Hey, chickie mama. What's shaking?"

"Not a whole lot. You back?"

"Not till tomorrow, but save your evening. There's a band we gotta see and men we gotta meet."

I grinned. Evidently, my fun-loving friend Farrah was "off" again in her longtime on-again, off-again romance. That suited me fine. I had a spell to test out. And meeting men with Farrah was the best test method I could think of.

Somewhere out there was the answer to my prayer.

CHAPTER 2

"I'll have a large coffee and a blueberry . . . No, make that a cranberry-walnut muffin." I dug into my purse, fumbling for some money, thoughts fixated on the delicious energy surge I'd soon be sinking into. The voice behind me, grating in its nasal familiarity, quickly burst my bubble.

"Tsk, tsk, tsk. *Coffee* and a *muffin?* Not quite the breakfast of champions I'd expect from someone as purportedly health conscious as young Ms. Keli Milanni."

I forced a polite smile before turning to face my tormentor, the tall, stiff, ginger-haired thorn in my side.

"Good morning, Crenshaw."

He followed me to the condiment station. "I'd expect a super-vegan marathoner like you to be ordering wheatgrass shots at the juice bar. Not *coffee* and a *muffin.*"

"It's all about balance, Crenshaw. You know, throwin' in a little sweet with the spice." I edged toward the door. "Besides, this is a vegan bakery. It's all good."

At least it was until you arrived, I thought. What was he doing here, anyway? And why was he hovering over me instead of ordering his own breakfast?

"How many miles will you have to run to work off that muffin? It must be at least three hundred calories, no?"

I took a sip of my coffee to avoid answering the inane question and promptly scorched my tongue. *Damn!*

"See you at the office," I said as I slipped out the door.

Crenshaw stood looking after me, a bemused expression playing across his pasty, bearded face.

I hurried down the sidewalk toward the town square, rolling my eyes. *What a dweeb.* Crenshaw Davenport III. *Esquire.* He probably wasn't much older than me—we'd started at the firm around the same time. Yet given the way he looked down his nose at me, the condescending way he spoke to me, he clearly felt he was my superior. And he was always angling to prove it at the office, with transparent attempts to move ahead of me on the partnership track.

I pushed aside pesky thoughts of Crenshaw, as my field of vision was filled with a much more pleasant sight. If I wasn't mistaken, the hot young thing holding the door to my office building had just done a double take when he caught sight of me.

I turned on a soft smile as I approached, doing that top-to-bottom, automatic insta-scan practiced singles did in a flash. Twentysomething, slicked hair, tight bod. Cute.

His scan of me wasn't as subtle. In fact, it was more of a leer. As I paused before him, his gaze seemed to stick to my chest area, and I swore he was unbuttoning my shirt with his eyes.

Okay, maybe this guy wasn't the one.

"Thanks," I said, passing through the door. I chuckled to myself. Was I going to have to put up with this all day? I was wearing a bit of my love potion from the night before, smudged onto my pulse points like perfume. It was sweet and musky, but not too strong—at least, not strong smelling. It did seem to be strongly magnetic, though, if the attention I'd received on the way to work was any indication. First, the paperboy, then the guy walking his dog, then the random driver who stopped at a green light to wave me across the street.

Then . . . *oh, Lord.* Was *that* why Crenshaw had acted all weird and in my space at the bakery? Well, he was always weird. But if I had attracted *him* with my love spell, I might have to rethink this whole proposition. Crenshaw was *so* not Mr. Right.

I was about to step onto the elevator when another figure caught my eye, coming from the stairwell to the left. I glanced over, ready to do another insta-scan, and gasped involuntarily. *Beefy, hulking, massive* were a few words that came to mind. This was one imposing dude, and that was even before I saw his face: squinty eyes, flattened nose, jagged scar across his right cheekbone. The guy seemed to be walking right toward me, and my eyes widened even as I managed to summon up a pleasant smile.

To my surprise, the stranger looked right at me and nodded, apparently in response to said pleasant smile. And then he kept on walking, right out the front door and down the block. I stared after him for a second, then shook myself back to the present. Time to go to work. I rode the elevator to the second floor and stepped into the polished but comfortable business suite that was my home away from home.

Olsen, Sykes, and Rafferty was a small law firm with a long, distinguished history. The culture was an interesting mix of modern and conservative. The senior partner was a woman, and we had a lot of diversity among the attorneys, as well as the clients. In recent years, the partners had implemented some attractive contemporary changes, such as flexible work schedules and the most modern technologies. On the other hand, a good portion of the clientele was from Edindale's old-school country club set. No matter how progressive, they still expected a certain amount of traditional formality. We wore suits to work, participated in local charity fund-raisers, and maintained a quiet deference in all our client interactions. It was just expected behavior.

"Hey, baby. Stop by my office when you get a chance. I want to ask you something."

And then there was Jeremy. Jeremy Bradson was the newest and youngest lawyer here. He was certainly smart. He had been top in his class, and he was a sharp lawyer. Even so, it still kind of surprised me that he had been hired. When he started about a year and a half ago, Jeremy brought a certain element of . . . youthful irreverence to the place. He wore jeans on casual Friday; walked around munching on caramel corn, even in front of clients; and laughed boisterously at small amusements.

He was also *really* cute. Tanned, toned, and trendy, with a blondish-brown haircut, he had a disarming tendency to wink at people.

I would never forget the first time he winked at me. I was explaining our office's computer database system at the time—this was, like, his second or third day on the job. He was in a chair next to my desk, looking over my shoulder at my computer screen. I couldn't even recall what we were talking about exactly, but that wink I remembered. I suddenly became warm all over, and I swore my heart skipped a beat. *How blatantly, deliciously, inappropriately flirtatious*, I thought. From that moment on, I couldn't help regarding him in a more . . . interesting light. That devilish grin, the mischievous twinkle in his eye . . . Sometimes when our eyes met, I felt an embarrassing flush rise up all over again.

But I would *never* date him. No, no, no, God, no. There were *so* many reasons why that would never happen.

For one thing, I was his supervisor. I reviewed his work, gave him assignments, approved his vacation requests. No matter which way you looked at it, that whole superior-subordinate line was one I definitely would not cross. I liked my job way too much.

For another thing, Jeremy really wasn't my type. He was a bit too juvenile, a wee bit careless. And there was the tiniest suggestion of the slightest bit of smarminess. The winking thing could get tiresome. He winked at nearly all women: waitresses, clients, colleagues. Most people found it charming. Not Beverly, though. The first time he tried that with our senior partner, she'd called him on it. "I would prefer it if you would blink with both eyes," she had said.

Yeah, Jeremy was not an option for me. In my head, I called him "the Untouchable." I really had no business checking him out in those Friday jeans or even allowing him to drift into my idle fantasies during boring meetings. It was pointless.

Still, I couldn't help wondering if he had noticed my special perfume. After booting up my computer, making a quick check of my appointment calendar and messages, I walked down the hall to Jeremy's office. He stood up when he saw me and brushed caramel corn crumbs off his shirt.

"Hey there, Ms. Milanni! Wow. You look fantastic today. Did you do something different to your hair?"

I'd told him a hundred times to call me Keli. We weren't *that* formal around here. On the other hand, maybe the formality was his way of balancing out all the "babes" he let slip out.

"Thanks, Jeremy. What's up?"

"Oh, I was wondering . . . I mean, out of curiosity, does the firm ever cut our paychecks early? Or, you know, give advances upon request or anything like that?"

"I don't think so. Not that I'm aware of. Would you like me to check with Beverly?"

"No, no. That's okay. Forget about it. Hey, it's almost time for the meeting. I'll see you in there."

He slipped past me, heading toward the men's room. I shook my head, wondering what kind of financial difficulties Jeremy had gotten himself into. Probably just shopping for a flashy new car. Or maybe this was about the student loans he was always bemoaning. Whatever. Not my concern.

I went back to my office to grab my coffee and a notebook, then went to Beverly's "conference lounge." One of the cool things about working at the firm was that our meetings often happened in the comfortable room outside Beverly's corner office. Instead of gathering around the long table in the conference room, we settled ourselves on sofas and stuffed chairs. Beverly's grandfather, the original Olsen and the founder of the firm, had outfitted the space with a fully stocked bar and a cigar cabinet to treat his more important clients. We usually had just fruit or cookies.

"Okay, people. Let's get started." Beverly took her usual seat in the leather high-back chair by the window.

The other partners, Randall Sykes, a wiry forty-something with a closely trimmed Afro, and Kris Rafferty, a slender woman with dark, silky-straight bobbed hair, sat in the circle of chairs with us associates, six in all. Not only was Beverly the senior partner, but she was also like our beloved Queen Mother. Her silver-streaked auburn hair was wound in a high bun, lending even more height to her striking five-foot-ten-inch figure. Even more impressive than her appearance, though, was her integrity. No doubt about it, Beverly commanded our respect and affection and returned it tenfold. She'd go to bat for any of us.

"Keli, why don't you go first?" said Beverly. "I think you may have the most interesting client this week."

This was our regular Thursday morning conflicts meeting, where we all briefed each other on the cases we were working on. It was called the conflicts meeting because it was meant to keep the firm from accidentally taking on cases where our representation of one client might conflict with the interests of another. Of course, we used law office software programs to keep track of clients and avoid conflicts, but these meetings also helped maintain our sense of community.

"Well," I began, "my new client is Eleanor Mostriak. Eighty-four years old, widowed. I'm preparing her will, which is pretty standard. However, for the not so standard part, I'm also assisting her with the sale of a major new asset. You might say that she discovered a treasure in her attic."

Everyone leaned forward a little as I told them about Eleanor's discovery of the long-lost Shakespeare folio. When I described the book and its condition and mentioned the appraisal value, I could hear impressed murmurs all around. Someone whistled. I glanced at Jeremy, whose eyes were gleaming. He winked at me. Naturally.

Crenshaw, apparently, was about to faint.

"The . . . the First Folio, you say? The original, complete . . . all thirty-six plays? In very good condition? Those were the exact words of the appraiser? *Very good condition*?"

"That's right," I said.

"Extraordinary."

"Yes. I—"

"Do you realize what we're talking about here? You were an English major. You should know. The First Folio is *the* most important book in all of English literature. Just think of the historical value, the cultural value—not to mention the monetary value. And rare! If I recall correctly, there are only around two hundred complete copies known to exist throughout the world today."

As Crenshaw gushed, Pammy Sullivan, who sat next to Crenshaw on a love seat, kept interjecting, "Oh, *my*," after nearly everything he said.

Pammy, a good lawyer and a nice lady, was nevertheless unceasingly, and unintentionally, entertaining to me. She liked to color coordinate her makeup, her fingernails, her jewelry, and her suits. Today's ensemble featured a coral- and yellow-striped skirt suit, a matching jumbo bead necklace, a bracelet, earrings in coral, and shiny coral fingernails. I was endlessly fascinated by her outfits and couldn't even imagine what her dressing room at home must look like. I had to force myself to direct my attention away from her and back to Crenshaw, who was still hyperventilating.

"Has it been authenticated? Was it bound? Was it

embellished? What was it doing in your client's attic?"

I couldn't help grinning at his unreserved enthusiasm. "It is bound, yes. A local rarc-books expert gave Eleanor his initial assessment of the value, as I mentioned," I said. "Eleanor will have it officially authenticated next week, when she flies to D.C."

Before Crenshaw could pepper me with more questions, Beverly raised her hand. "Let's move on, okay? Keli will keep us updated as this matter progresses. This will be a high-profile sale and good for the firm. It will benefit us all. Good work, Keli."

I sat through the rest of the meeting reveling in Beverly's praise yet feeling I didn't really deserve it. What had I done? I had just interviewed a client and prepared a will. On the other hand, I supposed Eleanor had chosen me based on a referral from a friend of hers. I had made another client happy enough to recommend me.

That afternoon Eleanor came back to finalize her will. Normally, I allowed at least a week to put together a will, but Eleanor was anxious to have hers in place before her trip to D.C. So I made an exception and worked quickly that morning to prepare all the papers. When she arrived, she had the First Folio with her in a large canvas book bag with a single-button flap closure.

"Eleanor!" I said, ushering her into my office. "Haven't you put that thing in a safety-deposit box yet?"

She showed me her dimples and set the bag gently on the floor. "Well," she said, a little breathless, "it got too late last night. I had to get home after I left here. Darlene and the boys were coming over for supper. And, of course, the boys wanted to see the treasure."

Her eyes twinkled as she said it, and I smiled in spite of myself. "What about this morning? You haven't been doing your errands while lugging around that four-hundred-year-old treasure, have you?"

"Oh, heavens, no!" said Eleanor, laughing. "Well, maybe just one. Anyway, I have to go back to the bookseller after I leave here. He's going to take pictures of the book and give me some directions to that Shakespeare library in Washington, D.C."

"Okay, Eleanor. But after that, you have to promise me you'll go straight to the bank," I said. "Also, no more talking to Mr. Satterly. If you really think he's the one you want to sell the Folio to, then you've got to let me handle the negotiations. Although, I still think you should consider using an auction house," I added.

"I did think about it," said Eleanor. "I want to keep the Folio closer to home, at least for now. I know Mr. Satterly will sell it in no time, of course, but still . . . Oh, that reminds me. We have to hold off on the sale until after I have my book club meeting next month. I can't wait to see the looks on those ladies' faces." Eleanor crinkled her eyes, and I could only shake my head. "Anyway," she continued, "I like Mr. Satterly, and I also like the idea of supporting a small local business. You know, it's important to me to keep the money right here in our community."

I nodded. "I understand perfectly. So, that's what we'll do—assuming Mr. Satterly can pay a fair price. And you won't set the price until after the second appraisal you get in D.C. Now, let's review your bequests."

We went over the details of her will again, and I answered all her questions. Finally, I asked her if she wanted to have a family member look over the will, but she said it wasn't necessary.

"I talked to Darlene last night, and she's just fine with being the executor. She expected it would be her, being the oldest."

"All right, then. Let me just go grab a couple witnesses and a notary." I stood up, strode over to my office door, and pulled it open—only to be knocked sideways by a heavy, flailing weight that had evidently been pressing on the other side of the door.

"Ohh!" I staggered to my feet and gaped at the intruder. "Crenshaw! What in the world?"

"Oh! Er . . . I . . . I beg your pardon!" He clumsily grabbed my arm to assist, which was only more of an annoyance, as I was already standing. "I was just, er, stopping in to offer my services as a witness to the last will and testament of this, er, your client. My timing was, ah, most unfortunate. Do accept my apologies. I beg of you." Even through his stuttered apology, Crenshaw bounced from side to side, trying to get a glimpse of the First Folio.

Eleanor raised her eyebrows and looked from

me to Crenshaw and back. Crenshaw, for his part, finally stood still and hung his head.

"I'm afraid," he said, "to quote a phrase, I 'have seen better days.'"

"Who said that?" asked Eleanor.

"That would be Duke Senior in the Shakespearean Comedy *As You*—" He stopped cold when he saw my expression. "Right. I'll bid you adieu now and take my leave." With a halfhearted flourish, he backed out of the room.

CHAPTER 3

"Oh, my God, that is too funny," Farrah said, nearly choking on her rum and Coke. "What a piece of work! He was actually listening at your office door and then *fell* into the room?"

"He's a piece of work, all right. At the time, I was more embarrassed than amused. I was with a client!"

"This is the guy who wears three-piece suits all the time, right? Satin vests, bow ties?"

I nodded and winced. "That wouldn't be so bad if it weren't for the rest of his personality. He spent, like, one semester in England or something, and he acts like he's related to the royal family." I took a sip from my drink and leaned forward. "You know how he insists on always tacking 'the Third' onto the end of his name? Well, I found out his father isn't even named Crenshaw."

"What!" Farrah burst into laughter again. "That is too much. This guy is single, right? You know what he needs. . . ."

I laughed with her and reached over to snatch a stuffed mushroom from Farrah's plate. We were having snacks and drinks at the Loose Rock, one of our favorite hangs in Edindale. The Loose was a hip and relaxed scene in the early evening, great for predinner dates or catching up with friends. Around nine o'clock it became a popular venue for indie rock bands, and by the end of the night it was a hopping dance party. Farrah and I enjoyed all three aspects of the club—often on the same night.

We'd been coming here since our grueling law school days, when we really needed to blow off steam. I had met Farrah on day one of school, at an orientation seminar. The professor had been going on and on, in dour tones, about how rigorous the competition was going to be and how our grades were going to affect "our entire professional careers." He told us that there was room at the top firms for only 5 percent of our class and that these coveted jobs would be won only by the best, brightest, and most hardworking among us. The auditorium was quiet as a tomb. Then he told us to look around at each other and see not our classmates but our competitors—the ones who would determine if we would be winners or losers. At that moment, there was a loud snort at the back of the room. All heads turned to see this cute, sparkly blonde stand up and head for the door at the front of the room. "Thanks for the warm welcome, Houseman," she said brightly. "See ya in the lecture hall."

I loved her immediately. I found her afterward and told her she was my hero. She laughed and asked if I wanted to get a beer with her. It wasn't long after this that we decided to be study partners. When we learned we shared an eclectic taste in music, a fondness for old movies, and a love of long-distance running, we became best buds, as well.

Oh, and in spite of her inauspicious start, Farrah graduated in the top 5 percent of our class. She worked for a huge law firm for one year and then quit to be a sales rep for a legal software company. It gave her more time to "have fun." Everything was fun with Farrah.

Now I was about to ask her why she and Jake were on the outs again, but I was momentarily distracted by a vision of tall, dark handsomeness near the entrance to the bar.

"Whoa," I said. "Who is that?"

She swiveled in her chair. "Who? Rock Star over there? He looks like he just rolled out of bed, doesn't he?"

"Yeah," I sighed. I always was a sucker for the bedroom look. This guy had dark, tousled hair and a five o'clock—no, make that a six o'clock—shadow. He wore faded jeans and a navy blue music festival T-shirt that stretched perfectly over well-toned muscles—not too big, not too small. A bold tribal-style armband was tattooed around his left bicep.

I tried not to stare, but this guy pulled my gaze like a steel magnet. Farrah laughed and waved her fingers in front of my face.

"It *has* been a while since you've dated anyone. You've been working too much, Kel." She turned to check out the new dude again. "Hey, he's talking to Jimi now," Farrah said. Jimi Coral, an energetic guy with a goatee, was the owner of the Loose. We knew him pretty well, with us being regular customers and all.

"Um, you know," I said, rising from my seat, "I think there's something I need to ask Jimi, like, right now. Isn't there?"

"Yes. Yes, I do believe there is. And I think I see Katie and Dawn, so I'll just catch up with you later."

I smiled sweetly at Farrah, and she wrinkled her nose at me and got up to join some friends at another table. She and I used to do this to each other all the time. We both understood that some opportunities were meant to be jumped on. So to speak.

Casually, I strolled over to the other side of the bar. "Hey, Jimi," I said.

The two men stopped talking and turned to face me.

"When are you gonna start singer-songwriter night again? Farrah and I were just talking about how much we miss that."

"Hi ya, Keli. Soon, I promise. I've got some interesting acts coming up next month."

I looked at Rock Star, who was even hotter up close. His dark brown eyes met mine, and I felt my heart quicken in my chest. Jimi, bless his soul, didn't miss a beat. He quickly introduced us.

"Keli, meet my friend Wes. He's my old college buddy. He just got back from New York." Jimi clapped Wes on the shoulder briefly, then made like he had to run. "Keli, maybe you could chat with Wes for a minute. I've got to check on something in the kitchen." Jimi took off before the word "Sure" was out of my mouth.

Wes smiled at me, then indicated a nearby booth. "Have a drink with me?"

We slid into the booth, and a waitress appeared to take our orders. For a few seconds, Wes studied me like he was trying to place my face.

I spoke first. "Have we met before?" I asked. I was pretty sure I would never have forgotten a man who looked like this. All the same, I did feel an odd sense of having known him.

"I was just trying to figure that out," he said. "Where'd you go to school?"

We chatted for a few minutes about college, but I had gone to undergrad back in my home state. And by the time I'd come to Edindale for law school, Wes was already in New York.

As we continued making small talk, I found myself liking this guy more and more. I especially appreciated how he gave me his full attention. He didn't look around the room, like some guys I'd dated.

When the waitress brought our drinks, Wes said, "You know what? I'm starving. Think I'll order some chicken wings, too. You want something to eat, Keli?"

"Oh, no thanks. I already ate."

"You can share my wings," he said. "If I remember right, Jimi's kitchen is generous with their appetizers."

"Thanks," I said. "But, actually, I don't eat meat."

"Oh, you're a vegetarian?" He seemed genuinely interested, which was a good sign. I'd had this conversation a million times before. Most meat eaters fell into one of two camps: those who found my diet a fascinating curiosity and those who found it not only weird but also somehow threatening. That second group liked to challenge my food choices as a personal affront to their own way of life.

I nodded. "Vegan, really. Just plant-based foods for me."

"I knew some vegans in New York," he said. "They seemed real healthy, and I admired their sense of conviction. I just think I'd starve, though, you know? I can't see me getting enough protein from nuts and beans or whatever."

"You might be surprised," I said good-naturedly.

He smiled and cocked his head at me. "How long have you been vegan?"

"About fourteen years," I said. "I was a teenager, still living at home. I saw an anti–animal cruelty video at school, and that was it for me. I was really impressionable, I guess. My parents about flipped. They thought I had an eating disorder or something."

Wes laughed with me, and I suddenly wanted to know everything there was to know about him.

"So, what were you doing in New York?" I asked. "Besides hanging out with very cool vegetarians."

"Well, for the past year and a half I worked at the Met. That was pretty awesome, being around all that art on a daily basis. But what I really—" He frowned and pulled out his cell phone. "Sorry. I gotta take this."

I watched as Wes put his phone to his ear and said, "Hey, what's up?" The conversation was brief, and then Wes stood up and reached into his pocket for some money. There was no trace of his earlier joviality as he put a few dollars on the table. "I'm really sorry. I have to go."

And then he was gone.

I sat there feeling bewildered, staring at the door through which he'd exited stage left. As the seconds ticked by, I realized he wasn't coming back. And he hadn't even asked for my number.

Then the waitress brought a basketful of chicken wings. I scrunched my nose at them and looked at the dollar bills on the table. Not even enough to cover two drinks plus the food.

Great.

I was about to go find Farrah, so we could ponder together all the dire scenarios that might possibly have pulled away such a promising guy, when I was startled by a familiar—and unnecessarily loud— voice.

"Hey, sexy! What are you doing, sitting here all alone? Buy ya a drink?"

Good God, it was Jeremy. He stood in front of me with his spiky hair, shining eyes, and a boyishly goofy grin. He held two brimming shot glasses, one in each hand.

"Jeremy! Hi. . . . Uh, what are you—"

He sat down in the seat vacated by Wes and slid a glass toward me, the original intended recipient of the drink apparently forgotten. "Come on, Ms. Milanni. A toast!"

I sniffed the caramel-colored liquid and smelled hot sweetness. Butterscotch schnapps maybe? I looked at Jeremy and pursed my lips into a reluctant smile. *What the heck.*

He winked at me as we raised our glasses. "To Thursday nights," he said.

Indeed. I downed the shot and felt the hot bite dissolve into a warmth that slid from my throat to my toes. I had licked my lips and opened my mouth to make some conversation when a crazy-hopping, drum-heavy dance tune filled the club and Jeremy reached for my hands.

"Come on, boss! Let's dance!"

And so that was how I found myself—three or more dance songs and at least one slow song later—in a shadowy corner of the club with the Untouchable . . . our arms entwined, our mouths inches apart. We were so close, I could practically taste the cigarettes on his breath, which was actually pretty repulsive. Yet, at the same time, I couldn't help being drawn to the animal heat radiating from his whole body.

The shots we kept downing between dances might have had something to do with this predicament.

I was certainly feeling warm and fuzzy. Even so, I was also aware that he seemed even farther along than me toward complete, sloppy drunkenness. *Yet another reason I should extricate myself from this situation at once,* I told myself sternly.

"Wanna go for a walk?" he whispered.

"Sure."

He put his arm around my waist and led me toward the door. I let myself be led, doing my best to ignore the devil and the angel duking it out on my shoulders.

What are you doing?

Shut up. It's just a walk!

The pavement was wet and shimmery under the streetlamps. It must have just stopped raining, and I'd had no idea it even started. For some reason, this bothered me, the fact that it had rained without me knowing about it. We had gone a few steps in the direction of Fieldstone Park when the phone in my purse rang.

"Hold on," I said to Jeremy. The rain-scented air and the absence of noise were clearing my head a bit, and I was glad for the excuse to pause.

I didn't recognize the number. "Hello?"

"Hello, Ms. Milanni?" It was a woman's voice, sounding strained.

Jeremy looked impatient and started to shift from foot to foot.

"Yes," I said. "Who's this?"

"This is Darlene Callahan, Eleanor Mostriak's daughter."

"I gotta piss," mouthed Jeremy, turning to head back to the bar.

I furrowed my eyebrows, wondering why Eleanor's daughter was calling me at this hour of the night.

"I'm sorry to call you so late, but I felt it was important to let you know." Darlene paused, and I felt a sinking sensation in the pit of my stomach. "M-mother passed away this evening. She had a heart attack."

CHAPTER 4

I awoke with morning-after remorse like I hadn't felt in a very long time. Not only was I hungover (stupid shots), but I also felt sad about Eleanor, disappointed about Wes, and horrified about Jeremy. What had I been thinking? After I heard the news about Eleanor, my desire for Jeremy had evaporated like the steam rising from the black street.

After some slow yoga stretches, I threw some colorful veggies in my juicer to concoct the most powerful detox blend I could think of. I drank it slowly and purposefully, intoning an improvised healing spell for good measure. Then I showered quickly, coaxed my hair into a semi-messy French twist, dressed in my most comfortable cotton pantsuit—gray and black, to match my mood—and headed out the door. As I walked to work, I made sure to breathe slowly and deliberately, doing my best to feel normal. All the while, I told myself I was getting too old to party like a college coed.

In fact, I must be *really* old to use a term like *coed*. When I entered the office suite, I said a quick hello to Julie Barnes, our young receptionist, and tried to scuttle straight to my office.

"Oh, Keli, hang on a minute," Julie said. She peered at me over her rectangular glasses with an appraising look. "You're in a hurry this morning," she said.

"Sorry," I said. "Um, I had a client die last night. Eleanor Mostriak. I wanted to look over her file."

"Oh, I'm so sorry! That sweet old lady? She was just here, like, yesterday!"

"Yeah," I said. "Thank goodness we finalized her will. It would be a shame to have the court distribute her estate when she'd already settled on all her last wishes."

The door opened behind me, and I almost did a double take when I looked around. Crenshaw came in, swinging his briefcase and sporting a clean-shaven face. Gone was the beard he had cultivated the whole time I had known him—and now revealed was a surprisingly strong jawline. I couldn't help staring.

"Rough night?" he questioned. When I didn't answer, he directed his eyes to the ceiling and stalked to his office.

Julie didn't seem to notice Crenshaw. Still fixated on Eleanor's death, she shook her head from side to side. "Wow, oh, wow. Here one day, and gone the next. Sure makes you think, huh?"

I smiled weakly at her. Julie had been with the firm for four years, but she was only twenty-two years old. She'd applied for the job right out of high school, and Beverly had been so impressed with her drive, she decided to give her a chance.

"Did you have a message for me, Julie?"

"What? Oh, yeah. Jeremy called in sick. He sounded awful. He asked me to let you know."

Coward. Well, at least I wouldn't have to go out of my way to avoid him. I thanked Julie, then went to my office and shut the door. I pulled out Eleanor's will and set it aside. I would go file it with the probate court clerk later in the day and then would contact Darlene to let her know. As she was the executor, I would talk to her about selling the Folio and settling the estate. These things couldn't be put off too long, but I didn't need to hassle her first thing after her mother passed away.

For the rest of the morning, I drafted documents for other clients and made a couple of phone calls. By 12:30, I was ready to come up for some air and take a break. Before grabbing some food, I needed to stop in at one of my favorite places in Edindale, Moonstone Treasures. It was a cute gift boutique around the corner from the law office, and it sold all kinds of goodies: books and cards, candles, crystals, jewelry, and CDs. And, behind a gauzy purple curtain, psychic readings. By appointment only.

A chime over the door jingled as I entered the shop, and I felt like I'd walked into a fairyland. A light blend of jasmine and citrus oils perfumed the air, while Native American–inspired flute music played softly in the background. Overlapping fringed throw rugs in warm jewel tones softened my steps, and from the ceiling delicate wind chimes, oriental paper lanterns, and shimmering spiral decorations swayed gently in the breeze that had followed me in. The atmosphere felt mystical. At the same time, the large picture windows in front kept the shop bright and open.

Just being in the shop was a restorative experience. But it was the set of shelves in the far back corner that interested me the most. This was where I could find special tools and supplies for the craft. There were mortar and pestle sets, chalices and athames, as well as candles, herbs, and oils. There were also tools for divination: tarot cards, runes, tea leaves.

I was in heaven.

I was admiring some new moon- and stars-adorned frames when the proprietor came in from the curtained back room.

"Hi, Mila," I said, looking up.

As always, Mila Douglas was a vision—boho chic meets Audrey Hepburn, with the slightest punk edge. She wore indigo skinny jeans and a simple cream-colored peasant shirt with three-quarter sleeves—the better to show off the charming triquetra tattooed on the inside of her right wrist. Her brunette hair was cropped in a short, easy shag, the tips dip-dyed pink. Dangly crystal earrings were her only jewelry.

Mila's style was what I imagined I might try if I didn't work in a law office five days a week. And who knew? Maybe I'd wind up like her yet. She had once told me she was forty-something, though she didn't look a day over thirty-five.

"Keli, so nice to see you. How are you liking the vanilla-berry candle? Is it working for you?"

Mila, of course, knew of my Pagan proclivities. Although we'd never gotten together outside the shop, I'd spent enough time there that I considered her a friend.

"It's great," I said. "Um, this is kind of embarrassing, but there's something I'm dying to tell you."

"Oh, do tell," said Mila, dropping her voice conspiratorially. "Do you want to go to the back room?"

"No. Well, not yet, anyway." I lowered my voice, too, even though there was no one else around. "I cast a love spell the other night."

"Which night?" Mila whispered.

"Wednesday," I said, somewhat surprised by the question.

"Hmm," said Mila. "You should have waited until Friday. Friday is better for love spells."

"Really?" That was new for me.

Mila consulted a calendar near the cash register. "At least the moon was waxing on Wednesday night, though the spell would've been more powerful if you'd waited for the full." She turned and smiled warmly. "Anyway, the *most* important element is you, and what's in your heart. How did you feel about the spell? Did it feel good to cast it? And how do you feel now?"

"A little confused," I confessed. "I'm afraid maybe I wasn't specific enough."

Mila nodded. "What was your intention exactly? Not a specific person, I assume." She opened a mini fridge behind the counter and took out a glass carafe. "Lemon water?" she said, reaching for two glass tumblers.

I accepted the drink and flopped into a cushioned wicker rocking chair in the book section of her store. Mila sat cross-legged on an oversize velvet ottoman and waited for me to answer.

"No," I sighed. "Not really a specific person. Just Mr. Right, I guess." I looked at her with a wry smile. "My intent was to attract my perfect mate. It felt right at the time, so to speak."

"And now?"

"Well, the next day I did seem to attract a lot of attention—which gave me a certain amount of confidence, I suppose. I even met someone new."

"How did you meet him?" asked Mila. She held her glass in both hands and regarded me intently.

I laughed. "At a bar. He was like the dark and mysterious stranger who rode in on a stallion. New in town and everything. And *very* nice to look at, let me tell you."

"But?" Mila prompted.

"But he bailed," I said. "Got a call and left." *Without asking for my number.* I couldn't bring myself to say it.

"Hmm," said Mila. "Spells do take time, you know. It's not like rubbing a magic lamp, and— *poof*—a genie appears to make your wish come true."

"I know," I sighed. "But I've actually been contemplating this spell for a long time. Kind of saving it as a last resort, I guess."

Mila raised her eyebrows.

"Not that I'm desperate or anything," I hurried to say. "It's just that . . . Well, I'm turning thirty in a couple weeks."

"Oh, when's your birthday?" asked Mila, all lit up like a child on her own birthday.

"June nineteenth."

"A Gemini," she said, nodding her head. "Of course."

"What do you mean, 'of course'?" Astrology was a little over my head. Interesting to a point, but just complicated enough to make my brain hurt if I thought about it too long.

"The twins," said Mila. "The duality. You know, the two sides of your personality—the straitlaced lawyer on one side and the free spirit on the other."

Mila hopped up from her seat and went to a nearby cabinet, talking to me over her shoulder. "I've got something for you. An early birthday present."

While she rummaged through the cabinet, I got up and strolled over to the front window. Sunlight streamed through the glass, reminding me of late spring school days when it looked like summer outside. I used to gaze out the window, longing to be outside in the sun instead of cooped up in a stuffy classroom, learning algebra or some such subject I'd never used since. The memory made me reluctant to go back to the office.

Just then, I became aware of a couple walking down the sidewalk. I glanced over, then quickly jumped back and darted to the side of the window. It was Pammy and Crenshaw.

I peeked cautiously from the edge of the window to see where they were going. *Please, not in here.* I couldn't imagine why they would, especially together, but stranger things had happened. Based on the take-out bag Crenshaw carried, I guessed they were on their way back from lunch. I watched as they passed by, Pammy decked out in turquoise and silver, Crenshaw dapper as usual in pinstripes and a bow tie, his shiny new chin jutting out before him. What a pair. Thankfully, they crossed the street and headed away from the shop.

"Who are we spying on?" Mila whispered, coming up behind me.

"Coworkers," I replied. "Muggles." I turned and grinned at Mila, and she rolled her eyes.

"Here," she said, taking my hand. She pressed a small smooth object into my palm and closed my fingers over it. "This is for you. It's a wishing stone I found in a creek bed a few years ago. It's really unique, heart shaped and tinged pink. I knew this had to be a love charm, so I drilled a small hole and threaded it with a slender chain."

"Then what?" I asked. I was itching to look at the stone, but Mila still held my hand shut with hers.

"I wore it around my neck for a couple days. But it was kind of heavy, not very comfortable, really. On the third day, I took it off at home and plunked it on the coffee table with a groan. 'This thing is hurting my neck,' I said to my husband. He came up behind me and started rubbing my neck. 'Why are you wearing it, then?' he asked."

"Yeah, really," I said. "Why *were* you wearing it?" I had heard Mila speak of her husband before. I knew they had been together happily for years.

"Well," she said, "that neck massage I got from my husband was really nice. It turned into a shoulder massage, then my back. And then one thing led to another." Mila arched her eyebrows suggestively, and I laughed.

"Ah," I said. "So it worked?"

"You bet. I mean, the love was always there. But that little charm helped draw it out even more." Mila let go of my hand and gave me a quick hug. "It served its purpose for me. Still, I held on to it, knowing it would have another purpose someday. It's yours now."

"Thank you," I said, feeling touched.

"You know what to do," she continued. "Imbue it with your energy. Feed it your intention. And carry it with you as a reminder, a touchstone. Then let the magic happen."

I closed the door of Mila's shop, a smile still on my lips. Mila was a good friend; I felt lucky to know her. However, when I turned around and looked up, my smile quickly dropped away. Across the street, gleaming brown-and-white wing tips planted in nearly the exact same spot as before, stood Crenshaw. Staring at me. It was so unexpected, I felt flustered. What was his deal, anyway? He must have dropped Pammy off at the office and then continued around the block again. Maybe he was doing laps, speed walking or something.

Crenshaw moved on, but I lingered on the sidewalk. I wasn't quite ready to go back to the office. Instead, I walked to the end of the block and turned right instead of left. Two doors down and I was at Callie's Health Food Store and Juice Bar, where I ordered a fresh six-veggie blend with ginger. Two juices in one day seemed totally called for today. For good measure and some crunch, I also grabbed a package of nuts. Thus fortified, I was prepared to work quietly at my desk until quitting time.

No sooner had I typed "aphroDite17" into my computer's password field than I heard the sound of robust male laughter from down the hall. From Jeremy's office.

Sick, eh? Maybe I'd better go see just how sick, the lazy bum.

Leaving my lunch on my desk, I checked my hair in the mirror beside my door and then popped over to Jeremy's office. There he was, chill as ever, leaning back in his chair, tossing caramel corn into the air and catching it in his mouth. Crenshaw was relaxing in one of the client chairs, long legs crossed elegantly. Randall Sykes, arising from the second chair, was speaking.

"Odds are three to one, fellas. We may want to re-think this one after tonight." Chuckling, he turned to me. "Want in on this, Keli? I'm collecting for the office baseball pool."

I shook my head. "Thanks, anyway. I'm not much of a gambler."

Crenshaw stood quickly, gave me that obnoxious half bow, and motioned to the chair vacated by Randall. "Have a seat, Keli. Tell us, does fortune smile upon you?"

I ignored the chair and the allusion and leaned against the door frame. "I've got to get to work. I just wanted to see how Jeremy's feeling." Turning to Jeremy, I said, "I thought you weren't coming in today."

Before he could answer, Pammy poked her head

in the room. "Oh, Crenny, there you are. I wanted to ask your opinion on this case I'm working on."

Crenshaw motioned to the empty chair again but stayed seated. "We were just having a brief postprandial chat. Not much else this hour of the day is good for."

Jeremy snorted and leaned forward to grab a pen from the plastic beer stein he used as a pencil cup. He began doodling on the oversize blotter calendar in the center of his desk.

Pammy walked around me and sat down in the empty chair. "Keli," she said, "I was really sorry to hear about your client passing away. She seemed really sweet."

"Thank you," I said. "She was eighty-four yet so youthful. I guess she'd had heart troubles before. Still, it was quite a shock."

"Is the funeral all arranged?" asked Pammy.

"There's a visitation tomorrow from five to eight. I plan on stopping by."

"Where's the First Folio?" asked Crenshaw. "You don't have it, do you?"

"No," I said. "Eleanor was having so much fun with it, showing it off. It's probably still at her house. I'll try to talk to her daughter about it if I get an opportunity."

"She still lived in her own home?" Pammy asked.

"Mm-hmm." I nodded.

"Gosh, what a blessing," said Pammy. "My siblings and I are in the process of looking at nursing homes for our mother."

I gave Pammy a sympathetic look and was about to say something more when Crenshaw cleared his throat. Affecting a pose, he projected his voice as if he were on a stage. "'But age, with his stealing steps, Hath claw'd me in his clutch.'" He looked at each of us as if he had uttered something profound. "That's Shakespeare, of course. *Hamlet*, act five."

For a moment, we all stared at Crenshaw. Then I slipped out without a word.

CHAPTER 5

The sun was still bright in the western sky when I arrived at Carlston Funeral Home, a whitewashed colonial-style mansion. I stood for a moment on the broad porch before the closed front door, and I took a slow deep breath. And then another one. With my feet planted firmly on the Berber entrance mat, I mentally grounded myself to the earth and centered myself in the present. It took only a moment, but it worked. I felt calmer and stronger as I pushed open the door and crossed the threshold. People milled about, somber and quiet. The muted colors, floral arrangements, and soft organ music in the background gave the place a churchy feel. Spotting the guest book, I signed my name. Then I made my way to the viewing room to pay my respects.

After placing my flowers among the others, I went over to introduce myself to Darlene. Darlene was a petite, youthful-looking woman in her fifties with highlighted auburn hair. She had Eleanor's dimples, which she flashed briefly, putting on a determinedly brave and gracious face for the public. I recalled Eleanor telling me that Darlene's husband, Bill, was retired from the army but had recently taken a job with a military contractor. He was currently somewhere in the Middle East, heading up some sort of infrastructure project. I wasn't surprised he hadn't made it back for the visitation.

While I talked to Darlene, we were joined by Eleanor's son, Kirk, who came in through a side door, picking cottonwood fluff out of his hair. An attractive man with graying temples and deep laugh lines, Kirk was just a little taller than me and appeared to be in his late forties. He put his hand on my arm and said by way of greeting, "Is it over yet? All this sympathy is giving me hives." Darlene shushed him affectionately, while another woman nearby chuckled softly. I gathered that Kirk was the comedian in the family.

After offering my condolences, I wandered over to the reception room. I had no appetite for the store-bought cookies and fruit punch, but I did want to look at the picture boards. There was Eleanor throughout the years, in black and white, faded Kodak, Polaroid, and digital. I smiled as I perused the photos: Eleanor as a little girl and as a young lady, Eleanor and Frank on their wedding day. Children, grandchildren, birthday parties, Christmas celebrations. Posed shots and silly candids. *What a sweet life*, I thought.

I grinned at one family portrait, so recognizable in its universality. Every expression was a story in itself: the determined cheerfulness of the harried mom, the bored smirks on the teenagers, the goofy faces on the overstimulated kiddos, the screaming baby. One person always with his eyes closed. And in the middle, a beaming Grandma Eleanor and Grandpa Frank, so proud of their brood.

Hang on a minute. My glance went back to the bored teenagers, apparently two brothers. These would be the grandsons Eleanor mentioned in her will, Wesley and Robert.

Hmmm. There was something familiar about the older one. I searched the boards for a later photo. There it was.

Oh. My. God. Dark hair, warm eyes, sexy smirk. Wesley was Wes! He was the hottie from the bar. The disappearing hottie. It must have been the news of Eleanor's death that had caused him to leave the bar so abruptly.

I stood a little straighter as the next realization hit. He could be *here*! In fact, it was highly likely that he was. I swung around and gave the room a sweeping glance. No sign of a dark-haired hottie.

I was about to go prowling through the other rooms—Was that wrong? That was so wrong—when someone gasped to my left. I started guiltily and glanced over to see who the mind reader was. A middle-aged woman with short, frizzy hair peered at one of the photo boards.

"I forgot all about that picnic! Look at Aunt Eleanor in that yellow minidress and sixties flip. And Uncle Frank in that plaid suit! That's me, the scrawny little kid in braids."

She turned to me, smiling and misty eyed. "They

were doing Shakespeare in the Park, the university theater troupe. Uncle Frank and Aunt Eleanor thought it would be fun to get dressed up and to bring a picnic basket with wine and cheese and fruit. Apple juice for us kids, of course. Don't we look like we're straight out of some European film?"

I looked at the picture with her, murmuring in agreement. She pointed out her mom and dad and her cousins, which would be Darlene and Kirk. The kids, squinting into the sun, sat cross-legged on a blanket. Eleanor looked so young and elegant, standing with one hand shading her eyes, the other draped at her side. She looked as if she had just been laughing.

"And here we are with Santa." The woman had moved on to another photo.

"Such a beautiful family," I said. "The love and warmth really shine through in these photos."

"Yes," the woman agreed, nodding. Then she turned to me again. "I'm Sharon, by the way."

I stuck out my hand. "Keli Milanni," I said. "Eleanor's lawyer."

"So nice of you to come," Sharon said. She reached over to touch my arm and lowered her voice. "Say, as a lawyer, maybe you can help. I told Darlene she needs to request an autopsy before it's too late, but she's not real keen on the idea."

"An autopsy? That's not really necessary, is it?"

"Look at this," Sharon said, pointing to one of the more recent photos on the display board. "Look how healthy Eleanor appears, years younger than her real age. This was taken less than a month ago."

"But she did have a history of heart issues, didn't she? And high cholesterol?"

"Yes, but we don't know for sure what happened. The coroner said she had probably passed away a few hours before Darlene found her on the kitchen floor. I'd just like to know the exact cause of death."

I nodded slowly without saying anything. I knew it was natural for family members to want answers.

"You know what?" Sharon said. "I'll ask her doctor tomorrow. I work at the hospital, which is right next to the clinic where Eleanor always went. Her doctor can ask for an autopsy." She turned back to the photo board and shook her head. "I just have a hard time believing she up and had a heart attack out of nowhere."

Clearing my throat, I decided to change the subject. "There seems to be a big turnout today. Was the whole family able to come?"

"I think so, except for Bill. Poor Darlene. I guess she's used to being an army wife, but it's a shame her husband has to be so far away, he can't even fly home for things like this. Most of the cousins from out of state made it in this afternoon."

"Of course, much of the family lives right here," I said, thinking of Wes again. "Like her grand-children, I think."

"Mm-hmm, some of them. Darlene's boys are here, and two of Kirk's kids are in nearby towns. Kirk's youngest daughter is in L.A., but she got here this morning."

"I think I'm actually acquainted with Darlene's

son Wesley," I said, pressing on. "I'd like to offer him my condolences. Do you know if he's here?"

"Well, he *was* here, but he left." Sharon's disapproval couldn't be more apparent if she'd worn a sign.

Uh-oh. The guy ditched his own grandmother's memorial service?

"He had to work?" I ventured.

"Work?" said Sharon, fairly scoffing. "No. He had to avoid being in the same building as his own brother, apparently. Two grown men still acting like children. Shameful, if you ask me. Just shameful."

Maybe it was the memory of our first encounter, cut short just as it was getting interesting. Or maybe it was his second aunt's insinuations. Either way, I couldn't get Wes out of my mind. I think I dreamed about him that night after the visitation, but the memory of it vanished with the early morning fog.

Still, I kept thinking about him as I jogged through Fieldstone Park and over to the old rail trail, lightly populated on this Sunday morning by a few other joggers and cyclists. I guessed most people, or at least most of the college students I often saw on this trail, were sleeping in after a typical Saturday night of partying. Others might be at church. Edindale had something like twenty churches, so that would be a safe bet.

As for me, I *was* at church. Nature was my church. The trees formed my cathedral; the birds made up my choir. The fresh scent of the earth was better than any incense. And the sun streaming through the clouds, and the gentle breeze on my face, were like heaven itself.

I was feeling pretty good, running at a brisk pace and basking in the holy environment, when I thought of Wes again. What would he think if he knew I was a Goddess-worshipping, Earth-loving, tree-hugging nature girl? Would he be cool with that? Or would he run screaming for the proverbial hills?

My first impression of him was that he seemed to be a laid-back, open-minded kind of guy. He probably wouldn't be scared off too easily. Yet . . . would it matter to him if I told him a love spell had brought us together?

Um, perhaps I wouldn't be telling him that anytime soon. In fact, who knew if I'd even see him again? Those chocolate eyes, that chiseled chin . . .

Whoops! My toe caught on a stone sticking halfway out of the dirt, and suddenly, after a split second of useless flailing, I was on my hands and knees. *Guess I really am a Holy Roller*, I thought wryly as I dusted myself off. I sat on the edge of the trail for a minute, checking to make sure nothing was twisted, ripped, or broken. Luckily, I was all in one piece, just a little scuffed and bruised. As I pondered how I'd managed to trip on the only loose pebble visible on the whole trail, it hit me.

Loose Rock.

This was a sign. If I wanted to see Wes again, I needed to go back to the place where I first met him.

I walked for a few minutes, then gingerly began to run again, heading back the way I'd come. With a new sense of purpose, I fairly flew through town.

Of course, I still had a few hours before the Loose would open up, so I slowed down when I got home. I stretched and sipped water. Then I made myself a refreshing green smoothie consisting of frozen banana, a big spoonful of peanut butter, a couple of handfuls of fresh spinach from my tiny backyard garden, and a healthy splash of soy milk. *Delish.*

Then I showered, shimmied into a lime-green sundress and strappy sandals, and applied a touch of bronzer, a swipe of mascara, and a kiss of lip gloss. I was ready to go.

At 11:00 a.m. Jimi would just be opening up the Loose. I hoped to catch him before he got too busy and grill him about his old college buddy. He ought to be able to share some useful information, such as Wes's phone number.

As I suspected, the place was nearly empty. While my eyes adjusted to the dim lighting, I made my way over to the bar to ask for Jimi. The bartender was leaning down, stocking some bottles, so I took a seat and waited, contemplating what I would order if I were inclined to order a drink before noon on a Sunday. Bloody Mary? Mint julep? Cold beer? I had no idea.

I started idly drumming my fingertips on the bar as I squinted at the labels along the shelf. The bartender stood up and started apologizing.

"Oh, sorry. I didn't see—" He stopped when he recognized me, and I nearly fell off the stool when I recognized him. It was Wes . . . daylighting as a bartender?

"Hey!" he said, a smile lighting up his face. "It's good to see you again, Keli."

He remembers my name, I thought with relief. "Wes! Hi. You bartend here?"

"Oh, well, I'm filling in today. Helping Jimi out. What a nice surprise to see you! What can I get you?"

"Hmm . . ." I hesitated, furrowing my brow.

"Oh, are you . . . uh, are you waiting for someone?" Was that disappointment I detected on that dreamy face of his?

"Actually, I was looking for you. I wanted to tell you how sorry I am about the loss of your grandmother."

Now Wes looked really surprised and a little perplexed. For a second, I let him wonder. It was fun to be the mystifying woman, but I couldn't play the part for long. I came clean.

"I was your grandmother's lawyer," I said. "I didn't know you were related to her until I saw your picture at the memorial yesterday. And then I realized the phone call you got Thursday night was probably about your grandma."

Wes absentmindedly grabbed a towel from behind the bar and started wiping the scratched wood. For a minute I was afraid it was too weird that I had come. Maybe he didn't want to be reminded of his grandmother's death. Then he shook his head in wonder.

"That is so wild. What a coincidence." He stopped wiping the counter and looked at me again. "Oh, hey, I'm sorry about cutting out on you so abruptly the other night."

"Oh, gosh, don't be sorry. I mean, it's perfectly understandable, under the circumstances."

Wes regarded me for a minute. "Hey," he said suddenly. "Why don't we finish that drink now? You had rum and Coke, right?" He reached under the bar, pulled out a bottle of Bacardi, and placed it in front of me. As he turned to grab a glass, he paused and looked over, waiting for an answer.

"Okay," I said agreeably. "But put it in a tall glass, please. And with lots of ice."

Wes grinned. "Of course." I watched as he pulled out two highball glasses, filled them with ice, and deftly mixed the cocktail. He garnished each glass with a wedge of lime—a nice complement to my dress—and pushed a glass in front of me. "Your Cuba libre, senorita."

I picked up my glass and swiveled around on my stool, while Wes walked around the bar to join me. He motioned to the waitress to come get him if she needed help with any customers, and we went back to our table from the other night.

As soon as we were seated, Wes lifted his glass. "To second chances?"

I touched his glass with mine and felt an unexpected rush of happiness. I knew there was something special here. It must be fate—helped along with a tiny, little heartfelt love spell.

"So, how long have you been Gram's lawyer?" Wes asked.

"Oh, about two days," I said regretfully. "But I spent all afternoon with her on Wednesday and a couple hours on Thursday. I really liked her. I wish I could have known her longer."

"She was the best," Wes said softly. "I only wish I had come back from New York sooner."

I started to ask him about his years in New York and why he'd come back now. But he beat me to the punch with questions about my law practice. He seemed impressed and kept asking me about myself. Still, I was eager to know more about him. When he paused to sip his drink, I tried again.

"I really liked looking at your grandma's pictures at the memorial. Such a cute family. You have one brother, right? Does he live here in town?"

"Yeah."

"His name's Rob, right? You two must be pretty close. Aren't you just, like, a year or two apart in age?"

Was that a shadow that just crossed Wes's face?

"Mm-hmm. Do you have siblings? Any family around here?"

"My family's mostly back in Nebraska. I'm the youngest of four," I said. "But it's not what you think," I added, seeing he was about to tease me about being the baby. "I wasn't spoiled or anything."

"Sure," joked Wes. "Whatever you say."

"Really," I insisted, smiling along with him. "Actually, I was pretty much left to my own devices. My two older sisters are eleven and twelve years older than me. They were rivals slash best friends, more interested in sports and friends and themselves than in their baby sister. And my brother, who is four years older than me, was *really* the baby. I mean, he was a good kid, more or less, but always up to something. After keeping up with those three, my parents allowed me a lot of independence."

"So why'd you pick Edindale?" Wes asked, keeping the conversation on me.

Before I could answer, Jimi came by. He stood at our table with arms crossed, toe tapping the floor. "Sitting down on the job already?" he said in a mock-disapproving tone. At least, I was pretty sure he was joking. "And drinking, no less. Am I going to have to fire you on your very first day?"

Wes looked up at his friend, grinned devilishly, and took a big gulp of his drink in return.

Jimi sighed loudly and rolled his eyes. "Well, I guess I'll forgive you this time, considering what pulled you away." He touched my shoulder and gave me a quick nod, then walked over to the bar to take the position vacated by Wes.

"If you need to go—" I began, but I was cut off when a phone started buzzing. Wes pulled his cell from his pocket, glanced at it, and hit IGNORE.

"Sorry about that," he said. "So, you were telling me—" His phone buzzed again.

"Someone's persistent," I remarked.

"It's my mom," said Wes, hitting IGNORE again. "She probably wants to lecture me about not being in church this morning."

Um, wait a minute. "You—you didn't go to your grandma's funeral?"

"It's not like that," said Wes. "There wasn't a funeral. Grandma was like me. Neither of us cared much for church. Anyway, the memorial last night was it. Her body was cremated. There was no burial. My mom has the urn. I think the plan is to have a scattering ceremony in the fall, when my dad is back from his job overseas."

The phone buzzed again.

"Please," I said. "Go ahead and answer it. I don't mind."

Wes shrugged and put the phone to his ear. "Hi, Mom. Sorry I missed you earlier. I was . . . What? No, I . . . of course not. Yeah. I'll head over now."

Wes put the phone in his pocket and stood up. "I'm sorry to do this again, but I have to go."

No way. "Is something wrong?"

"Maybe," he said. "My mom can't find the book."

"The book?"

"The Shakespeare book. Apparently, it's missing."

CHAPTER 6

It didn't take much prodding for me to get Wes to take me with him. After all, I reminded him, I was Eleanor's lawyer. And I wanted to help. I could help look for the Folio—Eleanor had probably stashed it in some secret hidey-hole—and I could also talk to Darlene about the will and ask if the family still wished me to assist with the sale of the book. On the drive over to his grandmother's house, I asked Wes about the family lore surrounding the First Folio, and he told me pretty much the same thing Eleanor had said, that Frank inherited the rare book from his uncle. Sometime later, it was lost.

And now it was lost again.

When we arrived at Eleanor's house, a yellow Cape Cod with a stone walkway leading to a welcoming red door, we were greeted by a very frazzled Darlene. From the entryway, I could see a room to the left that seemed to be in a state that matched Darlene's. It was a combination office/library/sitting room with a desk and filing cabinets on one side and comfortable chairs and reading lamps arranged on the other. Floor-to-ceiling bookshelves lined the wall facing the doorway. It would have been a lovely, cozy room, but drawers were pulled out, papers and books littered the floor, and cushions were all cast aside. One of the chairs was turned on end.

"Wes, we've turned this place upside down, but maybe with a fresh set of eyes . . ." Darlene trailed off hopelessly. Then she noticed me standing behind Wes. "Oh, Miss Milanni! I'm glad you're here. We have a bit of a crisis, I'm afraid."

She didn't seem to realize I had arrived with Wes. Since Wes kept his mouth shut, I decided to do the same. Darlene closed the door behind me and began introductions, starting with the person who had driven me there.

"This is my son Wes. And this is my cousin Sharon."

Sharon stood in the living room, to the right of the foyer, wearing a worried expression. From the look of things, she had started pulling cushions off chairs in this room, too.

Darlene touched my arm. "This is Mom's lawyer, Keli Milanni."

Sharon spoke up. "Oh, sure. We met at the visitation. Keli, maybe you can help us solve a little mystery. The mystery of the missing manuscript." She tried to keep her voice light to break the tension in the room, but Darlene looked as if she were about to crumble. I was beginning to second-guess my assumption that the Folio was just hidden away. "Why don't we go into the kitchen and sit down?" Sharon said.

She guided Darlene down the hall and directly to a kitchen chair. I followed them and, trying my best to instill a calming presence, sat down next to Darlene. Wes went to a cabinet for a glass and poured some water for his mother.

I glanced around the room, which was tidy and modest, with a comfortable country style, complete with gingham curtains and a hen-shaped cookie jar. Recalling that this was where Eleanor had died, I looked up from the maple-wood flooring and cleared my throat. "When did you last see the book, Ms. Callahan?" I asked.

"Call me Darlene," she said automatically. "It was . . ." She closed her eyes and rubbed her temples. "Yesterday. Before the memorial. Around four o'clock, I think. I stopped in to get a dress for Mom to be laid out in."

"She changed her mind about the dress she originally gave to the funeral home," explained Sharon, who leaned against the kitchen counter. "It was black, with pleats. Very formal. We decided a flowery print would be nicer."

"What was it like when you arrived today?" I asked. "Was the house locked? Was there any evidence of a break-in? Anything disturbed?" Inwardly, I cringed at the last question, remembering the look of the front rooms, where *everything* had been disturbed.

"No, I don't think so," Darlene said uncertainly. "Sharon and I got here about an hour ago, after Kirk went back to Indiana."

"We were going to do a walk-through," Sharon

offered. "Water the plants, check her messages and mail. It may have been more than an hour ago."

"I knew the book was in the den," Darlene continued. "Like I said, I saw it the day of the memorial service. I had passed by that room on my way upstairs, and I saw it in there, in Mom's old messenger bag. I even thought to myself that we should get it to the bank. Or, at least, someplace else besides Mom's den. But at the time . . ."

"You had a lot on your mind, Mom," said Wes. "I think everyone else had forgotten about it."

"We were in such a rush," said Darlene. "Rob was waiting in the car. Then you got here, Wes, and we had a big—" She stopped suddenly, looking upset. I noticed Wes look away and stare absently out the window above the sink.

I turned to his mother and asked gently, "Did you lock the house when you left?"

"Yes, I'm sure I did. I remember unlocking the front door again when we came by later to get the extra sodas and chips and cookies from the pantry."

"When was that?" I asked.

Darlene looked at Wes and Sharon. "It must have been after eight thirty, right?"

Sharon nodded and turned toward me. "The visitation ran long. There was a meal over at the church hall, but most of the family didn't get over there until pretty late. We stopped in here on the way, my husband, Dennis, and I and Darlene."

Darlene continued, "I knew Mom had all this food in her pantry, and I just knew she'd want us to get it. So we hurried in and gathered it up. And I—"

Her eyes widened, and she looked helplessly around the room. Her voice dropped to a whisper as she continued. "I glanced in the den in passing. And I noticed that the Folio wasn't sticking out of the bag anymore. I assumed that Sharon or Kirk or someone had moved it. Maybe put it in a safer place. Like I should have."

"Darlene, don't blame yourself," said Sharon. "We were all preoccupied."

Wes spoke up at last. "Mom, did anyone else have a key to Grandma's house besides you?"

Darlene shook her head. "I have two keys, actually, the spare I have always had, plus Mom's keys. They're in her purse, which is back at our house." She had a pained expression on her face. "Mom's purse, with its spare change and hand lotion, I managed to protect. Yet a priceless seventeenth-century artifact, I somehow overlooked." She sighed heavily.

Wes looked thoughtful. "Didn't Grandma keep an emergency key hidden in the front yard? Under a rock or something?"

For a moment, the family looked at one another in silence. Then, all at once, they got up and headed for the front door. I started to follow, then paused at the library—the den, Darlene had called it. It was in such a state of disarray, I realized it would be futile to look for any evidence at this point. I wandered back to the kitchen to take a look at the back door. Not that I had any clue as to what I was looking for. I could still hardly believe that someone had actually stolen the Folio right out of

Eleanor's home. I also couldn't help remembering what Sharon had said at the visitation—that maybe Eleanor hadn't died of natural causes, after all. The thought gave me goose bumps.

After opening and closing the back door, I looked up to see Wes coming into the kitchen by himself.

"The key was still there," he said. "Took us a couple minutes to find the right stone. Hard to say for sure, but it didn't look as if it had been used lately. The key was pretty crusty."

Just then, Darlene came into the kitchen with a guy I recognized from the photos at the visitation, Wes's younger brother, Rob. In a T-shirt and jeans, he resembled Wes. He had the same build, only slightly shorter, and the same chiseled jawline. He was cute. Instead of dark hair, he had sandy hair, which was sticking out from beneath a blue baseball cap. Seeing me, he immediately came over and stuck out his hand.

"Hi there," he said with a friendly smile. "I'm Rob."

"Keli," I said, shaking his hand.

Wes took a step closer to me and gave his brother a warning look. *Interesting.* Then he addressed Darlene. "Mom, we need to call the police. We've got to report that the Folio was stolen."

"Oh, no," said Darlene, looking around the room. "I can't believe it. I just don't believe it. I can't—"

"Mom," said Wes, cutting her off. "Want me to call?"

She nodded and fell into a chair.

Rob perched himself on a stool, looking pensive. "Guess the next call will be the insurance company, huh? Well, at least we don't have to worry about selling the old book. Now it will just be the insurance proceeds to divvy up."

I suddenly had a horrible thought. Had Eleanor added the Folio to her insurance policy? If she hadn't, there was no way her homeowner's insurance would cover the loss of a million-dollar valuable the insurer knew nothing about.

Wes looked at Rob incredulously but didn't say a word. Flipping through a phone book on his grandmother's counter, he found a number for the local police station and placed the call.

Sharon had to leave for work—the second shift at Edindale Medical Center, she said—but the rest of us waited in the backyard, which was lush and fragrant in the warm afternoon sun. It was a sizable yard, dotted with maple trees and fruit trees, lilacs and rosebushes. It was the kind of paradisiacal yard that tempted me to leave my cozy town house for greener pastures.

Darlene, who looked like she wanted to keep busy, emptied the birdbath and turned on a hose to refill it. Then she started pulling weeds from the vegetable garden. Rob sat in a lawn chair on the small patio, eyes glued to his smartphone. I watched as Wes ambled around the yard. He stood on the back steps and then walked slowly down the path that led to an old toolshed and then to the wooden fence along the alley. He went through the gate, passed the garbage cans, and looked up and down the alley.

I started wandering around myself, tracing the perimeter of the house and pondering how someone might have gotten in without a key. There was no cellar door, no other entrance, and all of the first-floor windows looked intact. On the north side of the house, I looked up and noticed a window was slightly open. But it was out of reach without a ladder. The closest tree, a towering, bushy pine, was a good eight feet from the house. Besides, pines were difficult to climb. Too sticky.

I walked back to the patio, where Wes was talking with his mom.

"Who are the neighbors?" I asked, pointing to each side of Eleanor's house.

"That's Mrs. Ross there," answered Darlene, nodding toward the house on the pine tree side. "She's a widow. She was at the visitation. The other side is the Perrys. They were at the visitation, too."

The police arrived, two middle-aged officers named Buchanan and Shakley. They dutifully took notes while Darlene gave them the same account she had relayed to me. The officers looked at the front and back doors and walked through the house, but they didn't stay long. They said they would talk to the neighbors, and then they left. They weren't gone thirty seconds before Wes grabbed my arm.

"Let's follow them."

"What?"

"I want to see who they talk to, find out what they learn. Come on."

Admittedly, I felt silly. It was comical, really, the way we were trailing two cops, trying to be nonchalant as we sauntered down the sidewalk in this peaceful, leafy neighborhood. We tried to stay back a good half block while keeping the officers in our sight. Every time they turned to approach another front door, we turned quickly to face the other way or ducked behind a tree or a parked car. I didn't know who was more conspicuous, a couple of uniformed police officers going door-to-door or the two goofballs behind them.

Secretly, I was having a blast.

"Too bad we don't have a dog to walk," Wes murmured from the corner of his mouth. "It would be the perfect cover."

"Do you have a dog?" I asked. Hey, I wasn't going to miss an opportune "getting to know you" moment, crime-fighting mission or not. I was a practiced multitasker.

"Nah. Too much responsibility. And I'm not home enough. Maybe someday, though."

Intriguing. I was about to ask a follow-up question when Wes suddenly pulled me off the sidewalk and alongside an SUV that was parked in a short driveway. We crouched down and peeked through the vehicle's side windows. Shakley and Buchanan were walking to the front of a nice two-story frame house painted pale blue, with manicured bushes in the front yard.

But it wasn't the house or the cops Wes was eyeing. I followed his gaze and saw a girl of fifteen or sixteen standing like a statue behind a juniper bush on the side of the house. She regarded the cops with wide eyes.

I looked at Wes questioningly. He shrugged and whispered, "She was walking around from the backyard and practically dove behind that shrub when she saw them. I'm pretty sure she didn't notice us."

The cops stood on the front porch, speaking to a ponytailed woman wearing cargo shorts and a white polo shirt. We could hear indistinct voices, punctuated by the occasional "Oh!" and "No, I don't think so."

Before I realized what was happening, the officers stepped aside and the woman, ponytail swinging, trotted down the steps and made for our direction. I tensed up and grabbed Wes's arm, ready to bolt. Though to be seen running away would probably have proved more embarrassing than getting caught.

Wes placed his hand on my knee and gave me a warning look, but his eyes sparkled. I had to stifle a sudden urge to giggle out loud.

"Brandi!" the woman called out loudly as she rounded the corner of the house.

The girl behind the bush started backing up. She looked like she was ready to bolt, too.

The woman spotted her and stopped short. "Brandi! What are you doing back there?"

"Mom!" the girl hissed. "I don't want to be seen like this!"

I couldn't blame her. She had on a string bikini, which wasn't so bad in itself. But for a cover-up, she wore a tentlike gray painter's shirt. Her legs were bare, except for the shiny oil she'd slathered on.

And on her feet was a pair of clunky orange Crocs. A crooked topknot fell limply over her forehead.

As the officers came up behind her mother, she quickly pulled the band off her head and shook her hair loose. Then she pulled her shirt closed.

"Brandi," said the woman sternly. "There was a robbery over on Willow Street, just across the alley from our garage. These officers are asking around to see if anyone saw anything. Probably last night."

The girl held back, doing her best to stand behind her mother as the police officers questioned her. I watched as she shook her head and muttered one-word responses. Even from where we hid behind the SUV, I could see Brandi darting her eyes, looking anyplace except at the officers. She looked so guilty, I almost began to wonder if *she* had stolen the Shakespeare book.

The cops must have thought the same thing.

"Where were you yesterday between four and eight thirty?" asked Buchanan.

Brandi glanced at her mother, who answered for her. "Brandi was grounded yesterday, so she was in her room reading all evening—except for when we had dinner from six to six thirty or so. I don't suppose she would have seen anything, unless it was out her bedroom window." She turned to her daughter. "Did you see anything?"

Brandi shook her head quickly and examined her cherry-red fingernails. The officers stared at her for a second. Officer Shakley handed a business card to Brandi's mother.

"Give us a call if you think of anything," he said.

They left and moved on to the next house, and Brandi followed her mother into their home.

I looked at Wes, eager to speculate about what little Miss Teen Spirit was hiding. But he stood up with a groan and stretched his back.

"Time to get back," he said. "I guess those cops know what they're doing."

The walk back to Eleanor's house was much less fun than before. Wes didn't say a word. I imagined he was thinking about his grandma or maybe his mom. But something about the telltale worry lines around his eyes made me wonder if little Miss Brandi wasn't the only one with something to hide.

CHAPTER 7

Monday morning I started the day at a mortgage company's office, representing the buyer at a real estate closing. It was pretty routine; I'd done a million of these, so no big deal. But I felt distracted and anxious. Every time someone mentioned insurance, I got this uneasy flutter in the pit of my stomach.

My worst fears were realized when I returned to the office. Darlene Callahan was waiting for me in the reception area. Although she was dressed neatly in slacks and a short-sleeved blouse, the dark circles under her eyes and the neglected gray roots made her appear drawn and harried.

Julie gave me an apologetic look. "She didn't want to make an appointment," she said quietly. "She's been here about twenty minutes."

"That's okay. Ms. Callahan. It's nice to see you again. Let's go back to my office." I tried to keep my voice bright, but I felt uncommonly nervous. The worried look on Darlene's face didn't help.

Darlene followed me into my office and sat down

in one of the two armchairs facing my desk. I set down my briefcase and took my seat. Sometimes I sat on the same side, next to a client, but this time I felt like having the protective barrier the desk provided, at least psychologically.

"I didn't expect to be going through my mom's things so soon," Darlene began. "But between searching for the book and then looking for the insurance policy, I feel like I've turned that place upside down and inside out two times over."

"No luck?" I said, not knowing what else to say.

"I found her bank papers and the safety-deposit box key. I just came from the bank. But all that was in the box was the deed to her house, the title to her car, and her marriage certificate. So, that's why I came here next. I figured you must have a copy of the insurance policy for the Folio." She looked at me hopefully.

Crap.

I swallowed hard. "Well, no," I said as gently as I could. "Eleanor was taking care of the insurance. She didn't ask me to . . ." I trailed off, feeling extremely lame.

A deep mottled flush rose from Darlene's neck into her cheeks. She took a slow, ragged breath. "Ms. Milanni, this is a multimillion-dollar piece of property we're talking about here. You were handling Mother's affairs, taking care of all the business involving that Folio. You were representing her in the sale, and . . . and . . ." She stood up, her voice rising. "What do you mean, she didn't ask you to? Was she supposed to *ask* you to cross every t and dot every i? Isn't that your job? To protect her interests? Didn't you have a *duty* to her?"

By this time, I could feel that my face had to be as red as Darlene's. I understood why she was so upset, but all I could think of at that moment was that I had to get her out of my office. This was not a pretty scene, and I had to put an end to it.

She continued shrilly, "You don't drive out of a used car lot until the vehicle is insured, for Pete's sake! And something this valuable . . . Shouldn't you have kept it in your custody?"

"Darlene," I said as calmly and firmly as possible. "Please don't be so hasty. Let's not jump to conclusions until we have all the facts." I stood up, as well, and walked around my desk. "I'll go see the appraiser right away. Maybe he'll know something about the insurance."

Darlene's eyes still flashed, but she didn't say anything. I grabbed my briefcase and headed for the door, which stood ajar. *That's just great.* The whole office had probably heard this mortifying exchange.

"Besides," I said, "it's been only two days. The Folio may turn up yet. The police are working hard to track down the thief." As if I had any insider knowledge of what the police were doing.

I held the door open for Darlene. She hiked her purse on her shoulder and took another deep breath.

"Okay," she said. "Let me know if you learn anything useful."

As soon as she left, I rushed over to my file on Eleanor and grabbed the paper on which I'd written the local appraiser's name and address. Then I hightailed it out of my office, trying not to see which of my colleagues were staring at me from their own office doors.

Satterly's Rare Books was a short drive from the office. That is, if you had a car. Since I lived so close to the square, I usually didn't have my car at work. Luckily, Edindale's bus system was pretty reliable. I walked the three short blocks to South Central Illinois University, waited about five minutes, then hopped on the bus. Four stops later, I stood on the corner of Main and Whitney, looking at the piece of paper I'd grabbed from Eleanor's file. Then I crossed my fingers, walked two doors down, and entered the dimly lit, climate-controlled bookshop owned by one Theodore Cornelius Satterly.

With a name like Theodore Cornelius Satterly, I imagined the proprietor to be a neat, bespectacled gent in tweeds. Crenshaw's long-lost twin maybe. So when I saw a portly fellow sporting faded jeans, an even more faded Smokey the Bear T-shirt, a bushy mustache, and one courageous gray comb-over walk in from the back room, I thought I must be meeting the janitor.

"Howdy, miss. What can I do you for?" he said, squeezing past a sky-high stack of books to fit himself behind the counter.

"Hi," I said, putting on my friendliest face. "I'm looking for Mr. Satterly. My name is Keli Milanni." I pulled a business card from my purse and handed it to ole Smokey.

"You're lookin' at him," he said, glancing at my card. "I'm not being sued, am I?"

I was opening my mouth to respond when Satterly burst out in melodious laughter. "Just kidding, just kidding." He hefted himself onto a stool, eyes twinkling and mustache twitching. I had a feeling this man liked to find amusement in the smallest things.

"Mr. Satterly," I began.

"Call me T.C.," he said. "Everyone does."

"T.C.," I said, trying again. "I represented Eleanor Mostriak. She brought in a copy of Shakespeare's First Folio for your appraisal. I'm not sure if you heard—"

"Oh, yes, yes," he said, sobering instantly. "So sorry to hear of her passing. Saw the obituary Saturday and couldn't believe it. Such a nice lady. Seemed healthy, full of life." T.C. shook his head and examined his fingernails.

"Did you hear about the theft, as well?" I asked.

"Theft?" He looked up questioningly.

"Yes. Um, unfortunately, on Saturday someone broke into Eleanor's home. At least, I think they broke in. Anyway, it appears they took the Folio and nothing else."

T.C.'s eyes widened, and his gray eyebrows rose halfway up his broad forehead. "Good Lord! Someone stole the Folio? It wasn't locked up in a bank?"

I shook my head sadly. "It wasn't in a bank," I said.

I watched him closely as he processed the information. He did seem to be truly surprised. After a moment, he stared wistfully out the shop window behind me. Almost to himself, he murmured, "The First Folio. Amazing condition. I held it in my hands. Right here, in my hands."

"You were confident it was legitimate, even though it hadn't been authenticated yet?"

"Oh, yeah. I've been in this business a long time. It looked like the real deal to me, and I was very interested in acquiring it. Mrs. Mostriak told me she wanted to keep the sale local." He heaved a sigh and shook his head again.

"I've never been so close to owning something so special as that. I wish to heck I could've purchased it before . . ." He stopped himself and looked at me. "Of course, my loss, if you could call it that, is nothing compared to the family's. First, they lose their mother, their grandmother. And then they lose their inheritance. What a blow, huh?"

"I know," I agreed glumly. "I feel terrible about it, too. Um, I take it Eleanor didn't mention anything about an insurance policy to you?"

"Well," T.C. said, "I know for a fact the Folio *wasn't* insured as of the time she was last here on Thursday. She asked me for an extra copy of my appraisal letter for her to give to her insurance agent."

"Then she was probably going to go with her current agent," I said half to myself. So much for the hope that there might be some unknown insurance policy out there.

For a minute, neither of us said anything, each feeling the weight of the loss.

If only the Folio would just reappear.

"T.C.," I said suddenly. "How easy will it be for the

thief to sell the Folio? And, for that matter, *where* could he or she sell it?"

"Well, now, that all depends," T.C. mused. "If it was a professional, someone with contacts in the art and antiquities world—and someone who's willing to travel anywhere in the wild blue yonder—it could be done relatively quickly. But if it's a small-time thief, they might hold on to it longer. They'll want to be careful about who they talk to. As for *where*, well, a place like my store here might be a good start."

Now it was my turn to raise my eyebrows.

T.C. chuckled. "Not because I'm a known dealer in stolen books, let me assure you. I mean a place *like* mine. Any dealer in used books would be a potential buyer for the Folio. Or a potential broker— someone who could put the thief in touch with interested private buyers. Of course, you know the first question any bookseller worth his salt will ask is, 'Where'd you get it?'"

I pondered what T.C. had said. "It seems unlikely to me that it was a professional book thief," I said. "I mean, first of all, how would they know Eleanor even had the Folio? She had just found it and wasn't making it widely known. She took it to you initially on Tuesday, and—"

"I didn't tell anyone, except my wife," T.C. cut in. "No sense in drumming up competition."

"She came to see me on Wednesday," I continued. "She mentioned she had made some phone calls to arrange a trip to the Folger Shakespeare Library in Washington, D.C., but I don't think she had actually made an appointment with anyone yet."

My wheels were spinning, but I decided I'd taken enough of T.C.'s time. "Well, I guess the police will check out all the angles," I said. "Come to think of it, though, I'm a little surprised they haven't been here to see you yet."

T.C. stroked his mustache and slowly shook his head. "I've been here all day. Haven't seen any cops, that's for sure."

I frowned. Weren't the cops trying to find the Folio? You'd think the book dealer who had valued the thing would be top on their list of people to question.

T.C. must have read my thoughts. "On Saturday I was at my in-laws in K-Town, trying to install a new dishwasher most of the day, or so it seemed like. But we went out to an early bird dinner. Good pie. But I really should have passed on that second helping." He patted his belly and broke out into another trill of laughter.

I smiled at T.C. and thanked him for his time.

Back on the bus, I stared out the window and pictured Eleanor's last days. In less than a week, she had discovered a historically significant family heirloom, carted her thrilling find around town, changed her will, and made plans for showcasing the treasure. Had the excitement been too much for her? Was that what had led to her heart attack?

Or, as Sharon intimated, had someone killed Eleanor to get the book? It was a troubling idea, but I supposed it was possible. Still, if that were the case, why not take it right away, instead of waiting until the visitation? Unless the killer had been inter-rupted and hadn't had time to look for it . . .

Ugh. If there had been any indication of foul play, surely the police would have noticed. I shook away these unpleasant thoughts and wondered what to do next. I couldn't bear to go back to the office. I pulled out my cell phone, checked the time, and sent a text.

Meet me @ the Loose in 10?

Maybe Farrah could get away for an afternoon break. Two seconds later, she replied.

Be there in 15.

Awesome. I couldn't wait to unload some of this burden onto my best bud. Gazing out the window again, I suddenly caught my breath. Was that Wes wandering into an adjacent alley? Quickly, I pulled the cord and hurried to the front of the bus. When it pulled over at the next stop, half a block from the alley, I hopped off and ran back to the place where I'd seen Wes. I was sure it was him. He even had on the same T-shirt he'd worn the night I met him.

But there was no sign of him now. I walked the length of the alley, which ran between the backside of the public library to the east and the Cozy Café and Brickman's Shoe Store to the west. At the end of the alley was a road that ran along the length of a half-empty private parking lot used by the utility company. I looked both ways and didn't see anyone in the road. Turning back, I studied the back doors of the library, the café, and the shoe store. None of them were open to the public, but I felt sure Wes must have gone into one of them.

After making a quick decision, I sent another message to Farrah.

Make it the Cozy Café instead.

Then I walked around the corner and entered the café through the front door. By this time it was mid-afternoon and the lunch rush was well over. My stomach reminded me I hadn't eaten since 7:00 a.m., so I grabbed a booth by the window and ordered right away. I got the black bean burger, no cheese, and sweet potato fries. After placing my order, I moseyed on back to the ladies' room to wash up and peek in the window to the kitchen. I could see a couple of cooks and a busboy bustling about, but there was no sign of Wes.

Farrah came in just as I got back to the table. "I already ordered. Sorry," I said. "I was starving."

"You okay?" she said, taking the seat opposite me. Then, to the waitress, she said, "I'll just have an iced tea. Thanks."

I leaned forward, propped my elbows on the table, and began rubbing my forehead. "I've had better days," I said. I filled her in on the scene with Darlene. "I just came from seeing the appraiser dude. He told me he didn't think Eleanor had insured the book yet."

"Well, that's not your fault, of course," said Farrah, defending me at once. "All you were hired to do was draw up a will, right?"

"Yeah," I said. "And I was going to represent her

in the sale of the thing, too. And I *was* looking out for her interests." I remembered Darlene's accusations and felt my face getting hot again. "I advised Eleanor to take the Folio to the bank. And I would have told her to have it insured . . ." I trailed off and shook my head.

Farrah reached over and patted my hand. "I'm sorry she died, sweetie. And it really sucks that somebody stole her Shakespeare book. I mean, who would do that? Who even knew where it was?"

The waitress, a college student with short strawberry-blond hair and a tiny nose ring, arrived with my food and Farrah's tea.

Addressing the waitress, I said, "Do you happen to know Wes Callahan?"

She tilted her head, nose ring flashing in the sunlight. "Wes Callahan," she repeated. "I don't think so. Should I?"

"I thought he might have come in here a little while ago. Was there a good-looking guy here? About six feet, dark hair, blue T-shirt. Tattoo around his arm."

"Not lately," said the waitress. "I think I would've noticed. Too bad, though. Sounds nice."

After she left, Farrah looked at me accusingly. "Is that why we're here? You're stalking Rock Star now?"

I bit into my burger and shook my head. Farrah snatched a fry from my plate and waited for me to answer.

"I saw him in the alley behind here," I said, then took a sip of water. "I just thought it might be nice to run into him, you know? We've hung out, briefly, only a couple of times. But each time, I've felt like there could be something there."

"Oh, there's something there, all right," said Farrah, nodding. "You don't have to explain yourself to me."

I laughed shortly, then frowned again. "Well, there's not going to be much of a chance for anything if he blames me like his mom does." I heaved an exaggerated sigh. "I just wish that book would turn up."

"Turn up?" echoed Farrah. "That's not likely, is it? It could be anyplace, right? I mean, like, in a million possible hiding places from here to Belarus."

"Yeah, but wait," I said, leaning forward. "I've been thinking about this. There may be a million possible hiding places, but there aren't a million possible suspects. Not very many people knew about the book."

Farrah raised one eyebrow. "Go on," she said. "What are you getting at?"

"Eleanor had the book for only five days. *Five days.* And it's not like she went to the press or anything. She told very few people, I'm pretty sure. Let's see." I raised my thumb as I started counting. "There's her family, of course. And the book dealer, this T.C. character I just met. And me. And, well, my law office knew about it."

"Okay," said Farrah. "What about friends? Neighbors? Acquaintances?"

I shook my head. "I don't know," I said. "I really don't think she was spreading it around that much. I don't remember hearing anyone talking about it at the memorial service. I kind of think she was keeping it as a surprise for her friends."

"Hmm," said Farrah thoughtfully. "I suppose we know she didn't tell her banker or insurance agent, because she didn't lock it up or insure it."

"Right." I winced. "Don't remind me."

"Sorry," said Farrah. "But, you know, you may be right about the short list of suspects. Too bad you can't talk to her daughter about who else knew about the book. What about the cousin you were telling me about? Sharon?"

I shrugged. "I'm really not sure where I stand with the rest of the family. But I've got to assume they're all about as happy as Darlene. Honestly, I'm not in such a big rush to talk to her again."

"Okay," said Farrah, stirring her tea with a straw. "So, do we know when exactly the Folio was taken? You said the family called the police yesterday?"

"Yeah. But here's the thing. Darlene remembered seeing it before the visitation, at around four o'clock or so. And then, afterward, she noticed it wasn't where she had seen it before. That was around eight thirty, I think. The family was heading someplace for a late potluck dinner or something."

"So the robbery occurred during the visitation?"

"It looks that way," I agreed.

"Unless Darlene was lying," said Farrah. "She may have conveniently manufactured her own alibi."

I shook my head. "I don't think so. I mean, anything is possible, but I'd bet my next paycheck she was being sincere. If I were a betting woman, that is."

"Okay. Then does that mean the whole family is off the hook? Weren't they all at the visitation?"

I pondered these questions. "I'll have to make a list of all the family members who were in town. I believe Eleanor's will names all of them. I don't know if it's possible to get ahold of the guest book from the funeral home. I imagine Darlene has that. Anyway, it wouldn't really prove anything. People were coming and going throughout the whole thing." I stared out the café window as I recalled all the people I'd met and observed at the visitation. And the ones I hadn't seen.

"What is it?" said Farrah, reading my thoughts.

"There were two family members who left early. And from what Eleanor told me, they were among the first to see the Folio after she found it."

"Who?"

"Darlene's sons. Wes and Rob."

CHAPTER 8

The next morning, when I arrived at my office, I was surprised to find a bouquet of pink and purple roses in the middle of my desk. No card. Puzzled, I lifted the flowers to my face, closed my eyes, and inhaled the heavenly sweet scent. I didn't know who had left the gift, but I was cheered by it. I took it as a sign that this day wasn't going to be as bad as I thought.

I walked up to the reception area to see about a vase. Julie was already pulling a large mason jar out from under her desk as I approached. She handed it to me with a pleased expression. "You have a secret admirer," she said teasingly.

"Did you see who brought them in?" I asked. "And was he dark-haired, well built, and sexy-scruffy?" I wanted to ask.

"Well . . ." She shrugged, with a sly grin. "Some people might call him a brownnoser, but I'd call him supersweet." She tilted her head toward the hall and rolled her eyes toward Jeremy's office.

All morning I kept looking for an opportunity to

catch Jeremy alone, but it never happened. Between that and worrying about Darlene and the Folio, I was finding it hard to concentrate on work. But I did manage to photocopy the pages from Eleanor's will that listed all her living relatives. I put a line through the ones I knew weren't in town Saturday evening, based on what Sharon had told me. After hesitating for a second, I went ahead and put a line through Darlene's and Sharon's names, too. I started to cross out Kirk's name, as well, assuming that both of Eleanor's children would surely have been at the visitation the whole time. But then I remembered he had come in from outside while I was talking with Darlene. Better hold off on ruling him out.

I finally had a chance to see Jeremy that afternoon at the in-house seminar the partners had arranged. As all the attorneys gathered around the long table in the conference room, I snagged the empty spot next to Jeremy. He glanced at me and winked. While Crenshaw set up his PowerPoint presentation and began introducing himself—as if we didn't all already know everything we wanted to know about him—I opened my notebook and wrote the words *Thank you* on the first line. I slid the notebook in front of Jeremy, and he looked down at it. I was watching him, expecting to get another wink. Instead, he leaned over to whisper in my ear.

"You had a rough day yesterday, with that bitch screaming at you and everything. I thought you could use some cheering up."

Okay, now I was confused. The flowers had

nothing to do with the other night? These weren't "I'm sorry I made a drunken fool of myself and created a totally awkward work situation" flowers?

Before I had time to analyze it, a couple of latecomers squeezed in at the table, causing Jeremy to move his chair closer to mine. Then the lights dimmed and the presentation began.

Five minutes later I nearly jumped out of my seat when I felt Jeremy's knee touching mine under the table. *What the holy hell?*

I kept my eyes fixed firmly on the screen and noticed in my peripheral vision that Jeremy seemed to be watching the screen, too. Then he started taking notes, as casual as can be. I waited for him to move over, and he did, all right— even closer. Our thighs were touching now.

Okay, I reasoned to myself. *This is probably just that guy thing, where they gotta spread out and let their boys have some breathing room. Right?* As oblivious as Jeremy often was, he probably wasn't even aware he was encroaching on my space.

I was so irritated with myself for not moving away. Even worse, I was sort of liking it. *Damn. Damn. Damn.* Here I was, touching the Untouchable. I really needed to get myself a boyfriend.

The second the presentation ended, I scooted my chair back and darted out of the room. I was nearly to my office when I was stopped by a sharp voice behind me.

"Keli! Could I see you in my office, please?"

Oh. Shit. How could she have seen what happened under the table? Was it that obvious? Burning with embarrassment, I turned to see Beverly already walking away, expecting that I would follow her.

We passed through her cozy lounge and went directly into her spotless office. The mahogany desk gleamed under orderly stacks of legal documents. Souvenirs from her travels decorated the room, including a large African mask, which now seemed to stare reproachfully down at me. Judging me.

Beverly took her seat behind the desk, and I sat down in one of the client chairs facing her. She regarded me over red-framed bifocals.

"Keli, you didn't tell me you had a visit from Darlene Callahan yesterday."

"Oh." *Of course.* "Well, there wasn't much to tell."

"That's not the way I hear it," Beverly said. "A number of your colleagues informed me that Ms. Callahan was quite upset."

"She *was* upset, understandably. She just lost her mother and then the Folio. And, unfortunately, her mother passed away before having the Folio insured." I tried to keep my voice steady. If I didn't make a big deal over this, maybe Beverly would let it go.

"Yes," said Beverly. "These are unfortunate circumstances. Also unfortunate is the fact that another client overheard your exchange with Ms. Callahan."

I cringed. "I am so sorry, Beverly. I should have closed my office door."

"That might have been a wise idea. However, it wouldn't have solved this problem. The fact is, not only is Ms. Callahan upset, but it also sounds like she blames you."

"Beverly—" I began, but she held up her hand, cutting off any excuse I might offer.

"You need to get a handle on this, Keli. You need to undertake major damage control. Fix things with the family."

"I know Darlene's son," I offered. "Maybe if I talked to him . . ."

"If you think that might make a difference, then by all means talk to him. The sooner the better."

I glanced at the clock behind Beverly's desk. It was only 3:50 p.m.

"Go ahead," said Beverly, looking grim. "Go home early if you need to. Just nip this in the bud."

I walked home quickly, the scene in Beverly's office looping in my mind. She might not have reprimanded me, not officially, but I still felt scolded. I hadn't felt this way since my parents chewed me out in the ninth grade for skipping school. It was not a good feeling.

I let myself in, dropped my bag by the door, kicked off my shoes, and headed straight for the living room couch. After flopping down on my back, I stretched out and closed my eyes. *Breathe*, I commanded myself. My house was so quiet, I could hear the clock ticking in the small guest room I used as an overflow closet. *Maybe I should adopt a cat*, I thought halfheartedly. I longed to call Farrah, but I didn't want to bother her at work.

What should I do? After a couple more long breaths, I sat up and rubbed my temples. Then I reached for my laptop on the coffee table, propped it on my knees, and started typing. *Wesley Callahan, Edindale*. Bingo. He had a Facebook page, and, damn, what a cute picture. I stared for a second, then shook my head and clicked. Private. It figured. Did I want to send a friend request? Um . . . maybe later.

I searched the other Callahans and found an address and a phone number for Darlene. I wasn't about to call her. I also found an address, but no phone number, for Wes's brother, Rob. I recognized the address, an apartment complex called Woodbine Village. As I recalled from one or two parties I'd attended during law school, it was occupied mainly by older university students. It was in a woodsy area near the campus lake. The rail trail passed behind the place.

But forget Rob. Wes was the guy I really wanted to see. Might as well return to the place where I'd found him twice before. I took about ten minutes to freshen up, trade my trousers for skinny denim capris, and remove my blazer. The black cami would do. Then I ran a brush through my hair, slipped on some cute beaded sandals, and walked out to find my silver-blue Fusion where I'd left it parked on the street.

It was just past five o'clock when I arrived at the Loose Rock, and happy hour was already well under way. I went straight to the bar, hoping to get lucky again, but Wes was nowhere to be seen. I would have chatted up the bartender, Gary, but he was clearly too busy to talk. Instead, I walked toward the back and peeked through the kitchen door to look for Jimi. No sign of him there, so I went around to a door marked PRIVATE and rapped loudly. A couple of seconds passed, and the door swung open. Jimi wore a scowl, which he promptly dropped when he saw me.

"Oh. Hey, Keli. What's the matter?"

"Hi, Jimi. Nothing's the matter. I was actually looking for Wes. Have you seen him?"

"He's not here. Sorry."

Okay, this was really awkward, but I had to do it. Swallowing my pride, I pressed on. "Could you give me his number? I really need to talk to him."

Jimi hesitated, then shrugged. "Sure, I guess." He pulled out his phone. "Ready?"

I took my phone from my purse and entered the number as Jimi read it. It had a 212 area code, which made me wonder if Wes would eventually be going back to New York.

"Thanks a bunch," I said. Then, as an afterthought, casual as can be, I added, "Hey, so where is Wes staying, anyway? Not with his parents, right?"

"Uh, no." Jimi looked away, stroked his goatee, and glanced at the floor.

What's with the evasive maneuvers? I wondered.

He shrugged again. "He's staying with some friends or something, I think. Look, Keli, I gotta finish up with inventory and check on things in the kitchen. See you later, okay?"

"Yeah, okay." I said it to myself, as he had already closed the door. *Strange.*

But I didn't waste any time worrying about Jimi. I hurried out to my car, where I could sit quietly and call Wes. Nervously, I punched in the number and waited. Two rings, three rings, four.

"Hi. This is Wes. Can't take your call right now. Leave me a message and I'll catch up with ya later." *Beep*.

With my heart in my throat—What was I? Twelve years old?—I left a message. "Hi, Wes. This is Keli Milanni. Give me a call when you get a chance. I'm calling from my cell. Um, I know your mom is upset with me. And, uh, I was hoping I could talk to you. Bye."

Ugh. I felt like such a dork. I immediately called Farrah, but she didn't pick up, either. So I started driving, no clear destination in mind. Sitting at a stoplight, I absentmindedly fingered the charm Mila had given me, which now dangled from my keychain. When the light changed, I turned left and soon found myself heading toward Woodbine Village. It seemed doubtful that Wes would be staying with his brother, considering the chilly relationship they seemed to have. Still, maybe I would learn something from Rob.

From the outside, number 103 looked like a lot of the other apartments. Except this stoop had a lawn chair instead of potted flowers. The worn welcome mat looked like an artifact from the 1970s, and the black handrail suffered from rusty measles. A crushed beer can lay forlornly on the ground by the steps. *Classy*.

On the other hand, the trees surrounding the complex were mature and beautiful. Before knocking on the door, I fixed my gaze on the leafy branches and took a deep, centering breath. Now I was ready for whatever reception I might get from this Callahan son.

Rob opened the door as I raised my arm to knock a second time. For a moment I felt a little flustered, as I took in how cute he looked, standing there barefoot, in gym shorts and a fresh white T-shirt. His sandy hair was damp, as if he'd just gotten out of the shower.

"Hi," I said brightly, recovering myself. "Rob, I'm sorry to drop in unannounced like this. I'm Keli Milanni. We met at your grandmother's house on Sunday."

"Sure. I remember," he said. Was that an amused look in those crinkly blue eyes? "You're the lawyer, right?"

"Yeah," I said. "I was wondering if I could talk to you for a minute."

"Uh . . ." He paused, looked over his shoulder, then ushered me in. "Sure. Uh, don't mind the mess. I'm barely home long enough to clean." Moving quickly, he cleared off a fuzzy brown armchair, tossing a stack of newspapers to the floor and wadding up a wrinkled shirt, which he then lobbed into an open doorway around the corner. "Have a seat."

"Thanks," I said, trying my best not to look at the crumpled tissue lying on the floor by my feet. "Is this a bad time?"

Still dashing around the room, Rob gathered an armful of empty cans and tossed them noisily into a kitchen trash can. He spoke to me through an opening under some cabinets built over a countertop bar that divided the living room from the kitchen. "No, it's fine. I just got home from the gym a little bit ago. I worked just a half day today. The job was slow. Want a beer?"

"Oh, sure," I said. Might as well be sociable. "What kind of work do you do?"

Rob came around the bar with two cans of beer. He handed me one, then sat on the couch and popped open the other. "I'm a CPA," he said. "I work for Boone, the tax preparation service. It's pretty seasonal, as you can imagine."

"Oh, sure," I said, nodding my head. I took a sip, feeling increasingly self-conscious. Now that I was here, I had no idea what to say. And Rob, with that disconcerting twinkle in his eyes, stared at me, not making this any easier.

I cleared my throat and tried for honesty. "So, Rob, I feel really bad about the Folio being stolen. Your mom came to see me yesterday, and she seemed really upset."

Rob looked at me and raised his eyebrows. Then he nodded his head slowly, so I went on.

"Um, so the other day I was talking to Wes, and he said he was going to try to track down the thief." At least he had implied he would. Hadn't he? "I'd really like to help, if I can. Is, um . . . Wes isn't staying here, is he?"

Rob snorted. "No," he said flatly. "Big brother is not staying here."

"Anyway, do you have any theories about the theft?"

Rob looked down at his hands and slowly shook

his head. "No idea. I mean, it was really valuable. It shouldn't have been just lying around Grandma's house. But, of course, she didn't expect to die so suddenly. I guess she didn't have time to put it someplace safer."

"Yeah," I agreed. "I guess not."

I looked around Rob's apartment, trying to figure him out. Evidently, he was employed, and he must have graduated at least five years ago. But from what I could see, his place was decorated much like a college dorm. Art posters covered one wall, and a large CD collection filled metal shelves on another. Directly opposite the couch, a flat-screen TV perched upon an overturned milk crate. In the short hallway, which presumably led to the bedroom and bathroom, I spotted an interesting wood carving hanging next to a small collection of felt sports pennants. I stood up and walked over to read the message on the carving. LORD, WHAT FOOLS THESE MORTALS BE.

Coming up behind me, Rob flipped on the hall light. "It's probably dusty," he said, wiping a finger along the top of the carving.

For a second, the scent of Rob's aftershave made me slightly woozy. Or maybe it was his proximity. I took a step back. "This is nice," I said, pointing to the carving.

"It was my grandpa Frank's. It was one of his favorite sayings. He said it all the time. Somebody made this for him, I think. He had it hanging in his study."

"Did he quote Shakespeare a lot?" I asked.

"Shakespeare?" said Rob, his face a blank. "I thought it was from the Bible."

I suppressed a grin. "I'm pretty sure it's Shakespeare," I said.

Rob shrugged. "Well, whatever. It was pretty funny whenever Grandpa said it."

"Who made it?" I asked.

Rob shrugged again. "No idea."

"May I?" I took the carving from the wall and turned it over. Sure enough, there was a name written in black pen in the corner. "Wendell Knotts," I read out loud. I glanced up at Rob, but he just shook his head.

I didn't think I was going to get any useful information from Rob, so I replaced the carving and walked back to the living room.

"I should get going." I fished a business card from my purse and handed it to Rob. "But please give me a call if you think of anything that might lead to the Folio. I really do want to help, and I'm not sure how much success the police are having at the moment."

"Yeah, okay," said Rob, holding the door open for me. "It would be nice if the book turns up, but I'm really not losing any sleep over it. I mean, finding the book won't bring Grandma back. Plus, we were gonna sell it, anyway. It might take a little time for the insurance company to pay up, but they will eventually. So, it's all the same."

Rob gave me a reassuring smile, as if I shouldn't be worrying my pretty little head over such a nonissue. I guess he didn't speak to his mother often. Well, far be it for me to set him straight.

I was stepping onto his front stoop when I turned back for one last question. "By the way, do you know where your brother's staying?"

Rob scoffed in reply. "Sorry," he said. "What's that saying? I'm not my brother's keeper. Is that Shakespeare, too?"

I allowed a rueful smile as I shook my head. "No," I said. "That one, I do believe, *is* from the Bible."

CHAPTER 9

It was super early when I left for work Wednesday morning—like "sun barely up, dark reception area" early. Still, Crenshaw's office light was on, and the door was slightly ajar. I also heard someone else's voice down the hall, possibly on the phone or maybe dictating into a recorder. I slipped into my office, flipped on the light, and shut the door. I wanted to work in peace for a while.

After turning on my computer and pulling out the thermos of hot orange pekoe I had brought from home, I listened to my voice mail. I had four new messages: an old client calling to make an appointment to update her will, a potential new client about to buy a house, a colleague asking if I'd had a chance to review the contract he sent me . . . and a surprise phone call from a familiar voice.

"Hello, Ms. Keli Milanni! T.C. Satterly here. Satterly's Rare Books. Listen, I cannot stop thinking about the Folio. The police never did pay me a visit, and, well, time is precious. Now, you asked me where somebody might try to locate a buyer for the

Folio. I've already called all my book-dealer peers all over the area, telling them to keep a lookout. But that's about all I can do. I'm no Perry Mason, you know. Heh-heh. But if I did want to poke around some—or if Perry Mason were here, ha-ha—I'd tell him he might want to pay a visit to the university. The university English program, I'm pretty sure, has a course on Shakespeare, and one of the professors there is a Shakespeare expert. Max Eisenberry's the name. An expert like that would know all about the Folio and might have some ideas on the market for such works. Anyhoo, just wanted to pass along that suggestion. Bye now."

I sat there, looking at my phone, for a full minute after hearing T.C.'s message. Then I shook my head and grabbed a file folder from the top of a nearby cabinet. I had a contract to review and phone calls to return. Shakespeare was going to have to wait.

No sooner had I taken out my red pen than the phone rang. Caller ID told me it was Beverly. I swallowed hard and picked up.

"Good morning, Beverly."

"Keli, could you please come to my office?"

"Uh." I looked at the contract on my desk, and the words blurred together.

"Now please." *Click.*

"Shit." I muttered under my breath, closed the file, and walked reluctantly to Beverly's office. When I got there, I found Beverly, Randall, and Kris in the lounge, having coffee and talking quietly, like they were in some secret meeting for senior partners only. Except that Crenshaw was there, too.

Beverly looked up when I entered and set down her coffee cup. "Keli, I need to ask you something."

I sat on the edge of the couch and didn't say anything. The room was hushed, except for the sound of light raindrops that began to patter against the window behind Beverly.

"Did you have a retainer agreement with Eleanor Mostriak?"

"No," I said, meeting Beverly's stern gaze. "I was charging her the standard flat fee for preparing a will. She paid it the first day."

"And the book?"

"She said she'd like me to assist her with the sale, but we didn't discuss details. She was eager to complete the will. I planned to define my scope later. . . ." My voice trailed off, and my palms felt moist. The words sounded lame, even to my own ears.

Beverly picked up a piece of paper lying on the end table next to her chair. It appeared to be a letter. "This is from Pella Schumaker," she said. "Darlene Callahan's lawyer. It's a demand letter."

"Wh-what does she want?" Now I felt short of breath and wished desperately for a glass of water.

Randall answered, "Oh, just the value of the Folio, that's all. Either we pay to cover her loss, or else they slap our firm with a malpractice action."

"That's crazy!" I exclaimed. "I didn't do anything wrong. And Eleanor was my client, not Darlene. She has no basis for a malpractice claim."

Crenshaw cleared his throat. "I think the point, if I may, is the poor publicity. I had a disturbing conversation last night with Edgar Harrison regarding the loss of the Folio. He told me that, due to recent events, he is very concerned about our firm's trustworthiness. He is, in fact, on the verge of disassociating himself and his business from Olsen, Sykes, and Rafferty."

"Oh, no," I groaned. Edgar Harrison owned half of Edindale. The firm had practically been built on the backs of the Harrison family and their legal needs.

It was then that I noticed the file folder and legal pad on Kris's lap. She seemed to be taking notes on this meeting. What was going on? I felt a sinking feeling in the pit of my stomach.

Beverly was never one to beat around the bush. "Keli, I am not pleased to do this, but I feel we have no choice. For the good of the firm, we are asking you to resign."

Two things happened in the next moment. I felt the floor drop away beneath me, and the phone in Beverly's inner office began to ring. She ignored the phone, and while it rang, I sank back into the couch and looked around incredulously. Everyone was looking anyplace but at me. Crenshaw watched Beverly, a grim expression on his rigid face. Or maybe it was smug. Kris wrote furiously on her notepad. Randall scowled out the window. And Beverly glanced at the portrait of her grandfather above the mantel. When the phone stopped ringing, Beverly stood up.

"Keli, we had intended to call you in at the end of the day. But since you arrived so early, we decided it was much wiser not to delay. So, now I think you should clear out your office before the others start arriving."

My head was swimming. I could not comprehend what she was saying.

"Keli." Kris spoke up for the first time, pushed her short hair behind her ear. "We all agreed we wanted to give you the courtesy of allowing you to resign, rather than terminating your employment. So, if you'll just sign here."

I ignored the document she tried to give me and appealed to my mentor. My mother figure. My friend. "Beverly, please. I don't want to resign. This seems so rash, so extreme. Can't we just—"

The phone began to ring again. Beverly raised a finger, indicating we should wait for her, and went to answer the phone. While she was gone, I closed my eyes and took a deep, steadying breath. Exhaling slowly, I visualized the release of everything negative that was pent up inside me: the shame, the guilt, the fear. I took another slow, deep breath. *I am calm*, I told myself. *I am confident. I am competent. I am okay, no matter what.*

I opened my eyes and saw Crenshaw staring at me, eyes narrowed. *I am so screwed.*

Beverly returned but didn't sit down. "Well," she said, looking at her watch, "it's almost eight o'clock. Keli, I'm sure you understand why it would be best for the firm if you stepped down. I'm very sorry, but—"

"I have another idea," I said, cutting Beverly off. I sat up straight, trying to convey the confidence I so totally did not feel. But I rushed headlong, anyway. "What if I take a leave of absence instead?

Harrison, and whoever else might be worried, can rest assured that you're dealing with me and thoroughly investigating and addressing any perceived breach of trust. As for Darlene and that wacky letter, I'm sure that's her attorney blowing smoke, hoping we'll freak out and offer a nice big settlement. There's no way she really expects us to pay two million dollars."

Beverly frowned impatiently, but I thought I detected a slight softening in her countenance.

"Plus," I went on, "the Folio may be found. Efforts are under way to trace several leads even as we speak." Okay, that last bit might have been a slight exaggeration. But I, for one, would be tracing a lead as soon as I could hightail it over to the university.

Beverly looked at Randall, who shrugged, and at Kris, who shuffled through the papers on her lap.

"Keli has two weeks of unused vacation," Kris reported. "Unpaid leave is also an option."

"Okay," Beverly said abruptly. "You can use up that vacation time. Starting today. After that, we'll see where we are."

"Oh, thank you!" I stood up in a flood of relief. But Beverly was already turning back to her office. Randall and Kris headed to the door.

Before leaving, Kris looked back and said softly, "Good luck."

I was preparing to follow them out when Crenshaw again cleared his throat. He stood by the window, hands behind his back, brow furrowed wistfully. "Let us hope," he said, "that this unpleasant business will have been much ado about nothing."

"Yeah," I said, wanting to kick him in the "much ado." "Let's hope so."

"I was fired!"

"What!"

"Well, asked to resign. Same thing."

Farrah ushered me into her spacious apartment, where I followed her around while she got ready for work. She was going to be "in the field" today, visiting various law offices to demonstrate her company's legal research software, and she didn't have to be at the first location until 9:30 a.m. It was one of the many perks of her nontraditional law job.

"Nuh-uh," she said. "You were not fired. Impossible. They love you at that place. *Everybody* loves you."

"I *nearly* was fired. I swear!"

Farrah looked at me skeptically in her bathroom mirror. But by the time she finished putting on her makeup, during which I relayed the details of my awful morning, she regarded me with more sympathy.

"That really blows," she said. "And with no time to plan a proper vacation getaway. I take it you're not going away, right?"

"Of course not. I've got a thief to catch."

"Right." Farrah laughed. "Keli Milanni, girl detective. No problem." Farrah stepped into her bedroom for a pair of earrings and put them in while she walked to the kitchen. "Coffee?" she said. "I'm making it to go, but I'll brew some for you, too."

"No, thanks," I said, sliding onto a stool at her granite kitchen island. "Listen, Farrah, I'm serious. Like I said the other day, the suspect list isn't that long. Plus, I don't think the Folio is going to be that easy to fence. I had a call from T.C. Satterly, and he suggested I talk with a Shakespeare expert at the university."

"Hmm." Farrah popped a raisin bagel in her toaster, then turned to face me. "You really are going to play investigator on this, aren't you?"

I nodded. "I have to. It may be the only way to save my job."

"In that case," she said, "count me in."

"Really?"

"Yeah. I'll be the Cagney to your Lacey. The Velma to your Daphne."

"Um, don't you mean the Daphne to my Velma?"

"No way. I'm Velma. You're Daphne."

"You are way more—" I stopped myself and hopped up to give her a hug. "Thank you," I said. Then I opened a cabinet, grabbed a mug, and helped myself to some of her coffee.

"So, partner," I said, "any suggestions?"

"Well," said Farrah, looking thoughtful as she spread cream cheese on her bagel, "I know someone at the police station. A friend of Jake's. I'll make a call and see if there's any public info available. You go ahead and follow that lead you have today. Then we'll meet up this evening and do what any good detective would do."

"What's that?" I said.

"Return to the scene of the crime."

* * *

Without too much trouble, I found my way to McCallister Hall, a turn-of-the-century redbrick building in the original quad of SCIU's sprawling green campus. Unlike the shiny modern law school building, where I'd spent the bulk of my time at SCIU, McCallister Hall retained a quaint, traditional feel. It even had the musty aroma of old books and polished wood, like the old-fashioned county courthouse where I'd interned one summer. Without central air, the place was warm but not stifling. I climbed the marble staircase to the second floor, which housed the English Department, and located the office of Dr. Max Eisenberry. According to the sign on the door, Professor Eisenberry would be back for office hours in about twenty minutes.

To kill time, I wandered around, peeking into classrooms and perusing bulletin boards. Although the summer session had started a week ago, the halls were quiet and largely empty, save for two students reading in a small lounge area in one corner of the floor. I watched them for a second and felt a twinge of nostalgia for my own college days. All that knowledge just waiting to be lapped up. All those new ideas and theories to learn and research. All that reading. All the homework.

Okay, maybe I didn't miss it quite so much, after all. Besides, the education part was really only half the college experience. The other half was the newfound independence and pursuit of f-u-n. For the first two years of undergrad, this included a conscientious determination on the part of my friends and me to sample—er, date—a variety of new and interesting college boys. That is, until Mick came along. Once he and I hooked up, that was it. We were inseparable. We were in love. We were gonna take on the world together.

And then we weren't.

For a moment I stood in place, eyes ahead but unseeing, all my attention directed to the past. And then the past dissolved as the words on a flyer in front of me came into focus: SHAKESPEARE'S *A MIDSUMMER NIGHT'S DREAM*, PERFORMED BY THE SCIU DRAMA TROUPE. EDINDALE RENAISSANCE FAIRE, SATURDAY, JUNE 22.

Shakespeare. Right. The reason I was here. I turned back toward Professor Eisenberry's office as two people approached, presumably the prof and a student. Dr. Eisenberry was younger than I expected, and sported a trim brown beard, Dockers, and a short-sleeved, buttoned-up cotton shirt. The student was an earnest-looking redhead who wore a denim skirt and was carrying a patchwork hobo bag. They paused before the office door and glanced at me as I walked up.

"Dr. Eisenberry?" I said pleasantly.

The young man raised his eyebrows in surprise, while the redhead answered. "That would be me," she said.

"Oh! Sorry," I said.

I stood there like an idiot while she pulled some keys from her bag and unlocked the door.

She disappeared inside and returned at once with
a book, which she handed to the well-dressed guy.

"Thanks," he said to her. Then he threw a look my
way that was a mixture of disbelief and amusement.

Damn. That was two times in one week I'd pre-
judged a person based solely on their name. How
unenlightened of me.

"I'm really sorry," I said again to the professor. "I
thought Max—"

"Short for Maxine," she said. "Not a problem.
What can I do for you?"

I took a breath and plowed ahead. "My name is
Keli Milanni. I'm an attorney who represented a
woman who owned a copy of Shakespeare's First
Folio. Recently, my client passed away, and the Folio
was apparently stolen."

"Come on in," she said.

Her office was small but tidy. A large window
dominated one wall, offering a nice view of the
quad below. Bookshelves lined the other walls, surrounding a metal desk that was squeezed into the
corner. There were few decorations, just a wall calendar and a framed photo of the teacher and her
cute little family of three—teacher, hubby, and a
dolly of a baby with red hair like her mommy. I
smiled at the photo as I settled into the single guest
chair next to the desk. Professor Eisenberry took
her seat behind the desk and regarded me with interest.

"You don't seem to be surprised," I said.

"No. I heard about the Mostriak Folio," she responded. "Word gets around. It's a shame it wasn't

examined and authenticated before it disappeared. Otherwise, there would probably be more publicity around the theft. As it happened, we learned the Folio was lost before we even knew it was found. It's almost like one of Shakespeare's own dream scenarios, really."

Hmm. Okay. I didn't know about all that. But as far as I was concerned, the theft was going to cause a tragedy for my career if the plot didn't turn around real soon.

"Well," I said, "I feel terrible about the whole thing. And I was wondering if you might have any ideas about where someone might try to sell the Folio. Also, even if it does turn up, will it even be possible to know it's the Mostriak Folio, as you say? I understand there were more than two hundred copies."

"Actually," she said, "there were seven hundred fifty originally printed. Around two hundred twenty copies are known to exist today. But those aren't just floating around out there. Eighty-some copies are at the Folger Library in D.C. Several copies are at the British Library, and several more at a university in Japan. All the known copies have been indexed and described, down to the smallest detail. For example, there are differences in binding and condition, et cetera. So, if a previously unknown copy were suddenly to appear at an auction house, it *could* be the stolen copy. The coincidence of having an unindexed copy appear soon after one was stolen might lead you to presume they are one and the same copy. But, whether or not such a presumption would hold up in a court of law, I have no idea. You would know better than I."

"Right." I nodded glumly. Without some documentation on Eleanor's copy, something to identify it, it would be virtually impossible to prove that a newly surfaced copy of the Folio was *her* copy, rather than some unindexed copy. Unless . . .

"I wonder," I said, thinking aloud, "if maybe there was a description of this copy at one time. Eleanor Mostriak's husband, Frank, inherited the book from his uncle, who was a collector. Maybe the uncle had it authenticated. Maybe there *is* a record on this copy someplace."

"Well, I'd say that's a highly likely probability."

Yay! I brightened at the professor's words. But then I slumped in my chair again, as I realized I had no idea what to do next. Ever patient, the good Dr. Eisenberry had the answer for me again.

"You know who you should talk to? My predecessor, the former Shakespeare Instructor here. He retired after more than half a century of teaching, and even then I don't think he slowed down much. Now, here's a true-blue, dyed-in-the-wool Shakespearean scholar for you. If he doesn't already know the particulars on the missing Folio, he'll at least know where to turn. I have his number here somewhere."

While she rummaged through a desk drawer, I noticed a copy of the flyer about the Renaissance Faire lying on the edge of her desk. I turned it around and traced the black-and-white comedy and tragedy masks that adorned one corner of the flyer. "Is there always a play at the Renaissance Faire?"

I asked. "When I was in law school here, I seem to remember the festival being mostly about food and drink, with some juggling and jousting and merry music thrown in."

The professor looked up. "Oh, this is the second year the drama department has participated, I believe. They had a Shakespeare in the Park program some years ago. They switched to a more modern playbook for a while, and now they're back to Shakespeare. I'm helping out in an advisory capacity."

She turned back to her drawer and pulled out a yellowed business card. "Here it is," she said. Then she paused, rested her elbows on the desk, and stared at the flyer. "You know what?" she said. "If you want to find potential buyers for the First Folio, this would be a pretty good starting place." She tapped the flyer, and I followed her gaze. In smaller lettering toward the bottom, it said 12TH ANNUAL LITERARY CONVENTION, 9:00–4:00, UNIVERSITY BALLROOM.

"Literary Convention?" I said.

"It's a literary conference that coincides with the Renaissance Faire each year. Actually, it's not so much for students. It's more of a networking event for those in the rare-books business. The head of the English Department helps to organize it."

"Rare books, huh? Like Satterly's Rare Books downtown?"

"Sure. Dealers and collectors from all over the state tend to come to LitCon, as they call it. And I'm sure they'll be buzzing about the Mostriak Folio, authenticated or not."

"Wow," I said, halfway to myself. "I wonder if the thief knows about this."

"You might ask Dr. Knotts about LitCon. I don't think he's missed one yet."

I raised my eyebrows in question, and Dr. Eisenberry handed me the card she had retrieved. "The retired professor I was telling you about."

I took the card and glanced at the name with a start. The former professor of Shakespeare was none other than Wendell Knotts. The same name I had seen on the back of the carving in Rob's apartment.

CHAPTER 10

Farrah picked me up at 4:00 p.m. in her sporty blue hatchback, and we zipped on over to Eleanor's house. During the fifteen-minute drive, I filled her in on what I'd learned from Max Eisenberry, and she told me what she had found out from her police officer contact.

"Jake's buddy, Dave, was eager to help," she said. "He's married, has a young family, and wants Jake to settle down, too. He's hoping we'll get back together."

"Oh?" I'd been through a Jake breakup with Farrah before. I knew better than to comment on their relationship, one way or another.

"So I let him think it was a possibility. I told him to tell Jake hello from me, you know?"

"Nice touch," I said. "So, what could he tell you?"

"About Jake?"

"No, silly. About the case."

"Oh, yeah. Well, the police don't know much more than we do—which, of course, isn't much. It looks like they're referring this case to the state.

The state police have a Bureau of Stolen Arts and Antiquities, or something like that. Dave wasn't sure if the referral had actually been made yet, but he did say Shakley and Buchanan have moved on to other assignments."

Terrific. While I kept telling people the cops were all over this case, they were really dragging their heels and passing the buck. All the more reason to take matters into my own hands. But as we rounded the corner onto Willow Street and the big yellow house came into view, I felt the confidence seep right out of the bottom of my feet. "Farrah, I really don't know what we hope to find here," I said as she parked by the curb. "I guess it would be nice if we found some evidence of a break-in."

"Mm-hmm," Farrah murmured, shutting off her car and peering through the side window.

"Because," I went on, "if there was no break-in, then what we're looking at is an inside job, right? Somebody in the family. And I really don't want it to be somebody in the family."

"Speaking of which," said Farrah. "Whose car is that in the driveway?"

It was a dusty-looking black two-door, with a bug-spattered windshield. We stepped out of Farrah's car and ventured over to look inside it. Fast-food wrappers littered the passenger seat, and the back-seat so resembled a gym locker—with baseball bat and glove, tennis shoes, duffel bag, and other such guy stuff—that we could practically smell it through the windows.

"Something tells me this isn't Darlene's."

"Gotta be Rob's," I said. "I've been in Wes's car."

We looked at each other, and I shrugged. Up to the front door we went. Along the way I noticed that a few of the decorative stones lining the front path had been pushed out of place. And the lawn appeared to be several days overdue for a trimming. Farrah rang the bell. A few seconds passed, and then I saw a curtain move in the living room window. I reached over to press the bell again. Finally, the door opened and Rob stood there, looking a little sheepish and trying to cover it up. He had that cute college boy look going on again, with gym shorts, a rumpled sweatshirt, and a baseball cap pushed back to reveal mischievous blue eyes.

"Uh, Keli, right?" He looked from me to Farrah and back to me. "How—how's it going?" he said uncertainly.

"Hi, Rob. This is my friend Farrah. She's a lawyer, too. We're doing a little investigating, and I wanted to show her where the Folio was stolen." I said this like it was the most natural thing in the world. As if I had every right to investigate the matter or even be at Eleanor's house. I was counting on a certain level of naïveté I'd noticed in Rob, as well as the fact that he seemed to be more concerned with appearing natural himself. Then there was the disarming charm that Farrah could turn on anytime she so chose.

"Hi there," said Farrah, with a brilliant smile. She offered her hand to Rob for a friendly handshake. "I hope we're not intruding. Wow. What a beautiful house."

Rob held on to her hand a fraction longer than necessary, then stepped aside to let us enter. "No trouble," he said. "I, uh, was just checking on things, you know? Thought I'd make the place look lived in for a while. I was getting ready to watch the ball game. Grandma has satellite TV, so it's always better over here." Rob nodded toward the living room, which appeared dark and unused.

"Oh, the game!" said Farrah. "Want some company?" Farrah looked up into Rob's eyes and twirled a finger in her hair.

"Sure!" he said. "Um, I doubt if there's any beer here, but I bet there's some sodas in the pantry. And maybe some popcorn."

"Sounds great!" said Farrah. "You're so sweet!" Farrah went over to turn on the TV, while Rob went into the kitchen.

I met Farrah's eyes and smirked. "You rock," I whispered.

"Go find that evidence you were talking about," Farrah whispered back.

We heard the sound of popcorn popping in the microwave and the refrigerator door opening and closing. I zipped into the library and saw that someone had straightened it up since the last time I'd seen it. After a brief look around, I decided what I really wanted to see was the upstairs. So I tiptoed down the hall and padded up the carpeted stairs. When I reached the top landing, I heard Farrah say, "Keli went to go find the little girls' room. So, do you play baseball, Rob? Are you on a team?"

On the dimly lit landing, I found myself facing several wooden doors, two open and three closed. Quickly, I peeked into the rooms with the two open doors—a bathroom and what looked to be the

master bedroom. Then, one by one, I opened the
closed doors. There was a linen closet; a spare room
with purple and pink accents, probably Darlene's
when she lived here while growing up; and a
smaller spare bedroom in navy and red, Kirk's
room, no doubt. Each of the bedrooms looked to
be tidy and undisturbed, yet they felt stuffy and
closed in. The small windows in these rooms, which
faced the front of the house, were shut tight.

I went back to the master bedroom, Eleanor's
room, with some hesitation. It was also tidy and
quiet, but fresher smelling. I stepped inside and
gazed around. A queen-size bed, neatly made with
a colorful green, yellow, and blue quilt, dominated
the center of the room. To the side was a closet,
with door ajar, dresses, pants, and blouses hanging
neatly in a row. On a chair next to the bed was
draped a long cotton nightgown. A pair of faded
blue terry-cloth house slippers sat side by side,
expectantly, under the chair.

Seeing the nightgown and the house slippers, I
felt a lump rise in my throat. I felt like an intruder.
I was about to turn and leave when I noticed several
dresser drawers in the horizontal bureau were
pulled open. Upon closer inspection, I could see
they had been riffled through. Maybe Darlene had
been looking for something for the viewing?

I felt a draft of air and turned to the window,
which was open a couple of inches. A ruffled curtain fluttered in the light breeze. This was the
room, I realized, with the open window that I had
noticed the other day, while waiting for the police
to arrive. I walked over to the window and felt

the sill. It was slightly damp from this morning's rainfall.

Should I close it? I tested the sash, and it slid easily. Looking outside, I saw the big pine tree. It was too far away to reach from the window. To the right, toward the front of the house and about twenty feet away, was another mature tree. Its thick, leafy branches effectively shielded the window from the street.

As I turned away from the window, something on the floor caught my eye. I leaned over and picked it up. It was a piece of dried mud about an inch long. I looked out the window again, down at the ground below. The grass was sparse in that spot, and there was some mud. It didn't look very dry now, but maybe a few days ago . . . ?

I jumped when the TV downstairs roared in volume, then just as quickly became quiet. Then I heard Farrah emit a shrill laugh. "Sorry about that! Wrong button." I took that as my cue and darted out of the room. For good measure, I shut myself quietly in the bathroom, flushed the toilet, then rinsed my hands under the faucet. Then I hopped back downstairs. I reached the living room just in time to see Farrah stretch her arms above her head with an audible moan, simultaneously thrusting out her chest, where Rob's eyes, naturally, were glued. She spotted me and dropped her arms with a giggle.

"Keli!" she said. "Rob has a ball game tomorrow afternoon at Fieldstone Park. We should go."

"Sounds great," I said.

I wandered over to the framed photos on the

mantel, drawn to the ones that featured Wes. There was an old one of Darlene's family: she and Bill with big eighties hair, sitting side by side with stiff smiles while the two young boys clowned behind them. Wes and Rob looked like a couple of rascals who probably got into a lot of mischief together. And had lots of fun. I wondered when it turned sour. I turned back to the half of the dynamic duo sitting on the couch.

"Rob, I must have just missed you at your grandma's memorial service. I got there around six, I think."

"Huh?" Rob peeled his eyes from Farrah. "Oh, yeah. I stayed for a while, but then I had some business to take care of."

"What kind of business?" asked Farrah in her most girly "everything you say is fascinating" voice.

"Nothing too exciting," said Rob, patting Farrah on the knee.

"So, you didn't make it to the dinner with your family?" I knew I was pushing it, but I really wanted to know where he went that night.

"Nah. I paid my respects. I didn't feel like hanging out with my family anymore. They can be kind of stifling, if you know what I mean." Rob stood up, as if he was feeling stifled now, and took the popcorn bowl to the kitchen.

Farrah looked at me questioningly, her brows arched.

"Let's get out of here," I whispered.

We followed Rob to the kitchen and told him we had to take off.

"It was great to meet you," said Farrah, briefly

touching his arm. "Hopefully, we'll catch your game tomorrow."

"Yeah, see you later, Rob," I said. Then we scooted out the front before the situation could get awkward. Once on the sidewalk, I couldn't resist teasing Farrah.

"Well, well, Miss Marilyn Monroe. You seemed to be enjoying your little distraction role in there."

"Hey!" she protested. "I had to do something. You were taking forever up there." Then she looked at me and grinned slyly. "He was pretty cute, though. Who knew detective work was going to be so fun?"

"Ha," I replied, climbing into her car.

"Where to now, Chief?" she asked.

"Let's drive down the alley behind the house. I'm wondering how shielded it is back there."

Farrah rounded the corner and slowly entered the alley. We went past backyards and garages until we reached the back fence that belonged to Eleanor's house. Just as I thought, with the fence, the garage, the toolshed, and all the trees, you couldn't even see the back door of the house or any of the windows.

"Shame, shame," said Farrah. "Somebody's being naughty." I followed her gaze to the roof of a back porch on the other side of the alley. A girl sat on the rooftop, leaning against a window and smoking a cigarette.

"Hey, I know that girl," I said, narrowing my eyes. "She's what's-her-name. Brandi. The girl who acted all weird when the police questioned the neighbors."

"Interesting," said Farrah. "From up there, a

person might be able to see someone leaving out this back gate."

"My thoughts exactly."

Farrah shut off the ignition, and we exited the car, then strolled over to the short chain-link fence that marked the edge of Brandi's backyard.

"Hi there!" I called, causing Brandi to jump out of her over-tanned skin. "Can we talk to you for a minute?"

She looked nervously over her shoulder, then stubbed out her cigarette without a word. Farrah and I looked at each other; then I tried again.

"Don't worry," I said. "We won't tell your mom. We just want to ask you a couple questions."

Again silence. Brandi squinted at us suspiciously. "About what?" she finally said.

"About the other night," I replied. "We think somebody was here at the Mostriaks' house last Saturday evening. Did you notice anybody coming or going?"

Brandi stared at us for a second, then slowly shook her head.

"What's her deal?" Farrah whispered. "She's obviously hiding something."

"Maybe she's just feeling guilty about the smoking," I said quietly. In a louder voice I said, "Look, we're not the cops. We're just looking for some information. Why don't you come down from there so we don't have to shout?"

The girl hesitated, then looked behind her and through the window again. Making up her mind, she shook her head for the second time. "Sorry. I don't know anything. I gotta go."

"Hey!" yelled Farrah, causing Brandi to turn back, wide-eyed. "Don't you know that smoking is a nasty, unattractive habit? It totally makes you stink."

"Farrah!" I said. "We're trying to make friends here."

I turned back to Brandi to try to make nice again, but she was already gone.

"Dude!" I chided Farrah. "When it comes to the interrogations, I think you better stick to the boys."

CHAPTER 11

I wandered in a crumbling, overgrown cemetery full of weeping willows and brambles and weeds. It was night, and I was sure there were ghosts watching me. I wanted to escape, but I was walking in circles. Finally, up ahead I could see the way out through a large iron gate. Amazingly, I realized I held the key, a large skeleton key. I ran to the gate, but when I got there, it turned into a great wooden door, and I no longer had the key. Before I knew what was happening, I was in a car, making out with someone. We were going at it good, fogging up the windows. I pulled back for a moment to look into his eyes and saw that it was . . . Jeremy.

Ahhh! I jerked awake, feeling guilty and somewhat shaken by the weird dream. Rolling over, I looked at my bedside clock and saw that it was 9:00 a.m. *Crap!* I was late for work, too.

Oh, wait. I had no work. *Double crap.*

I heaved myself out of bed and walked zombie-like into the bathroom, where I splashed cold water on my face. I had stayed up late the night before, poring over all my witchy resource books, hoping against hope for a magical solution to my predicament. Unfortunately, this was the real world, not some supernatural TV show. Most of the spells I'd found were more about changing yourself than changing external circumstances. Darn New Age morality.

I had gone into the kitchen and had started pulling bags of frozen fruit out of the freezer and tossing pieces into my blender when I heard strange high-pitched singing coming from my backyard. Puzzled, I opened the patio doors and stepped onto my deck. Down below was Mrs. St. John, my next-door neighbor, who was making herself at home in my backyard, along with her yippy little pug, Chompy. I crossed my arms as I watched her drag her reclining lawn chair onto my lawn, settle herself down, and then toss a rawhide bone toward my vegetable patch. Chompy tore after it, kicking up the dirt in my garden in the process.

I cleared my throat loudly, and Mrs. St. John nearly fell out of her chair. "Oh! Keli, you gave me a fright!"

"Good morning, Mrs. St. John," I said, standing straight-backed with arms crossed in my best impression of a strict schoolmarm.

The poor woman, gray curls bouncing, scrambled to her feet. "I thought you were at work. What time is it? Why aren't you at work?"

"I'm on vacation," I said.

"Oh! Well, how long are you taking off? Are you going away?"

Now it was my turn to falter. "Um. Well, I'm just taking a few days off, I think. I haven't really firmed up my plans yet."

She wrinkled her forehead and opened her mouth to speak again, but then she was distracted by her husband, who was dragging his golf bag across the grass into my yard. She tried to wave him back. "Keli's home!" she whispered loudly.

"What?" he shouted, evidently not having turned on his hearing aids.

"Keli's home! Don't come over here!"

I turned and went back into my house to finish my smoothie. I couldn't deal with Mr. and Mrs. St. John right now. They probably spread out into my yard every day, the old stinkers. When I heard Mrs. St. John call their dog in that impossibly high-pitched voice of hers—"*Here*, Chompy! Here, little pooch! Come to Mommy!"—I rubbed my eyes with the heels of my hands. "Goddess, help me," I murmured. I had to get out of the house.

What to do? What to do? I knew I had some leads to pursue in order to learn more about the Folio. But I hadn't actually given up on the prospect of a magical assist. What I really wanted to do was talk to Mila. She had been practicing witchcraft a lot longer than I had, and she might have a spell or two up her sleeve.

The problem was, I was nervous about going downtown. I *really* didn't want to run into anyone from work. On the other hand, it was Thursday morning. I glanced at the kitchen clock. If I hurried, I could make it to the square while all my colleagues were safely ensconced in the conflicts meeting.

Quickly, I threw on some blue jogging shorts and a white and gold ribbed tank top, laced up my sneakers, and bounded out the door. It felt good to run. I fairly flew down the sidewalks, almost as if I could outrun my problems. Before long I found myself, only slightly sweaty, flushed, and out of breath, in front of Moonstone Treasures.

Before entering the store, I looked over my shoulder, as always. With the courthouse nearby, there was always the chance of being seen by attorneys from other firms, clients, or government officials—people who might raise an eyebrow if they knew I frequented an occult shop. Cautiously, I slipped inside and tried to act casual. There were a couple of other customers, so I played it cool, browsing the greeting cards, waiting for a chance to talk with Mila alone.

Of course, Mila didn't know my intentions.

"Keli! Hey! Come over here. Have a drink of water and meet my friends."

I looked up to see Mila standing by the checkout counter with two slender young women, arms draped casually around one another. They looked my way with polite interest, while Mila poured some water from her glass carafe.

"Hi," I said, walking up to them, with one eye on the door.

Mila touched my shoulder and addressed the couple. "This is Keli Milanni. She works in the law office around the corner. But I guess not today?" She indicated my jogging outfit.

"Nope. Day off."

Mila then inclined her head toward the two women. "This is Andi and Trina. They moved here from Chicago in April and joined Circle a few weeks ago." Circle was short for Magic Circle, the name of Mila's coven. She had invited me to their meetings several times, but I kept refusing. Even among friends, I couldn't risk going public with my beliefs.

"Nice to meet you," said Andi. She was the shorter of the two, with dark, pixie-styled hair and brilliant blue eyes.

Trina, who wore her blond-streaked hair pulled to the side with barrettes, nodded a hello.

"We were just talking about Litha," said Mila. Litha, I knew, was another name for the summer solstice. Also called Midsummer, it was an important holiday in many nature religions.

"Yeah," said Trina. "We're planning a solstice celebration in the woods near Briar Creek Cabins. We're going to have dancing, chanting, and drumming around a sacred bonfire. You should come."

"Oh, well, thank you. It sounds nice. But I'm a solitary practitioner," I said.

Trina shrugged, and Andi looked at me strangely.

To change the subject, I said, "Are you guys going to the Renaissance Faire on the SCIU campus? There's going to be a performance of Shakespeare's *A Midsummer Night's Dream.* Fittingly."

"We'll probably stop by the fair," said Trina. "We have mixed feelings about Shakespeare, though."

"Oh?" I said.

"You know," she said, assuming a didactic tone.

"In many ways, Shakespeare is responsible for the perpetuation of the negative stereotype of the witch as a demon hag. We're still dealing with it today."

"Yeah," Andi agreed. "'Double, double toil and trouble.' Still a strong icon four hundred years later."

"Hmm," I said, considering this. "I always think of the evil fairy-tale witch as just one more villainous storybook character. It's like in *The Wizard of Oz*—you've got the good witch and the bad witch."

Trina shook her head. "When someone says 'witch,' what do most people think of? And not only that, but there's a close link between society's view of strong women or elder women and the creation of the evil witch archetype. So I can't help it. I take offense at the denigration of witches, even in fiction. It's like they're creating an insulting caricature of women. Anything to bring us down."

Wow. This woman was intense. Still, I couldn't help liking her.

"Ooh," said Mila, rubbing her hands together. "This would be a great topic to explore at Circle. I'm going to find a book on this subject that we can all read together."

"I've got a couple you can borrow," Trina interjected.

"Keli," said Mila, "you really should join us sometime. Our Circle gatherings are always a lot of fun. We take turns hosting them in one another's homes."

I raised a palm and repeated my standard answer. "Solitary," I said, backing away from the counter. "Thanks, anyway."

A shadow fell across the room as someone walked by the window outside, and I instinctively ducked around the corner to the book section of the store. Andi and Trina completed their purchases and left. Then Mila came over and found me halfheartedly browsing the titles.

"Everything okay?" she asked.

"I've got a problem," I confided. "I desperately need to find something."

"Not true love, I hope."

"No. This time it's a missing object. Something that was stolen, actually. It's a long story, but my job depends on the recovery of this item. Maybe even my career." My voice hitched a little as I said it.

With a concerned look, Mila guided me over to the sitting area where we had chatted the other day. "This object . . . ," she said. "Have you tried a finding spell?"

"No. See, the thing is, the object isn't mine. I didn't lose it. It wasn't taken from me. It doesn't belong to me. None of the usual finding spells seem to fit the bill."

Mila furrowed her eyebrows and tapped her fingertips together as she thought about what I'd said. "Hmm. It shouldn't matter if the object isn't yours. Have you seen it? Could you draw it?"

"I've seen it, yes. I suppose I could make a rough sketch."

"Okay," Mila said decisively as she stood up. "I've got just the thing. Let me go grab a couple things for you and jot down a spell."

I followed her to the counter and chuckled as a

thought occurred to me. "If my mother were here, she'd tell me to pray to St. Anthony."

"Well, sure," said Mila, in complete seriousness. "That could work, too. But something tells me you don't have any statues of saints adorning your altar."

"True," I agreed. "So, you're saying that the deities we invoke—or the saints, as the case may be—have their particular power because we give it to them?"

"All I'm saying," said Mila as she handed me the paper bag she'd just filled, "is, 'What's in a name? That which we call a rose—'"

"'By any other name would smell as sweet,'" I said, finishing for her and nodding.

"Still," she said, with a twinkle in her eye, "I would recommend calling upon Persephone for this one. She can help you unearth the treasure you seek."

I took the paper bag and shook my head in wonder. I hadn't even told Mila what it was I was looking for. Yet here she was, quoting Shakespeare and talking about lost treasures. *That witch never ceases to amaze me*, I thought as I headed for the door.

Leaving Moonstone Treasures, I prepared to dash around the corner and head away from the law office. But in my haste, I nearly bumped into the opening door of the gallery next to Mila's shop. I skidded to a stop and gasped when I recognized the person exiting.

"Wes!" I felt a warm charge of pleasure at seeing

him again. Then I noticed his irritated expression. "How are you?" I ventured.

"I've been better," he said with a scowl, letting the door bang shut behind him.

"Oh." *Well, this is awkward.* While Wes clenched his jaw and muttered indecipherably, but probably profanely, under his breath, I stood there uncertainly on the sidewalk.

Then, quick as a sunburst, Wes softened. Running a hand through his hair—which was thick, tousled, and touchable, not that I noticed—he took a step next to me. "I'm sorry," he said. "It's just . . . nothing. So what's up with you? Out for a jog?"

Now, there was the look I remembered. That deeply interested gaze that held the promise of something . . . exciting. And perhaps steamy. I swallowed and tried to focus on the conversation.

"Uh, yeah," I said. "I'm taking the day off from work. Thought I'd get a run in before it gets too hot."

"Hey," he said, shifting his feet. "Let me ask you something. On Sunday I'm planning to drive out to this old farm my family owns. It's actually the place where my grandpa Frank grew up. We have an arrangement with a farmer to run the land, but it's good to check on it now and then, you know? I haven't been out there since I got back. Anyway, it's about ten miles outside of town, and it's a nice scenic drive. So I was thinking, if it's a nice day, would you like to come along? We could bring a picnic, stop off in the woods on the way."

"Yeah," I said without hesitation. "That sounds lovely."

"Wonderful." He smiled. "I'll give you a call later, and we'll figure out the details. I think I've still got your number in my phone."

As I jogged home, floating on cloud nine, I daydreamed about my date with Wes. This was perfect. I was finally going to have a chance to get to know him better. But as my mind wandered to our last couple of encounters and the whole mess surrounding the missing Folio, my pace became slower and slower, until my brisk jog turned into a languid walk. I could no longer ignore the elephant in the room.

Wes was a suspect.

And not only Wes. All the Mostriak-Callahan family members were the most likely suspects. The visitation might have provided an alibi for some of them, but the fact was that people had come and gone from the visitation. The funeral home wasn't that far from Eleanor's home. The family knew the Folio was there. And they knew how to get into the house.

The question was, who would do such a thing?

CHAPTER 12

"Ooh! Ouch!"

"Well, that's what you get for wearing such itty-bitty short shorts."

I made a face at Farrah and sat down gingerly on the hot metal bleachers. Her shorts weren't much longer than mine, but she propped her feet on the seat in front of us, bending her knees to keep her thighs raised. The bleachers were nearly empty, as most people were smart enough to bring their own chairs so they could sit in the shade.

Farrah studied the ball field for a minute, then turned to me and lowered her oversize sunglasses. "Where's our buddy Rob?"

Shading my eyes with my hand, I scanned the field, taking in each player, including the ones on the bench. It was the top of the fourth inning. Pop's Hardware was at bat against the Cozy Café—with one out and no one on base. Cozy was ahead five to one. Rob had told Farrah he was on Pop's team, but there was no Rob in sight.

"Huh," I said. "Let's go talk to the boys on the

bench." I stood up, grateful to leave the heat of the bleachers, and Farrah followed. Guessing that the players sat in batting order, we walked to the end of the line.

"Hey there!" said Farrah, turning on the charm.

The whole row looked our way. So much for not interrupting the game.

"We're friends of Rob Callahan," I said. "Any idea where he is?"

One of the players nearest us, a hefty guy with short curly hair, answered at once. "Ole Robby is MIA. Again."

"Well, how do you like that?" said Farrah. "He invites us to his game and then skips out on it."

"Has he missed a lot of games?" I asked.

"Games, practices. There's about a fifty-fifty chance he'll show up on any given day. I don't know how Coach puts up with it. Except that he is a pretty decent player when he does show."

"Does he at least have good excuses?" I said.

Curly Guy shrugged, and a long-haired guy next to him snorted. Farrah and I looked from one to the other questioningly.

"What gives?" said Farrah. "Where do you think we could find him now?"

Instead of responding, the players all shifted over on the bench as they neared their turn at bat. I noticed that they were one strike away from the third out, and then this whole team would be heading out to the field. I really didn't feel like sitting through another inning of this terribly non-exciting game, so I tried to get them talking again.

"Have you guys known Rob a long time?"

"Sure," said Curly Guy. "A while. We were on this team last year, too."

"I knew him from school," offered the other player, dragging his cleats casually in the dirt.

"Has he always been this unreliable?" asked Farrah.

Curly Guy shrugged his shoulders again, but the long-haired guy answered.

"Nah," he said. "I guess he developed this little problem some time later."

"Problem?" I echoed.

Now Curly Guy rolled his eyes. "Put it this way," he said. "Robby's got a little *fixation*. You might even call it an addiction. He should just admit it and get help already."

"Strike Three! *Out*!"

The boys on the bench all stood up and shuffled toward the field. Before they could get away, I grabbed Long Hair's arm. "Real quick," I said. "If you went to school with Rob, you must have known his brother, Wes, right?"

"Yeah, I know Wes. He was a couple grades ahead of us."

"Did you know he moved back to Edindale?"

"Sure. I've seen him around."

"Do you happen to know where he's staying?"

Giving me a look that said "I *really* gotta go now," Long Hair nodded and stepped away from me. Over his shoulder, he said, "Yeah. I heard he's staying with Jimi Coral, owner of the Loose Rock."

Farrah and I looked at each other, and Farrah raised her eyebrows.

"I can't believe Jimi lied to me!" I said. "Why would he do that?"

Farrah checked her Swatch and nudged me. "We don't need to talk to these baseball guys anymore, do we? I'm melting here, and I have to go home and shower before my date."

"Oh, who are you going out with?" I asked as we walked to my car.

She looked only slightly sheepish. "Jake. We're calling this a test date. If it goes well, we might start seeing each other again."

I laughed, unlocked my car, and lowered the windows to let out the heat. Anyway, I needed to get home myself. I had a date, too—with a certain Greek goddess called Persephone.

The shades were drawn; the candles lit. The altar was set. Walking clockwise—clothed this time—I cast the circle, pausing at each cardinal direction to invoke the spirits of the ancient elements:

God of the North, rooted in Earth, I call upon thee.
Goddess of the East, breath of knowledge, I call upon thee.
God of the South, light of truth, I call upon thee.
Goddess of the West, waters of purity, I call upon thee.

Then, kneeling before the altar, I held my hands, palms downward, above the sketch I had made of the First Folio. I closed my eyes, took three centering breaths, and intoned the words Mila had given me.

> *Goddess Persephone, Mistress of Life,*
> *From Hades's Realm you rose.*
> *Out of darkness, you brought forth light*
> *With blossoms 'neath your toes.*
> *Beloved Persephone, who comes and goes,*
> *As Nature lives and dies,*
> *Reveal for me the missing thing,*
> *Unveiled before my eyes.*

In the silence following the incantation, I kept my focus inward, my hands still hovering above the picture. I allowed my consciousness to expand as I observed whatever vision the Goddess would bring. Before long, the darkness behind my eyes lifted, as a fog lifted in a valley, and I saw a line of books. I saw shelves of books, row upon row, in all sizes and colors. A hall of books. Then the books disappeared and were replaced by a lovely garden, green and verdant, with flowering trees and shrubs. I saw roses and lilacs, and I realized it was Eleanor's garden. I saw Eleanor's cheerful yellow house. Then the house and gardens began to fade and were replaced by—

Knock, knock, knock!

My eyes flew open, and I fell sideways, knocked off balance by the jarring noise. I placed my hands on the floor to steady myself, feeling slightly woozy from being pulled out of the trance so suddenly. I was taking a deep breath and pushing myself to my knees when there was another round of loud knocks.

"All right, all right," I mumbled. Quickly, I grabbed the athame from my altar and cut an invisible doorway into my sacred circle. This was the safe way to exit a circle before it had been properly closed. Pulling my bedroom door shut behind me, I went to see who in the world was banging on my front door.

I peered through the peephole and saw a young woman I didn't recognize, pale blond hair framing her worried face. Curious, I opened the door.

"Oh, Keli!" she said. "I'm so glad you're home. I didn't know where else to turn."

"Um." I stared at her, trying to place the face. Nada. I had no idea who this was.

"Can I come in? It's about Jeremy. I need your advice."

Jeremy?

Seeing my confusion, she rushed to explain. "I'm Stacey, Jeremy's girlfriend. You and I haven't actually met, but Jeremy pointed you out at that museum fund-raiser last month. Hasn't he mentioned me at the office?"

"Come on in," I said, avoiding the question. "Can I get you anything? Water, tea, wine?"

"White wine would be great, if you have it." She followed me into the kitchen and plopped onto one of the cushioned chairs in my breakfast nook. I got out two glasses, poured the wine, and joined her.

"So . . . Stacey. What's up with Jeremy? Is he okay?"

To my dismay, I saw her lower lip tremble. "I

don't know," she said. Then, "I think he's having an affair!"

Oh, Lord. I nearly spilled my wine. "Wh-what makes you think that?"

Not that night at the Loose, I thought. Not those flowers, not the footsie under the table. None of that counted as an affair, right? I would *know* if I were having an affair. Surely.

"He's been going someplace in the evenings, and I don't know where. At first, it was once in a while, but now it's, like, a couple times a week. He always says he's going to the office to work on a big case or attend a night meeting, or something like that. But I went by the office tonight to surprise him, and it was completely dark. Locked up. Nobody there."

I furrowed my eyebrows, not sure what to say. Knowing Jeremy, he probably *was* having an affair. He had never once mentioned to me that he had a girlfriend.

"You're his boss," she said. "Do you know where he might be? Is there any business he might be doing at . . . at another office or something?"

I shook my head slowly and gave her a sympathetic look. I could tell she didn't really believe it even as she said it, poor girl. I felt sorry for her. Jeremy was a cad.

"I've *got* to find out what he's up to," she said, staring into her wineglass. "I hate not trusting him. And maybe it's nothing. . . ." She looked up at me, eyes pleading. "Will you help me? Find out where he's been going? Maybe you could, I don't know, give him an evening assignment. If he says he's busy, you can ask him what he's doing. Or . . .

or maybe there's something in his office that would indicate where he's going."

Taking a sip of my wine, I pictured Jeremy's office. It was kind of small and cluttered. Windowless. Somewhat boring, really. He did have that oversize blotter he liked to doodle on. As I recalled, he used it to jot down appointments, as well. Just maybe there *was* a clue there as to his nighttime meetings. Only problem was, I didn't currently have access to the office.

I shook my head. "I don't know, Stacey. I'd like to help you, but I don't see how I can. I'm actually on vacation this week, so I won't even see—"

"Please." She said it with a sob, and I could see that her eyes were brimming with tears. *Damn. Damn. Damn.*

"Okay," I said. "I'll check out his office. See what I can find out. I'm not making any promises, but I'll try."

"Thank you," she whispered.

I handed her a tissue, while inside I cursed Jeremy and his damn flirty ways. I *knew* I should never have touched the Untouchable. Now, thanks to my own guilty conscience, I was gonna pay the piper. That was karma for you.

It was nearly midnight, the witching hour, but this witch was wiped. When my bedside telephone rang, I was already snuggled in, dozing off, and inclined to ignore it. But just before voice mail picked up, I sighed and reached for the phone. It was Farrah.

"Hey, hippie chick! I didn't wake you, did I?" She sounded tipsy and jubilant. I guessed her date had gone well.

"No, no. I'm still up," I murmured, closing my eyes and resting my head back on the pillow.

"Guess who *I* ran into at the Loose?" she sang in a teasing voice.

"I've no idea," I mumbled. "Who?"

"Oh, just a certain hunky rock star type. Nobody you'd be interested in."

Okay, now I was fully awake. I sat up and propped my pillow behind me. "Was he with anyone? Did you talk to him?"

"Well, he wasn't on a date. In fact, it appears he's living there."

"What? I don't think I heard you right. Did you say—"

"Remember how we thought Wes looked like he had just got out of bed the first time we saw him? Well, he actually might have. He's sleeping on a cot in Jimi's office."

I scrunched my forehead, trying to make sense of this bit of information.

Farrah continued, "I saw him come out of there, and the door was left open—mostly—so I peeked in. I saw the cot and some bags and luggage and stuff. So I cornered Jimi to get the lowdown."

"What'd he say?"

"Well, he was cagey at first. But he finally admitted to it. Turns out Wes stayed at Jimi's house for a while. Then Jimi's wife kicked him out. Said she wasn't going to have a bum sleeping on the couch for a month." Farrah laughed, but I wasn't seeing the humor.

Wes? A bum?

"Jimi was all worried about getting in trouble with the city," Farrah went on. "It's not exactly legal to use a bar as a place of residence. So he's trying not to let people find out—especially us lawyers."

"Did you talk to Wes at all?"

"No. He took off. I couldn't exactly follow him in the middle of my date." I heard a muffled voice in the background and then Farrah's giggle. "One more minute," she cooed to the voice in the background.

"Good date?"

"So far so good," she said with a soft laugh.

At least somebody's having fun, I thought, sinking back onto my pillow. For some reason, Jeremy's face sprang to mind, followed quickly by the visit from his girlfriend.

"Hey," I said to Farrah. "There's something I have to do tomorrow night, and I could use your help." I told her about Stacey and my promise to snoop in Jeremy's office.

"And how do you plan on doing that?" Farrah wanted to know.

"Simple. I just have to sneak into the office after hours, when the place is empty. I have a key, so it shouldn't be too hard. I just have to make sure I'm in and out before the early morning cleaning crew. And I'll need a lookout. What do you say, partner?"

"Jeez. *Two* cases now? What are you? Keli Milanni,

PI? If the lawyer thing doesn't work out, you could start a whole new career as a detective."

"Yeah. Right." And how very not comforting at all. Laughing faintly, I told Farrah to go have fun with Jake while I drifted off to dreamland.

CHAPTER 13

On day two of my unplanned sabbatical, I decided not to stick around the house any longer than absolutely necessary. After an early morning run through the park, down the rail trail and back, I showered, dressed in my usual Friday business casual—skinny pants, a cropped blazer over a low-slung cami, and ballet flats—and called retired professor Wendell Knotts. When I told him Professor Eisenberry had suggested I contact him to discuss the First Folio, he eagerly agreed to meet me for coffee within the hour. He suggested the Cozy Café, which wasn't far from the university, and that suited me just fine.

Upon entering the restaurant, I spotted a slight man leaning over a newspaper at a window seat, his trim white hair encircling a perfectly round bald spot. His elbow-patched sports coat and horn-rimmed bifocals appeared to be circa 1979. *Too obvious?* I wondered, not wanting to jump to an erroneous judgment yet again. But when he looked up and saw me hesitating by the doorway, he lifted a hand in greeting.

"Keli Milanni, I presume?"

"Professor Knotts. So nice to meet you." I smiled warmly and took the seat across from him. "Thank you for agreeing to meet with me."

"Call me Wendell," he said, folding the newspaper and setting it aside. "I haven't been in a classroom for nearly a decade now."

The waitress appeared to take my order. It was the same woman from the other day, with the nose ring and reddish-blond hair. She snapped her fingers when she recognized me. "Oh! It's you! I was hoping you'd come in again. That guy was here yesterday, the one you asked about."

"Really? Are you sure?" Actually, I was surprised she remembered.

"Oh, yeah. Good looking, tattoo on his arm. He fit the description perfectly. I told him you were looking for him."

I nearly choked on the water I'd just sipped. "You did what? But how . . . ? I mean, what did you say?" Now I was all spluttery and embarrassed, not least of all because Wendell Knotts was following this exchange with great interest.

"Well, I didn't know your name," the waitress went on, oblivious to my concern. "I just said a pretty woman with long brown hair and a figure to die for was asking if he came in here." She grinned at me, clearly assuming I'd be flattered. But all I could think of was what Wes must have imagined when a random waitress told him I was asking about him. *Desperately Seeking Wesley*, maybe?

"Wow," I said. "He must have been surprised, huh?"

"I guess." The waitress shrugged. "To be sure it was you, he asked if you had hazel eyes. He also asked if you came in here a lot. So, what'll you have?"

He had remembered my eye color. Now I was slightly more touched than mortified.

"Ahem," the waitress said, interrupting my thoughts. "Do you need more time?"

"Oh, sorry. I'll just have coffee. By the way, what time was Wes here yesterday?"

"Late morning. Between eleven and eleven thirty, I'd say."

Probably came here right after bumping into me outside the gallery. *Terrific.*

When the waitress left, I turned to the professor with an apology on my lips. But before I could speak, he leaned forward and said softly, "'Love sought is good, but giv'n unsought is better.'"

"I beg your pardon?"

He gave me a charming, crinkly-eyed smile. "It's from *Twelfth Night.* When you live and breathe Shakespeare as long as I have, you find the bard had an insightful comment for just about every situation known to mankind." He paused. "In fact," he said, lowering his voice, "the secret to Shakespeare's longevity—his very genius—lay in his ability to recognize those universal traits that make us human, no matter what the time or place."

He sat back in his chair then, looking a little wistful. I didn't know if he was missing his teaching days or missing Shakespeare himself.

"So, speaking of Shakespeare quotes," I said, then paused as the waitress poured my coffee and refilled Wendell's cup. "I recently saw a wood carving you made that featured one. 'Lord, what fools these mortals be,' it said."

Wendell nodded and smiled that soft crinkly smile again. "*A Midsummer Night's Dream.* I've made several such carvings. It's a little hobby of mine. But given that you asked to speak to me about the First Folio, and given the rumors I've heard about the Mostriak Folio, I'm going to go out on a limb and say you saw the carving I gave to Frank Mostriak."

"You're right," I said, nodding. "I'm acquainted with the Mostriak family. Frank's grandson Rob has the carving now, and I was curious about it. Did Frank really quote that line a lot?"

"It *was* his favorite," said Wendell, chuckling softly.

I took a sip of my coffee. "So, Wendell, how did you meet Frank? Did you know him well?"

"I knew Frank for a good many years. And, believe it or not, it was Shakespeare who introduced us."

"Oh?"

"In a manner of speaking. I was a young professor back then, but already quite the Shakespearean scholar, if I do say so myself." Grinning boyishly, Wendell leaned back and continued, as if telling a story. "It was nineteen forty-nine, I believe, when this youngster, Frankie Mostriak, sought me out at the university. He had inherited the First Folio from his uncle, and he wanted to learn everything there was to know about it."

"Did *you* see the book?" I interjected.

"Mm-hmm," he answered. "I saw the Folio, and I saw the certificate of authenticity that came with it."

"There was a certificate?" This was news to me.

"Oh, yes. Frank's uncle was wise to keep the certificate with the Folio. It included a detailed description of the volume and attested to its provenance. The certificate was issued by a well-known expert appraiser out of New York City."

"Interesting. I guess the certificate must be lost now. Do you think there would be a record of it still, in New York? Is it possible the appraisal company still exists?"

"I could make some inquiries for you, if you'd like," Wendell offered.

"That would be *great*," I said enthusiastically. "I would really appreciate it. So, back to nineteen forty-nine. You and Frank bonded over Shakespeare?"

"Frank enrolled at the university for a semester and took my introductory course on Shakespeare. After that, he ended up leaving school to go to work and support his new family. But he would still drop by now and then, and I let him audit my courses anytime he wished. He was genuinely interested in the plays and the history—more so, even, than many of my students. So, of course, over time we became friends."

"Hmm. So you must know Frank's family pretty well, then?"

"Well, at one time, certainly. My wife and I would have dinner with Frank and Eleanor on occasion. And I've met their children, of course. Darlene and Kirk."

"Did you make it to Eleanor's memorial service?"

"I did. I was probably one of the first ones there."

"I must've just missed you. I was there later. After six," I said.

The waitress appeared again, but Wendell put his hand over his cup to decline a refill, and I realized our meeting was about over.

"So, Mr. Knotts . . . Wendell. Do you know anything about the fire that supposedly destroyed the Folio? I mean, did you know Frank still had it all these years?"

"Well, it's a funny thing," he replied. "About a month after Frank came to me, he did inform me he no longer had the Folio. He said that it had been lost in a fire. And yet Frank was no less interested in Shakespeare. Indeed, he did not exhibit a great deal of remorse over the loss. So, let's just say I was not greatly surprised to learn that Eleanor had found the prize hidden away all these years later. Truth be told, I imagine Frank had intended for her to find it long ago. But, for whatever reason, he never got around to cluing her in."

I nodded in agreement as we stood up. I tried to pay for Wendell's coffee, but he wouldn't hear of it. Instead, he left enough money on the table to cover my coffee, as well as the tip. I thanked him and handed him my card.

"I'm looking forward to hearing about the certificate. If the Folio is ever recovered, I think the certificate will be crucial to its identification. Don't you think so?"

"Yes, indeed. Yes, indeed." Wendell held open the door for me as we exited the café.

"Are you attending the literary conference next week?" I asked before we parted ways.

"I wouldn't miss it for the world," he said. With that, he gave me a quick wink and sauntered toward the bus stop on the corner.

Next on my list of interviews for the day was Sharon Baxter, niece to Frank and Eleanor, cousin to Darlene. When I last saw Sharon, at Eleanor's the day the Folio was discovered missing, she had mentioned that she usually worked the first shift at the intake desk at Edindale Medical Center. Last week she had been on the second shift to fill in for a coworker. I had no idea if she would be there now—or if she'd be of any mind to talk with me. But it was worth a shot.

Amazingly, when she spotted me walking through the sliding glass doors at the front of the hospital, Sharon greeted me like a long-lost friend. She stood up from her computer behind a broad counter and waved me over. "Keli, what a nice surprise! Did you come to see me? You're not checking in, are you?"

"Oh, no. I mean, yes. I came to see you. Is now a good time? I don't want to interrupt your work."

"This is a fine time, actually. We're slow this morning. The other two can man the ship for a few minutes." She nodded down the counter to two other women in hospital uniforms and placed a little CLOSED sign in front of her station. Then she led me to a quiet plant-filled alcove at the edge of the lobby.

"Any leads on the Folio?" she asked as we sat side

by side in connecting maroon-colored chairs. Seeing my surprise, she went on. "I saw Robby at Darlene's house the other day. He told me you were investigating the theft."

"Yes," I admitted. "I'm trying, anyway. So, um, did Darlene say anything about me? You know, my firm received a letter from her lawyer regarding the Folio."

"Well, I don't really know much about all the legal stuff," Sharon said. "But I did tell Darlene she ought to be thankful for your help. I also reminded her that having the book insured wouldn't have amounted to a hill of beans if it turned out a family member took the Folio. Wouldn't that be like insurance fraud?"

I was so grateful to Sharon for her candor that I could have hugged her. "Yes. I'd say collecting insurance for the loss of something that someone still possessed could definitely be construed as insurance fraud. Among other things." Proceeding cautiously, I added, "Do you think it *was* someone in the family?"

Sharon looked away and heaved a sigh. "I don't know what to think. Oh, I'm sure Darlene has no idea where it is. But I do know there was an awful lot of pride for Shakespeare in that family."

"What do you mean?"

"After Uncle Frank inherited the antique book, he was crazy for Shakespeare. Took college courses, took his family to Shakespeare plays. He even named his dog Hamlet."

I smiled with Sharon. "I actually just met Frank's old Shakespeare professor, believe it or not. He told me Frank didn't act very upset when the Folio was supposedly lost in a fire. Do you know anything about that? There wasn't insurance collected back then, I hope."

"No. I'm pretty sure there wasn't. Uncle Frank was a hard worker and did well for himself and his family, but he never had money to spare. No, that wasn't why he pretended it was destroyed."

"Do you have another theory?"

"Oh, my mom was sure she knew. My mom, rest her soul, was Frank's older sister. She never straight-up confronted him about it, as far as I know. But she used to say she had a feeling Frank still had that Folio hidden away."

"She did?" I was so fascinated by Sharon's tale. I was hoping she would keep talking and not notice the time—or the looks her coworkers were shooting in our direction.

"Oh, yes. Frank used to like to say, 'I once touched greatness. I once owned the First Folio,' as if that were enough for him to die a happy man. But my mom saw right through him. She figured he set the fire himself to keep the book out of the hands of Little Bo McPepper."

I yelped a short laugh, then clapped a hand over my mouth. "Little who?"

Sharon laughed. "Bo McPepper. His father was Big Bo. Bo Jr. was always called Little Bo. Now, there was a wily bunch, the whole McPepper crew. They were neighbors to Frank's people and regulars at the poker games Frank played every weekend."

"Right. I remember Eleanor saying the Folio was thought to have been lost in a fire or in a bet.

She was kind of vague on that point, come to think of it."

"Well, to hear Mom tell it, some people blamed Little Bo for starting the fire on account of he was mad at Frank. There was a high-stakes poker game one night, and the Folio ended up on the table. I guess Bo thought he had won, but then Frank did. Bo blamed him for cheating, but everyone else there backed up Frank. Anyway, my mother always suspected Frank set the fire to get Bo off his case about it."

I shook my head in wonder. It sounded like Eleanor had married a wild one.

"Oh, goodness," said Sharon, finally noticing the daggers her coworkers were sending her way. "Break time's over."

I had one more question before Sharon hurried off. "You said there was a lot of Shakespeare pride in the family. Did you mean currently, as well as back in the past?"

Sharon nodded her head slowly. "To some extent, yes. With Kirk especially. He was really close with his father. I think it was all those Shakespeare plays that inspired him to take up acting. When Eleanor told Kirk she found the Folio in the attic, he was against selling it. He said it should stay in the family."

"Really?"

"That's what Darlene told me. I guess they had a little family meeting about it. In the end, Eleanor decided it was wiser to sell it. Of course, so much for that. Now there's nothing to sell or keep."

After I left the hospital, I drove toward home. But when I got to the corner before my block and saw Mrs. St. John and Chompy in the front yard, I decided to turn and keep driving. I couldn't deal with them at the moment. Instead, I pulled my car up to the curb by Fieldstone Park, left my jacket on the front seat, and walked to a small grove of trees past the fountain. It was hot outside, and the park was fairly quiet. I imagined most adults were inside air-conditioned buildings, while most kids were probably at the swimming pool.

I made a beeline for a wide, sturdy oak tree and sat on the bench beneath it. Leaning back and staring up into the leaves, I asked the Goddess for guidance as I pondered the mystery. Who had taken the Folio, and why? Was it a sentimental family member who wanted to keep it secreted away, like Frank had for all those years? Or was it a down-on-his-luck family member who wanted the treasure for its monetary value? Or was it someone else entirely who knew the value of the book, knew Eleanor had it, knew Eleanor passed away . . . and jumped at the opportunity? Such as a Shakespearean scholar or a rare-books dealer?

I also couldn't help wondering again whether Eleanor's death really was from natural causes. It was Sharon, with her comments at the visitation, who had planted a seed of doubt about the coincidence of it all. So it was funny that she hadn't said anything about an autopsy during our conversation at the hospital. Maybe she had learned something from Eleanor's doctor. Or maybe she had just decided to let the matter drop. I would have to pay her another visit to find out.

"Ms. Milanni? Is that you?"

I looked over to the sidewalk and saw a petite, silver-haired woman walking toward me, leading a handsome Irish setter on a leash. The woman squinted, with a look of concern. "Is it true?"

"Hello, Mrs. Smith. Is what true?"

"That you've been . . . Well, I heard that you were suspended. From the law firm. Is it true?"

"No!" I said it so forcefully, I startled the dog, who let out a loud bark, then hid behind his owner. "Sorry, Buddy," I said, reaching out to pat his head. "I'm on vacation, Mrs. Smith. Who told you I was suspended?"

Mrs. Smith sat down next to me, then smoothed her cotton skirt and lengthened Buddy's leash. "I called your office the other day, because I wanted to talk to you about updating my will. Your secretary said you weren't in, so she transferred my call to Crenshaw Davenport."

Crenshaw. I should have known.

"He said he could help me with my will, because you might be out for quite a while. I asked him if you were okay. I mean, he sounded so dour, I was afraid you were on medical leave or something."

Under my breath I growled, but at Mrs. Smith, I tried to smile. "I'm perfectly fine, as you can see. So what did Crenshaw say?"

"He told me that you were on a leave of absence for an indefinite period of time, pending an investigation."

I closed my eyes and breathed deeply. The nerve of Crenshaw! Taking my client was bad enough. But implying that I was in some kind of trouble, that *I* was the subject of the investigation—that was just too much. And *an indefinite period of time?* What happened to two weeks? He had made it sound like I might not come back at all.

Well, I would be back, darn it. The sooner the better. And then I'd have a word or two to say to Crenshaw.

CHAPTER 14

Eleanor's house looked dark and forlorn, especially in contrast to the bright early afternoon sun. I had come straight over from Fieldstone Park, determined to keep searching for leads, for any clues at all, to the Shakespeare thief. Now I drove past slowly, noting the taller weeds and the collection of newspapers that had yet to be canceled. It had been only two days since Rob was there, ostensibly to make the house look lived in.

It sure didn't look lived in today.

Under normal circumstances, I could have helped the family settle the estate fairly quickly and put the house on the market before it languished for too long. But Darlene had her own lawyer now, and I was sure nothing would be finalized until there was some resolution regarding the Folio. I still felt bad about the whole thing and couldn't really blame Darlene for finding fault with me.

"I'm sorry, Eleanor," I whispered.

Rounding the corner, I entered the alley and

rolled to a stop behind Eleanor's garage. I peered over the gate, recalling my vision about her yard and wondering if the answer lay close to home. But there was nothing new to see. I turned and looked up at Brandi's window, half hoping she'd be up there, sneaking another smoke. No such luck. Well, I would have to make my own luck, then. If that girl had seen something, I was going to wheedle it out of her one way or another.

Just as I was about to return to the street and knock on Brandi's front door, the teenager came out the back, letting the screen door slam behind her. I watched as she spread a blanket on the lawn and settled herself down with a tall glass of iced tea and a paperback novel. The strong scent of coconut suntan lotion made me long for my own beach blanket, tall drink, and escapist paperback. Some "vacation" this was turning out to be.

"Hi, Brandi."

She sat up and frowned at me behind hot pink Wayfarer sunglasses. I entered through the garden gate and pulled a lawn chair up next to her blanket.

"My name's Keli. I'm a friend of the Mostriak family. I was hoping you would talk to me about the other night and what you saw from the rooftop."

She swallowed and glanced at her back door. I didn't know if she was planning to bolt or expecting someone to come outside. Either way, I figured I better talk fast.

"Look, Brandi. I don't know if you're protecting someone or if you're afraid of getting into trouble yourself. But I do know it's against the law to obstruct justice. If you have any information related to the burglary that took place across the alley, you're legally bound to disclose it." Of course, she wasn't legally bound to tell me anything, but I didn't let that stop me from asking. "Now, if you—"

"I don't know who he was, okay! It was getting dark. He was in the shadows. I don't have any useful information, anyway. I didn't see any harm in keeping quiet."

For a moment, I was so stunned that she'd opened up, I couldn't think of a response. But I recovered quickly. "So, you did see someone. What was he doing?"

"Nothing. He just came out of the gate over there, put something in his trunk, and . . . and left."

I had so many questions I wanted to ask the girl, I hardly knew where to begin. And my heart was palpitating so hard, I feared I would scare her away. I forced myself to take a slow breath and speak lightly. "Brandi, this is actually really helpful. Could you see anything at all of what he put in the trunk? The shape, the size?"

"Oh, it was a bag."

"What kind of bag?"

"Like a gym bag."

"Did you notice what color it was?"

"No. I told you, it was dark down there."

"Okay. No problem. So, what did this guy look like? Can you describe him at all?"

"He had on a baseball cap. I really couldn't see his face very well. But I could tell he was cute."

"Oh? Did he seem to be young?"

"Oh, no. He was definitely a man. Not a kid."

"A man?"

"Yeah. Like, the strong, silent type." I was beginning to guess why Brandi thought she wanted to protect this guy.

"Was he muscular?"

"Not, like, beefy or anything. But he had a nice body, from what I could tell. I don't know. He just seemed hot, you know? From his movements."

"Can you describe his movements?"

"Well, he seemed real sure of himself when he came out the back gate. Like, confident. Not like a sneak or anything. He put his bag in the trunk, and then he walked over to open his car door. That's when he noticed me."

"Up on the roof," I prompted.

"Yeah. He looked up and paused and, like, tipped his hat at me. Like a gentleman, you know?"

"Uh-huh."

"Then he put his finger to his lips like this, like he was saying, 'Shhh.' And then he did the gesture like you're zipping your lip and locking it, you know? Like, as if you won't tell a secret."

"Did you think he had a secret?"

"Well, at first I thought he was referring to my secret. Smoking up there. But then it kind of felt like we both had secrets. And he wouldn't tell mine, and I wouldn't tell his. At least that's what it felt like." She started to sound a little defensive, so I nodded encouragingly.

"Then what happened?"

"Then he blew me a kiss and got in his car and

took off." Brandi's face colored, and she looked away.

"What kind of car was it?"

She shrugged. "I don't know much about cars. It was just a regular car, not a truck or anything."

A regular car. Well, that was helpful. "Did you notice the color?" *Make, model, license plate number?*

"It was a dark color, I think."

"How about the guy's clothes? Or his hat? A team name or anything else descriptive?"

She shook her head. "His clothes were darkish, I'd say. The hat might have been blue or brown. Or green. I'm not sure."

I stared at her, finally at a loss. Did this girl need glasses?

"Brandi, who did you think he was? Any ideas at all?"

"I don't know. There are always people coming and going from the Mostriaks'. I guessed he was a friend of the family or a relative or something. He didn't act like somebody who had committed a crime."

"Right. I guess not. So, do you know what time this was?"

"Um, sometime after eight. I had just watched the sun set. There's a nice view on my roof."

I smiled at her. "I'm sure there is. Hey, thank you for confiding in me. Here's my card, in case you think of anything else. But you really should tell the police everything you told me." Not that they would do anything with the information, from what I could tell.

She took the card, looked at it, and stuck it in her book. "This guy I saw, he wasn't necessarily the thief, right?"

"No. Not necessarily."

"Mmm. Well, I hope they do catch the thief. Mrs. Mostriak was a nice lady. That's pretty messed up that somebody would steal from her after she died."

"Yeah," I agreed. "Messed up. You're right about that."

"Wow! You got an eyewitness report? This is huge!"

"I know, right?"

We were sitting in Farrah's living room, a bottle of wine on the coffee table between us, all set to premeditate our perfectly legal scheme to break in, enter, and search my law office in the dark of night. Of course, when I told Farrah about my coup with Brandi, we had to revel for a moment. And then analyze.

"I mean, she *saw* the thief."

"Well, the presumed thief."

"She interacted with him, could describe him."

"More or less," I said.

"Hey, we know it's a him!"

"Yes. This confirms my decision to rule out Darlene. We can also cross Sharon and all the other female relatives off the list."

"Okay. So, what else do we know? Tell me again. Exactly what did Brandi say?"

Farrah grabbed a pen and paper from a desk drawer and listened intently as I repeated my conversation with Brandi. When I finished, she still held her pen poised over the blank sheet. We looked at each other in silence, and then Farrah made a face and put down the pen.

"She didn't happen to take a picture, did she?"

I shook my head. "Her powers of observation are, admittedly, somewhat lacking."

"So, all we really know is that he . . . what? Has a *manly body?*"

I laughed in spite of myself.

"Which," Farrah continued, "to a teenage girl could mean anything from a twenty-year-old to a very fit fifty-year-old."

"Well," I said, trying to look on the bright side, "at least we can rule out T.C. Satterly, who runs on the heavy side. And Wendell Knotts, who runs on the elderly side."

"I suppose so. I guess it's a start." She finished off her wine, set the glass down, and pushed herself up from the couch. "Anyway, we should get going. Time to go catch us a cheater."

We took my car and parked on the street in front of the building that housed my law office. Farrah, who had insisted on wearing black tights, a black Lycra top, and a black stocking cap, even though she was staying in the car, whipped out her cell phone like it was a spy gadget.

"Synchronize watches," she whispered. "I got eleven-oh-eight."

"Right," I said, opening the car door. "Same

satellite, same time. Now, watch the entrance and buzz me if anyone enters the building."

Unlike Farrah, I wore the same outfit I'd put on to meet Wendell Knotts oh, so many hours ago that morning. Stifling a yawn, I crossed the sidewalk, my footsteps echoing in the silence. There were no nightclubs on this side of the square, no late-night hangs, and the street was empty. I was pretty sure the maintenance staff wouldn't arrive until 6:00 a.m. and I would be alone in the building. Still, I moved quickly and furtively. Catlike, in honor of Farrah and her *Mission: Impossible* fantasies.

Once inside the suite, I went straight to Julie's desk, where I retrieved the master key that unlocked all the interior offices. Lucky for me, this place wasn't exactly high security. Then I proceeded to Jeremy's office, let myself in, and flipped on the light. I glanced around, took in the clutter and general disarray, then sat down at his desk. Bits and pieces of spilled caramel corn lined the edges and filled the crevices in his keyboard. *Blech.* I'd have to talk to him about that.

Carefully, I set aside the legal pads, folders, and assorted papers, mentally noting their arrangement so I could replace them after studying the blotter. Then I leaned down and squinted at Jeremy's scrawls to see what I could make out among the coffee rings and the unidentified food stains. *Okay, Jeremy. Where ya been?* Meetings with clients, closings, court dates, a dentist appointment. Good luck with that, considering all the sticky caramel corn. But what about Thursday night, when Stacey showed up at my town house? I zeroed in on the calendar square for June 13 and . . . *Bingo*. There, in the corner, it said, *RQ 8:00.*

RQ?

I searched the other dates and found several more with the same cryptic notation, though sometimes with different times: RQ 7:00, RQ 9:30. *And coming up? Well, what do you know*, I breathed. For tomorrow night, Saturday: *RQ 6:30.*

I took out my cell phone, pressed the camera icon, and snapped a flash photo of Jeremy's blotter. Then I replaced his jumble of papers as best as I could and rolled back from his desk. Frowning, I looked around the room for any further clues. Who or what was RQ?

The desk drawers held office supplies. And more food crumbs. The filing cabinets contained files. The space under his desk hid gym shoes, a navy blue duffel bag, a box of case files, and a portable fan. The trash can . . . I shuddered to think what might be in there. But I knew I should check. Carefully, I tipped it on its side and, with a ruler from Jeremy's desk, stirred the contents, eyeing each piece in the mess. A wadded-up sandwich wrapper, an empty chip bag, a pop can—which, I noted to my chagrin, should really be in the recycling bin in the kitchen instead of in the trash—some junk mail, also recyclable, and a clump of folded receipts.

Hmm. Receipts. There could be evidence there of Jeremy's whereabouts. I grabbed them from the can and slipped them into my purse. I wanted to get out of there; Farrah was probably getting antsy.

After taking a last quick look around Jeremy's office, I righted the trash can, shut off his light, and left the room.

But once out in the quiet hall, I paused, struck by a thought. Maybe it was something about snooping around a deserted place in the middle of the night that put me in a suspicious frame of mind, but it suddenly occurred to me that all my colleagues here knew about the Shakespeare Folio. I tried to think back as to who might have known Eleanor still had the book when she died. Who might also have known the hour of the visitation—a time when Eleanor's house was likely to be unattended. Of course, anyone might have learned of the visitation from the obituary or even by inquiring at the funeral home. But I recalled three people I had told directly the day after Eleanor died: Pammy, Jeremy, and Crenshaw.

Pammy's office was right there in front of me, and Crenshaw's next to hers. After the slightest vacillation, I let myself into her room, flicked on the light, and gazed around a neat but crowded office. The lingering aroma of heavy floral perfume filled the air. Vases, picture frames, and knickknacks covered every surface, while stacks of files filled the corners. Under Pammy's desk were several department store shopping bags. I took a peek and found they held boxes of shoes and assorted articles of clothing with the price tags still attached. A cabinet in the credenza contained even more shopping bags. I raised an eyebrow and considered this for half a second. Then I shook myself. *What am I doing?* Brandi saw a well-built guy leaving Eleanor's place. Pammy did not fit the description.

But a newly shaven Crenshaw?

I slipped into his office next, opened drawers and cabinets, riffled through papers, searched under his desk and in every corner. At a minimum, I thought I might find evidence of him stealing my clients, but there was nothing of interest. Even his wastepaper basket was nearly empty. I was about to leave when something about Crenshaw's bookcase caught my eye. The second row of law books, which were lined up perfectly straight and flush with one another, stuck out a couple of inches from the shelf. I cocked my head, mentally measuring the space. Could there be something hidden behind the books?

I grasped *Black's Law Dictionary,* slid it out, and sure enough, there was another book tucked behind the others. Removing a couple more from the front row, I reached in to extract the hidden book and started when I made out the word *Shakespeare* on the cover. *For real?*

Of course, it wasn't the Folio. It wasn't nearly as large or as old. Plus, this book had a red binding. Still, it was an interesting find. I plopped myself down on the carpeted floor, folded my legs, and took a look at the book Crenshaw had so carefully hidden away: *Shakespeare's Sonnets.* I opened the cover, scanned the contents, read a few lines of poetry. It was no surprise Crenshaw was a Shakespeare buff. He quoted the bard any chance he got. So why hide this book away?

Then I noticed a piece of paper sticking out from

the book. Turning to the marked page, I found it was the section on love sonnets. I unfolded the paper to find, in Crenshaw's careful slanting hand, an apparent attempt at his own fourteen lines of iambic pentameter. There were strike outs and alternative rhymes jotted in the margins. The work was clearly unfinished. But I knew what was going on here. A slow grin spread across my face as a singsong chant floated through my mind. *Crenny's in love. Crenny's in love.*

I looked down to read his effort at poetry again, vaguely wondering about the object of his affection. Softly, I read aloud, "Your sparkling beauty I have long ador'd. With silken hair and eyes like—" A noise from the lobby made me jump.

Was that the door? Slowly, I closed the book on my lap and listened intently, eyes wide. Another sound, definitely from the lobby. After scrambling to my feet, I hastily shoved the book back in its hiding place and returned the law volumes to the shelf, doing my best to make them even. Then I shut off the light, hurried out of the room, flew down the hall, and skidded to a stop as I found myself face-to-face with none other than Crenshaw Davenport. The Third.

I squeaked out a gasp as my hand flew to my chest. For a moment, he looked as startled as I felt. Then his gaze slipped behind me to his own office door, which, I belatedly realized, I had failed to close tightly in my mad-dash exit.

He narrowed his eyes and looked at me accusingly. "What are you doing here?" he demanded.

"I work here," I answered, jutting out my chin defensively. "I *wasn't* fired, you know. I—I needed to get something from my office. Anyway, what are *you* doing here?"

"I saw that the lights were on."

"Oh."

"It seemed unusual, given the ripeness of the hour."

"Yes, well, I thought it was better to stop in after hours. You know, under the circumstances and all. But it is late, so I'll be going now. Good night." I scooted past him and rushed out the door before he could question me any further. I had never been a very good liar.

So much for giving Crenshaw a piece of my mind.

As I walked up to my car, I saw that Farrah was outside, leaning on the trunk and facing the alley adjacent to the office building. She was on her phone. I tapped her on the shoulder, causing her to jump, twirl, and drop the phone.

"Hey," I said "Lookout kid. You were supposed to be watching the entrance. I was caught!"

"What? Oh, no! Jeez. I'm sorry." She picked up her phone, saw the call had ended, and shrugged. "Jake called, and I got distracted. Who caught you?"

We got in the car, and I told her everything as I drove her home. Well, not quite everything. I filled her in on what I had found in Jeremy's office and on my little encounter with Crenshaw. But I skipped the middle part, where I poked around in Pammy's and Crenshaw's offices. I wasn't quite ready to accuse my colleagues of anything nefarious in connection with the Folio. Now that I thought about it, the idea that they could be involved in any criminal activity was pretty outlandish, and the fact that I had snooped in their things only made me look childish and disloyal.

After braking at a stoplight, I reached into my purse and handed Farrah my phone. "Check out the photo I took."

She squinted at the photo of Jeremy's calendar, then tossed the phone back in my purse. "I'll look at it after you transfer it to a bigger screen. So RQ, huh? Randy Quaid?"

I snorted. "That's better than the one I came up with—Ramona Quimby. Oh, see what this is." I fumbled in my purse again and dug out the wad of receipts.

Farrah took them and turned on the overhead light. "Contents of a man's pocket?"

"Probably."

"Roast beef sandwich, medium Coke."

"Skip that one. Anything else?"

"Box of Cracker Jack. Bottle of Gatorade."

"Next."

"Cash-out voucher."

"Cash-out voucher?"

"Yeah. For seventeen cents. Here's another one for twenty-two cents. No wonder he threw them away."

"But where did he get them?"

"Let's see. Ah. Interesting."

"We found RQ?"

"Yes, we did. Good work!"

"Tell me!"

Farrah laughed. "Get this. River Queen Casino."

"The River Queen? That steamboat casino on the edge of town?"

"The one and only."

"And that's where Jeremy will be tomorrow night. . . ."

I pulled up in front of Farrah's building and turned to face her. "Up for a little gambol tomorrow?"

"You are too funny," she said, exiting the car. "See ya tomorrow, partner."

CHAPTER 15

"What does one wear to a casino?" I stood before my closet, at a loss.

"You see everything," said Farrah from her perch on the edge of my bed. "For fun, we should go the LBD route. All the better to blend in with the cocktail crowd."

"LBD?"

"You know, little black dress. Come on. Pick one and let's go. We've got to stop by my place yet, and the clock's a-tickin'. Your boy's calendar said six thirty, right?"

"Yeah, yeah, okay." I grabbed a little satin number and matching strappy black heels and dressed quickly.

Farrah had stopped over this afternoon to coax me into watching a *Thin Man* marathon on the old movie channel. I was okay with her popping in—I always kept my bedroom door closed. But between the old movies and our usual gabbing, we had let the time slip away. So, when Farrah had stood up and said, "Come on. Let's find you an outfit for tonight," I couldn't argue with her. But I had insisted that she wait in the living room while I "made my bed."

"Oh, don't be silly," she had said. "I don't care if your bed is made."

"Just humor me," I'd said hastily. "I've got a thing. A hang-up. Just give me a sec." Then I'd dashed into my room to hide away several incriminating items. I'd had to make my altar look more like a decorative bedroom table and less like a Wiccan shrine.

Now, as I took a few essentials from my everyday purse and tossed them into my little black purse, I said to Farrah, "I hope we're not overdressed."

Forty-five minutes later, having left Farrah's car in the marina parking lot and having picked our way up the long gangway to board the triple-decker *River Queen*, we stood at the entryway, gazing into the main game room. Then we looked at one other.

"We are so overdressed," I said.

Everywhere we looked, at the flashing slot machines along the walls, around the poker tables, the blackjack tables, and the roulette wheels, were middle-aged folks clad mostly in jeans and shirtsleeves. The dressier ones, men and women, wore golf shirts and slacks. A few older ladies wore flowery prints. One such lovely, four feet tall and carrying a purse that must have weighed as much as she did, tapped Farrah on the elbow.

"This TITO over here took my ticket and didn't give me credit."

"I beg your pardon?"

"My ticket got stuck in the TITO machine. You need to come get it out. I had fourteen dollars on that ticket!"

"Um, I don't work here," said Farrah, furrowing her eyebrows. "Sorry."

The woman looked taken aback and turned to me next. Before she could get a word out, I pointed to a uniformed security guard. "Ask him," I said, steering Farrah toward the door.

"Why did she think I work here?" asked Farrah, still perplexed as we made our way to the promenade.

"Probably 'cause you look like you know what's what," I said. "Now, what say we take a tour of this place and see if we can spot Jeremy? You know what he looks like, right?"

"I met him at your office a while ago," she said, a teasing glint in her eye, "but I saw his backside recently, when y'all were dirty dancing at the Loose."

"We were not dirty dancing!" I protested, nudging my arm into Farrah's.

She only tossed her head back and laughed, while I fanned my face to cool the embarrassed flush.

For the next twenty minutes we strolled the whole ship, walking up and down stairs and through passageways, in and out of game rooms, restaurants, and souvenir shops. Finally, we stopped in at the lounge on the top deck and ordered martinis. We took them over to a tall round table facing the promenade and sat there, watching people walk by. As we sipped our drinks, a bachelor party filed in, followed shortly by a bridal shower group, all young and decked out. Now I didn't feel quite as out of place in my cocktail dress, but I was starting to feel edgy.

"What should we do?" said Farrah, playing with the olive in her glass.

"Let's make another round of the ship. He's got to be here someplace."

We circled the upper deck again, then wandered down into the large game room on the second level. By this time, Farrah was growing weary of the fox hunt with no apparent fox. She tugged my arm when we came to an empty seat at a flashing machine near the door.

"As long as we're here, I think I'll try my hand at the slots. I gotta see what this TITO business is all about," she said.

"All right. Just try to keep an eye out for any youngish men coming or going, okay?"

"You got it," she agreed. But I immediately saw the folly in this plan, as Farrah slid a twenty into the machine and pulled back on the crank. The hypnotic spinning images had pulled her in already. "Come on, triple cherries!"

"Oh, well," I sighed. This whole search seemed to be fruitless, anyway. As I roamed around the room, studying each glazed and dazed face, I wondered if there was some other way I might help poor Stacey.

No sooner had this thought crossed my mind than I rounded an ample gold-trimmed pillar and spotted him. Jeremy Bradson. There he was, settled at a poker table in a shadowy back corner, wearing an open-necked, button-down shirt and looking obnoxiously cute—especially in comparison to the other two players I could see, a grizzled older man with a potbelly and a scrawny, weathered-looking fellow, also with a potbelly. To Jeremy's right was another man, who was wearing a baseball cap, with his back to me. Jeremy leaned over slightly to say something to this guy, and when the guy turned his head, I could see who it was. Rob Callahan.

I jumped back behind the pillar and peeked around it in wonder. Jeremy and Rob were friends? Or at least acquaintances. And Rob was a gambler. . . . This must be the addiction Rob's baseball teammates were talking about. Did Jeremy have a gambling problem, too? Was this the big secret he was keeping from his girlfriend? Not some sordid affair?

As I pondered all these questions, I noticed Jeremy talking to Rob again and nodding toward the front of the room. Rob twisted around in his seat, then widened his eyes and rapidly turned back around. I craned to see what it was that had caused such a reaction, and nearly hit the floor myself. Striding down the center aisle was a very large, very determined dude, with a menacing glare and a mean-looking scar . . . on a face I remembered seeing at my office building the other day.

I turned back to the poker table and saw that Jeremy had remained in the game, unfazed. But Rob had vacated his seat and, cap pulled low over his forehead, had maneuvered around the roulette wheel toward a back exit. Making a split-second decision, I scurried over to retrieve Farrah.

"Come on!" I hissed. "He's getting away!"

She looked startled but stood up without hesitation. "Jeremy?"

"No. Rob." I grabbed Farrah's hand and pulled her through a throng of people surrounding the blackjack table.

"I was losing, anyway. Ticket in, ticket out, my arse," she grumbled. "More like money *in* the machine and *out* of my pocket."

We soon found ourselves in a passageway behind the game room. We passed some restrooms and the back entrance to a restaurant. I figured Rob must have ducked into one of those places. As we rounded the corner toward the starboard promenade, I saw a white-haired couple walking toward us, and they looked uncannily like my neighbors, Mr. and Mrs. St. John. I halted in my tracks, causing Farrah to bump into me. But as I realized that this couple was not, in fact, Mr. and Mrs. St. John, I caught a glimpse of a tall, attractive man coming up behind them. And this person *was* who I thought it was: one Wesley "Rock Star" Callahan.

I had done an about-face and had proceeded to drag Farrah in the opposite direction when I caught sight of Rob again. He looked over his shoulder at the shadow of a giant looming over him.

Caught between the two brothers and not knowing what in the heck was going on, I thought only to hide. Farrah, astutely picking up on this desire, was of the same mind. Together, we darted into the nearest souvenir shop and dove behind the heavy burgundy curtain that, conveniently, presented itself before us.

My heart thudded in my chest as I strained to see in the dark. Bumping into some boxes, I reached out my hands and felt a soft, filmy material. Suddenly, the tinny crescendo of a player piano filled the room at the same time that a bright light flared on overhead. I squinted at Farrah, who seemed to be wearing a feather boa. Then I looked down to see that I was holding a pair of black fishnet stockings.

"Go ahead and costume up, ladies!" boomed a voice from the other side of the curtain. "We're just opening up, but I'm ready when you are."

For a split second I feared we had found ourselves backstage at some kind of burlesque karaoke show. But as I looked around, I realized where we were. My exuberant friend was way ahead of me.

"Sweet!" said Farrah. "It's an old-timey photo parlor." She riffled through a box, donned a cowboy hat, and tossed me a lasso. "This could be handy for wrangling up those outlaws out there." She paused a beat. "Why are we hiding from them again?"

I shook my head. "I don't know. I feel like something weird is going on. I'm thinking it might be wise to keep a low profile right now, you know?"

Farrah flung an elastic garter at me, slingshot-style. "Suit up then, hippie chick. What's your alias gonna be?" She grabbed a couple more costumes and held them up, one in each hand. "Frontier hippie in a fringed skirt? Or steampunk in a lacy bustier?"

"'Bout ready, ladies?" called the voice on the

other side of the curtain. "I've got a washtub out here if you want to do a silly bathing scene."

I made an incredulous face toward the curtain and shook my head. "All right, let's put something on. Anything. I don't care." Then I turned and laughed at Farrah, who was now sporting a mangy beaver pelt hat. "Okay, anything but *that*."

Finally, we each selected a ruffled cancan skirt, a velvet bodice, and a feathered headpiece. Farrah added the boa she had had on originally, and I grabbed a feathery faux-silk hand fan. When we came out, our eager photographer, a slender man with long sideburns, gave us an admiring wolf whistle, then quickly scurried about, arranging the scene and posing us with props. The backdrop was an Old West saloon, complete with a long shelf of prop liquor bottles set up before a vintage oval mirror. Farrah and I sat back-to-back up on top of the polished wooden bar, our legs outstretched, with one knee bent. I held a six-shooter, while Farrah tipped back an empty whiskey bottle.

The photographer kept restarting the player piano, which appeared to be a genuine replica, if not quite an antique, and we actually had fun with the photo shoot. A few passersby stopped to watch, and a handful of guys from the bachelor party lined up for a turn in the booth. Farrah kept winking at them and tossing out Mae West one-liners, but I was too jumpy to flirt. I kept eyeing everyone who walked by, waiting to see a familiar face.

After taking several pictures, the photographer took his camera over to a computer to pull up the images and let us choose which ones we wanted to purchase. Farrah followed him, but I was ready to go change out of my costume. Just as I was pulling back the curtain, the photographer called over to me.

"Hey, would you be a doll and start up the piano again?"

Shrugging off the baby talk—I *did* feel like a doll in this getup—I wandered over to the player piano and found the ON switch. When I was done, I retrieved the fan I had set down and turned toward the dressing area. Just then, the back of my neck prickled, and I was certain someone was watching me. I could have slipped behind the curtain, but my curiosity was too strong. Instead, I unfolded the fan, brought it before my face, and slowly turned around.

I was right about being watched. Standing at the edge of the crowd, mouth open just a little in surprise, was Wes. Our eyes met, and my pulse quickened. Then he broke out into a wide grin. *Busted.*

I lowered the fan and used it to cool my face as Wes unchained the velvet rope that blocked the entrance to the photo parlor and let himself inside. He looked me up and down with mischievous eyes, and I began to wish there really were whiskey in the bottle on the bar. I could have used a stiff drink right about then.

"Nice dress."

"What? This old thing?"

"Did I miss the show?"

"'Fraid so." We looked at one another for a moment, and I started to feel awkward. The next line on the tip of my tongue was, "Come here often?" But I couldn't bring myself to say it.

Wes leaned his elbow on the bar. "Do you come here often?"

I chuckled inwardly and fluttered my lashes coyly. "First time, actually. Honest."

The photographer walked up then, and I looked over to see Farrah chatting with the guys in line. She didn't seem to be in any hurry to go get changed. The photographer reached over and took down a cowboy hat hanging on a peg on the wall and offered it to Wes.

"Shall we do a couple's shot now? I have a washtub if you want to do a funny bathing scene."

Wes raised his eyebrows, and I let out a nervous laugh. "I think I'm going to go get changed now," I said. Then, to Wes, "Do you want to go grab a drink at a real bar? I know a place upstairs."

With a backward glance, Wes bit his lip, apparently conflicted. "I would . . . but I'm kind of looking for . . . Don't get me wrong. I'd really like to." He looked meaningfully into my eyes, and I didn't doubt his sincerity. But I shrugged one bare shoulder, trying not to appear as disappointed as I felt.

Wes took a step closer to me. "Hey, we're still on for tomorrow, right? Country drive, picnic?"

"Sure. Absolutely."

"Good." With a glint in his eye, he put on the cowboy hat, tipped the brim at me, and nodded his head. Then he reached out with his left hand and touched my upper arm, while with his right hand, he tossed the hat onto the bar behind me. "So long, purty lady," he drawled.

I stood there, rooted to the floor, as I watched him disappear into the crowd. Part of me was vaguely concerned with how odd it was that he was there in the first place. But even more worrisome was the lingering sensation of his brief touch of my skin. I had it bad for this guy. And I didn't know if it was gonna turn out good, bad, or . . . real bad.

CHAPTER 16

Om. Om. Om, Shanti. Om. Breathe in . . . peace. Breathe out . . . love. Breathe in . . . Wes. Breathe out. . . . Damn. This wasn't working.

I opened my eyes, uncrossed my legs, and stretched my arms to the ceiling. Then I hopped up and decided to try something else to calm the butterflies in my stomach. I had woken up uncommonly nervous in anticipation of my date with Wes. I had already gone for a run, worked in my garden, taken a long shower. Now I tried to meditate, but even that wasn't working.

I still had more than an hour before Wes would pick me up. Today was Father's Day, and Wes had called to ask if we could do a mid-afternoon picnic, since he would be having brunch with his family and Skyping with his father. That was fine by me. It was only right that he should spend time with his family today. I had already called my dad and had a nice chat, deftly brushing off all questions about how work was going. It was a ten-and-a-half-hour drive to my hometown in Nebraska, so I saw my folks only two or three times a year. But we spoke on the phone or e-mailed at least once every couple of weeks, so it didn't take long to catch up. Dad was pleased with the books I had sent him, a trio of historical biographies, and he had hinted that I'd be getting a similar package in the mail for my birthday in a few days.

Now I was killing time, trying to get my nerves under control. As I sat on the deck, painting my toenails, I realized I hadn't been this nervous before a date since I got asked out by the star quarterback in the ninth grade. For some reason, this rendezvous with Wes felt extra significant. Maybe it was because of my love spell, which I had continued to nurture, with help from Mila's love charm. Or maybe it was just that Wes was so damn hot.

Or maybe it was the decidedly *intimate* nature of our date.

I couldn't stop thinking about the fact that this would be the first time we would really be alone together . . . side by side in a snug little car and then one-on-one at our private little picnic. It wasn't very likely he would be called away again. It would be just the two of us, alone, cozy, comfortable. Romantic.

I was excited, for sure. But I was also jittery, because of the missing Folio hanging over my head. For one thing, there was the not so small matter of Wes's mother, who had all but threatened to sue me. From what I could tell, Wes seemed to be in the same forgiving camp as Rob and Sharon . . . but still. I couldn't help wondering if he harbored any measure of blame toward me for failing to protect and insure the Folio.

Besides that, I was also dying to know what was going on with Wes and his brother, and what the deal was with the thug at the casino. Did Rob owe the guy money? If he was missing half his baseball games to gamble, then it wasn't much of a stretch to imagine he might be carrying some serious gambling debts. And that would be bad news for sure.

I wondered how much Wes would confide in me about the whole business. We would have plenty of time to talk.

As it turned out, having the time did not necessarily translate into taking advantage of it. After picking up some sandwiches from the vegan bakery, Wes and I were mostly quiet on the drive out of town. It was a clear, blue-sky day. Birds chirped, bees buzzed, and I felt pretty good. Wes played upbeat jazz on the radio and made intermittent small talk, but our conversation gradually tapered off after the first ten minutes. Wes didn't say anything about running into me on the River Queen. Nor did he mention the waitress at the Cozy Cafe who had told him I was asking about him. Zip about the Folio, too. Pretty soon, all the things unsaid seemed to hang in the air between us, and I wound up gazing out the window, feeling increasingly shy.

And speculating. When it came down to it, I knew more about Wes's family from Sharon and Eleanor than I did about Wes. I mean, I definitely had good vibes around him. He seemed kind and intelligent. But there was so much more that I didn't know. Who knew what secrets might be lurking beneath the attractive exterior?

I gave Wes a sidelong glance and thought back to

the night before at the casino. What was Wes doing
there, anyway? I had the impression he wasn't hanging out on the riverboat for fun. For all I knew, Rob
wasn't the only one with a gambling problem. Maybe
it even ran in the family, starting way back with
Grandpa Frank's Saturday night poker games.

As a matter of fact, if Wes was living in a bar, he
must be hard up for money.

After a while, the roadside cornfields gave way to
thickening stands of trees, and I realized we must
be near the state conservation area surrounding
Diamond Point Lake. One wooden sign pointed
the way to Briar Creek Cabins a mile west, while
others advertised boat rentals and pick-your-own
strawberry patches to the east. Straight ahead the
land became hilly, and another road sign told us
there was hiking, camping, and fishing not too far off.

But Wes didn't follow any of those signs. Instead,
he slowed the car and turned into a narrow un-
marked lane, nearly hidden from the road. We
bounced along under the overhanging trees for several minutes, until he pulled off the lane and into
a small hidden clearing. It would have been easy to
miss if you didn't already know it was there.

"There's a nice picnic spot near here," he said,
cutting the engine. He opened his door and exited
the car. I stepped out on my side and looked
around. There was nothing but trees in all directions. A crow called from high overhead, and then
it was quiet. It was peaceful . . . and secluded.

I looked back to see that Wes had gone around
to open the trunk. I thought maybe he had a blanket back there, but he pulled out a black duffel bag,

shut the trunk, and set the bag on top. I stayed by the open car door, keeping my eye on Wes as he unzipped the bag and fiddled with something inside. Our lunch was on the backseat. So, what was he messing with in the duffel bag?

Under the shadows, the air was cooler and very still. I could feel goose bumps rise on my arms as it suddenly struck me how this scenario might look to an outsider. *Girl meets boy. Girl falls for boy and goes off with him to a remote spot deep in the dark, lonely woods. Boy turns out to be . . .* What? A crazed killer? No way. Wes wasn't dangerous.

Still, here we were, all alone. Not a soul around. There was no place to run, even if I wanted to. No one to hear me scream

I swallowed hard and licked my dry lips. "Um, whatcha doing?" I asked, trying to sound calmer than I felt.

He looked up with a strange expression. "I finally have my chance," he said.

"Chance?" I echoed. I impulsively glanced into the car, hoping to find the keys still in the ignition, but he had taken them with him. I looked back at Wes, who stared at me with an inscrutable expression. My heart started thudding madly as Wes slowly began to raise his arm.

"A chance to shoot you."

I gasped sharply and stepped backward, stumbling over a fallen branch. Adrenaline surged as I prepared to fly off into the woods. Wes walked around the car toward me, and I let out a constricted squeak as he lifted his hand . . . and showed me the camera he held.

"What's the matter? Camera shy?"

He walked over to me, hanging the professional-looking camera on a strap across his chest. I exhaled heavily and slumped against the car. Trying not to let on that I'd just suspected him of wanting to attack me, I faked a small laugh. "Why would you want to take pictures of me?"

"Are you kidding? You're gorgeous. The camera will love you. Come on."

He headed into the trees, and I hesitated for a moment, looking after him. Then I shook myself, letting go of the residual fear. *See?* I told myself. I had been right all along. I should have listened to my instincts, which had liked Wes from the get-go. Taking a deep breath, I followed him down the path.

Before long, a bubbling creek came into view. As I got closer, I saw that it led to a meandering river lined by sycamores, elms, and white oaks. Wes walked over to a large flat rock and crouched down to photograph delicate flowering spikes of blue vervain on the water's edge.

"What a lovely place," I murmured, gazing at the river and the birds soaring and dipping.

I joined him on the rock and slipped off my sandals. Dangling my feet in the water, I took in the serenity of the scene and idly reached down to break off a sprig of the blue vervain. I knew it could be useful for its healing properties. Nearby, a pair of ducks bobbed for food, while a slender damselfly flitted from leaf to leaf. I tilted my face to the sun and closed my eyes for a moment, feeling so much calmer than before. When I opened them, I saw

Wes looking at me. He smiled and, without a word, crouched down and aimed his camera at me.

"So, you're a photographer, huh?"

"Yeah. Didn't I tell you?"

"Uh-uh. I thought you were a musician, actually."

Wes grinned at that. "I'm not that cool," he said.

He took a few shots, then sat down next to me. I could feel the warmth radiating from his body, and I suddenly longed to touch him. Imagined touching him. But I quickly checked myself, mentally shaking my head. I must be crazy. The relief at feeling safe again must be lowering my inhibitions.

I snuck another peek at Wes's profile, trying to figure him out. One thing I knew for sure, I really did like him. But I didn't know for sure how he felt about me.

More importantly, I couldn't forget he was a suspect. Even if he wasn't dangerous, he could still be a thief. I should be questioning him about where he was the night of the robbery.

"Wes?"

"Yeah?" he said, turning toward me.

"We forgot our lunch in the car."

A slow grin crept over his face as his eyes moved from my eyes down to my mouth and back. "You know," he said tentatively, "there's actually something I'd like to do more than eat right about now."

"Oh?" *Be still, my heart.* Without thinking, I looked at his lips, too, and leaned toward him ever so slightly.

Apparently, that was enough of an opening for

him. He leaned in, angled his head, and brought his lips slowly, gently, to mine.

Part of me was startled. The other part felt completely at ease.

I kissed him in return, feeling myself dissolve into his lips. He pulled back, looked into my eyes for confirmation and, seeing it, kissed me again. With eyes closed, I let myself surrender to the moment.

I guessed this answered the question as to how he felt about me.

Wes brought a hand behind my neck, and I found myself encircling his broad shoulders with my arms. I ran my fingers through his thick hair as we kissed, our bodies inching closer and closer together. All rational thought left my mind as I allowed him to ease me back onto the rock.

"Whoot, whoot! Yeah, baby!"

Wes lifted his head, and I looked over his shoulder to see a couple of kayakers not fifteen feet away. They laughed, and one lifted his camera phone to take a picture. Wes, apparently inclined to ignore them, turned back to resume his position. But I sat up and put my hand like a visor over my face to hide from the would-be paparazzi.

Wes grunted and sat back on his haunches. "Guess this place isn't as private as I thought."

I narrowed my eyes. "Have you—" I stopped myself before asking if he had been here at make-out point before. I knew I had no standing for jealousy, and besides, that was so beside the point right now. Actually, I was grateful for the interruption.

Okay, not all of me was grateful. Just the sane part.

"Should we get our lunch?" I suggested.

"Yeah. Sure." Wes stood up, looking embarrassed now.

Without further conversation, we found the path back to the car. My body still tingled, and I sort of hoped Wes would reach out to hold my hand. He didn't, but we did walk close to one another, our arms brushing now and then.

When we reached the car, he pulled out his phone to check the time. "It's getting kinda late," he said. "It's after five. Mind if we eat as we drive?"

I shook my head and got in the car. I unwrapped our food as Wes maneuvered the car out of the forest. Back on the main road, we continued toward the farm in a more companionable quietness. Locking lips had a way of bringing people closer together.

"You know," I said thoughtfully, watching the countryside, "I think this is the area where my aunt lived years ago."

"Oh, yeah?" he said.

"Yeah. On a commune, believe it or not. It was in the seventies." I looked at Wes, waiting for his reaction.

He raised his eyebrows and glanced my way. "That's cool," he said. "What kind of commune? Like an artists' colony or something?"

"I actually don't know," I admitted. "It's kind of a sore subject in my family. My aunt was only seventeen when she left, against my grandparents' wishes. She basically cut ties with them, never went back. She'd send a postcard every few years, letting them know she was still alive, but that was it. As far as I know, nobody knows where she is now."

"Wow," said Wes. "That's deep."

"To tell you the truth," I said, feeling comfortable enough with Wes to open up a little, "she's part of the reason I chose Edindale for law school. Although I never met her, I've always felt a special sort of connection with Aunt Josephine. I admire her renegade spirit. Plus, our birthdays are in the same week, exactly thirty years apart. She even sent a couple of postcards to me, one on my tenth birthday and one on my twentieth."

Wes smiled softly. "Well, I'm grateful to your aunt, then," he said. "If you hadn't come to Edindale, then I never would've gotten to meet you."

Awww. My heart melted, and I almost leaned over and kissed Wes again right there in the car. He was like a shot of butterscotch schnapps: hot, sweet, and apt to make me feel a little bit giddy.

Wes slowed the car, turned into a gravel lane, and picked up our conversation. "I can kind of relate to the connection you have with your aunt," he said. "I feel the same way about my uncle Kirk. He was kind of the black sheep, too, and ran off to New York after high school to be a stage actor. I always looked up to him as a kid, even though he probably wasn't the best role model." Wes chuckled to himself but didn't elaborate.

"I met him at the visitation," I said. "He seemed really nice. And funny too."

"Yeah, that's Kirk. Always lightening the mood, no matter what. He's had an unlucky streak this past year—laid off from his day job right after the local theater he was involved in shuttered its doors. But it hasn't seemed to bring him down, at least not that I've seen."

I remembered what Sharon had told me about Kirk's "pride for Shakespeare" and about how he didn't want his mom to sell the Folio. And that was in spite of the fact that he probably could have really used the money.

Of course, the money split among multiple family members—not to mention all the other beneficiaries Eleanor had had in mind—would have amounted to a lot less than the full jackpot for each. Whoever had the Folio now wouldn't have to share.

Wes left the gravel lane, such as it was, and steered the car down a dusty driveway that cut through expansive fields of wheat to our left and corn to our right. We slowed to a stop where the driveway ended, in a small grove of trees next to the foundation remains of what I guessed was an old farmhouse.

"Welcome to the Mostriak homestead," said Wes, opening his door. I got out, too, and followed him to the edge of the crumbling, weedy foundation.

"So, this was your grandpa Frank's home?" I asked.

"Yeah. He grew up out here. Him and his six brothers and sisters. He lived out here with his family pretty much until he met my grandma. After that, he got a job and a house in town, and they got married."

"It's peaceful out here," I remarked.

We wandered around the old yard. Wes snapped a few photos, taking advantage of the soft late afternoon light. We peeked in an old barn, which contained a tractor and other tools used by the farmer who managed the land. Then Wes showed me the place where the other barn had burned down.

"Do you know if that fire was ever investigated at the time?" I asked.

"Nah. No one was hurt, and my grandpa's family never asked for an investigation. At least I don't think so. Maybe they figured there wouldn't be any proof. I don't really know."

"But the story was that the Folio was destroyed in the fire?"

"Yeah. I mean, there were never any details about that part of the story. Grandpa talked about owning the Folio once. And then it was lost in a fire."

"Yet your grandpa really had it all along. Kept it hidden over the years."

"Yeah. It would appear that he did."

I thought about this as my eyes followed a brilliant dragonfly zipping through the air. We stood by an old three-board corral fence overlooking a meadow of native grasses and wildflowers.

"I wonder if he thought of it as some kind of grand inside joke," I mused. "You know? Maybe that's what he meant by that line of Shakespeare he liked to say. 'Lord, what fools these mortals be.'"

Wes looked at me curiously. "How did you know about that?"

Uh-oh. I hadn't really thought this through. I hesitated a second. "From Rob," I said in my most innocent-sounding voice. I hoped he would let it go. He didn't.

"Rob? When did you see Rob? *Where* did you see Rob?"

"Um, I don't know. The other day."

Wes blinked, and I could almost see the wheels spinning in his mind. "You saw that wooden carving he has. You were at his apartment?"

"Well, yeah. I stopped by, because . . . I was in the neighborhood."

Okay, that sounded lame. But I was afraid the truth would sound even worse. How could I tell Wes I had really been trying to track *him* down . . . because my boss was worried about the law firm's reputation and I was worried about keeping my job?

Wes looked at me for a moment, then looked away. "We better go," he said, swatting his arm. "The mosquitoes are starting to come out."

CHAPTER 17

It felt weird not to go to work on Monday morning. I spent much of the day moping about the house, fretting over my job situation. Was my work piling up? Would I even have any clients left when I went back? *If* I went back?

That is, I fretted over my job when I wasn't obsessing over Wes. I kept going back to our . . . interlude on the rock by the creek. It was such a perfect moment. The setting serene, the passion spontaneous and red hot. Even though we were interrupted, I felt like it could be the start of something promising.

But then I thought about how much of a bust the date had actually been. I hadn't learned a thing. I didn't know anything new about Wes—nothing about his photography, what had taken him to New York and what had brought him back, how and when he'd chosen his tattoo . . . if he had any more. If he'd been in any serious relationships.

If he knew where the Folio was.

And then there'd been that awkward moment

when Wes found out I had gone over to Rob's place. I didn't know if his reaction was due to some jealous sibling rivalry over me or to the rift already between them. Either way, the ride back to town had been much like the ride before, except the music had been even louder—which had allowed for even less talk.

Around lunchtime, Farrah called me for details about my date, and I pretty much told her everything. She laughed about my momentary panic in the woods. "Really? You thought the hottie had a gun?"

"Well, I was already a little on edge," I said defensively. "I just wish I knew for sure he didn't take the Folio. I wish he had an alibi for that night."

"Mmm." I could imagine Farrah frowning on the other end of the line. "Maybe you should hold off on dating any of the suspects for a little while. I don't want to see you get hurt. If you get too tight with Wes, and it turns out he was involved . . ."

I knew what she meant. Unfortunately, it was too late to follow her advice. I was already in too deep with Wes.

"How are we going to catch the thief, Farrah? I'm not really sure what to do next."

"Well, it seems to me we need to keep watching the family, right? Especially the male members. I'll see what I can dig up on Uncle Kirk. I find it interesting, what you told me about his possible sentimental attachment to the Folio."

"Okay," I agreed, sighing. This was all starting to feel a little Machiavellian, the way I was getting closer to the family at the same time I was investigating them.

"And maybe you can learn more about Rob through Jeremy," Farrah went on. "Just ask Jeremy out for a drink at the Loose. But be sure to bring up the gambling boat before y'all hit the dance floor." Farrah laughed, but I wasn't entirely sure she was kidding.

Lord. I still cringed whenever I thought about my poor judgment in getting drunk with Jeremy. It was especially regrettable now that I knew he had a girlfriend—and that she had turned to me for help. Stacey had called this morning to check on my progress. I had told her all about the River Queen and how Jeremy was apparently spending his evenings gambling. But Stacey hadn't been satisfied. When I'd told her I actually saw him for only a couple of minutes, she'd said it was still possible he was meeting someone there.

Talk about suspicious minds.

So, I was still on the case, though I wasn't sure what I would do next on that front, either.

As always when I needed some direction and encouragement, I turned to the craft. When I got off the phone with Farrah, I went into the kitchen to whip up a little herb magic. Standing in the center of the room, I closed my eyes, took a slow, deep breath, and set my intention: to find some inspiration as to where to look next for the answers that eluded me.

Opening my eyes, I knew just the thing. I walked over to the corner cabinet and pulled out the tools I would need for a Japanese tea ceremony: a matcha bowl, a bamboo scoop, a bamboo whisk and, of course, a container of tea—in this case bright green matcha tea. I set about boiling water, warming the bowl with the water, drying the bowl, straining the powdered tea, and carefully adding two delicate scoopfuls to the drinking bowl, all with slow Zen-like movements. Then I added boiled water and whisked the jade-green brew until it had a creamy froth. As I watched the swirling liquid, I repeated my intention, murmured a prayer to the Goddess, and took a healthy mouthful.

Mmm. Essence of summer.

I finished the tea, licked my lips, and nodded. *Of course.* If I wanted a sign, a trail to follow, I would have to leave the house.

After cleaning up the kitchen, I changed clothes and laced up my running shoes. I had plenty of time to make the 6:30 p.m. yoga class over at the gym near my office. I hadn't actually been to the gym since the weather warmed up in the spring, but I still kept a locker there. It was convenient for after-hours workouts in the winter.

After the two-and-a-half-mile jog to the gym, I grabbed my soap, shampoo, and towel from the locker and showered before yoga class. Then I rented a mat and entered the yoga room for forty-five minutes of strenuous asanas, followed by ten minutes of deep, relaxing shavasana, the corpse pose. I came out feeling tranquil, slack, and a little floaty. After turning in my mat at the front desk, I walked over to the water fountain for a cool sip, wondering how long it would take me to amble home in this state.

As I straightened up, the door to the men's locker room opened and out came Jeremy, freshly showered, gym bag in hand. *Ask and ye shall receive*, I thought, with a mental bow to the Goddess.

His eyes lit up when he saw me. "Hey, boss!"

Before I knew what was happening, he pulled me into a close hug, and I inhaled the fresh masculine scent of his body wash and shampoo. I gently pulled back.

"Hi, Jeremy. How are you? How's the office?"

"Same old, same old. We miss you, of course. When are you coming back?"

"Soon, I hope. What has Beverly said?" I tried to sound casual. This whole situation was mortifying enough as it was.

"Not much. She basically said she won't have any gossip around the office. But then she doesn't give us any information to combat speculation. I gather your absence has to do with your client who died, right?"

"Right. I'm actually trying to help the family recover the missing Shakespeare Folio." It was a true statement, even if it might lead one to infer the family had hired me for that purpose. Not my fault how Jeremy interpreted my response.

He raised his eyebrows. "Any luck?"

"Well, I am making progress, as a matter of fact. I've been talking to people, learning a few things. I think I'm getting closer."

Jeremy raised his eyebrows again, looking impressed. "That's awesome. So . . . what are you doing here?"

I laughed. "I needed a break from all that sleuthing.

I just finished a yoga class." Rolling my neck, I stifled a yawn. "But I'm so relaxed right now, I'm not sure I'm quite ready for the trek home. I came here by foot."

"Oh, let me give you a ride, then." He put his hand on the small of my back and turned me toward the door. "You crazy girl, walking all over town," he said in a teasing voice.

I shrugged my shoulders, feeling too weak to protest. Just then I became aware of another guy who must have just exited the locker room. He wore a red sweat suit and carried a matching red duffel bag. He blinked owlishly when I looked his way.

"Crenshaw," I said by way of greeting.

Jeremy turned to him, still with his hand on my back. "Good workout, buddy. I'll see you tomorrow." Then he turned back to me. "My car's right out here in the lot. Hey, do you want to go get something to eat first?"

Crenshaw stood immobile, watching us as we left. He was so weird. I noticed he was growing his beard again, the orange stubble making his face appear dirty.

As we walked to the parking lot across the street from the gym, I wrestled with whether it was really a good idea to go anyplace with Jeremy. But I did want to get some information from him about Rob—and about his own secret outings. Besides, I was sure it was no coincidence that I had bumped into him shortly after asking the Goddess for a divine clue.

"Maybe something light," I agreed. "How about the juice bar around the corner?"

"Sounds good to me. Let's still take the car, though. We already had our workouts."

Jeremy winked at me and unlocked his car. I got in, tossing some papers from the front passenger seat to the back, which appeared to be an annex to Jeremy's office. The backseat was covered with case files, legal pads, and assorted books, including a couple of fat phone directories from Chicago and St. Louis, as well as several days' worth of newspapers. I also noted a number of used lottery tickets littering the floor. Surprisingly, the scent in the car was a not unpleasant combination of caramel corn, faded cologne, and male sweat. I cracked the window as soon as he started the engine.

As we drove along in a comfortable silence, I glanced sidelong at Jeremy, trying to figure out how in the world I could bring up the casino without letting on that I was actually there. Spying on him. I couldn't think of any way.

At the juice bar, we ordered our drinks and took them out to the small patio in front of the shop. We sat at one of the round, umbrella-shaded tables with a view of the square. I took a seat on the attached bench that circled the table, and Jeremy sat down right next to me, within knee-touching distance. I scooted the other way, making an excuse about the sun being in my face, and eyed him warily.

"So, how's Stacey?" I asked.

"She's good. Always studying. By the end of the summer, she'll have earned her master's."

Nothing fazes him. Not a trace of guilt or even

surprise when I brought up his girlfriend. Maybe I was imagining him putting the moves on me.

I brushed off my worries, made an appropriate comment about Stacey's hard work, and sipped my juice. The sky was turning pink and violet, reminding me that this day was about over. I needed to stop wasting time.

"So, Jeremy, do you know if Darlene Callahan has had any more communication with Beverly or the firm?"

He looked at me blankly. "Who?"

"Darlene Callahan. Eleanor Mostriak's daughter. She's the one who came to the office and made a big scene last week." *Prompting you to buy me flowers,* I thought but didn't say.

He shook his head. "Not that I know of."

"The rest of her family is actually pretty nice. I've been talking to some of them, including her sons, Wes and Rob Callahan."

No reaction. Just a polite listening face.

"Rob Callahan actually plays baseball in the local men's league. He's probably about your age. You ever play baseball?"

"Not since I was a kid. Maybe I'll look into it sometime. Are you still running a lot?"

"Yeah." I sighed. "About every day, if I can manage it." This was getting me nowhere. Either Jeremy had a marvelous poker face or he really didn't know the name of the guy who was sitting next to him at the card table the other night.

Jeremy finished off his juice and squinted at the sky. "This was good, but it only whetted my appetite.

How about we stop off at the Loose Rock for a burger and fries?"

The Loose. That was the last place I wanted to go with Jeremy, undercover or not. I had to draw the line somewhere.

Two days later I began to regret not pressing Jeremy more about Rob and the riverboat. I should have just come out and said I was there with a friend, and I thought I saw him. Blah, blah, blah. At least then I could have asked him about the thug with the scarface.

As they said, hindsight was a crystal clear looking glass.

Now I was stuck again.

Worse, it was my birthday.

Here I was, thirty years old. Jobless, loveless, and darn near hopeless. *Terrific.* Who was I to think I could play detective and make everything right? I was starting to despair of ever recovering Eleanor's Shakespeare book. And lately I hadn't even had anyone to commiserate with. Farrah had been busy with work, and I was too embarrassed about my situation to call any other friends.

To shake my dark mood, I went outside to my garden right after breakfast. I pulled weeds, checked the moisture level, gathered vegetables. The spinach and lettuce were flourishing, as were the green onions and sweet peas. I was already planning the big salad I would have later. Amid the soil and plants, I felt exponentially better. Everything would be okay.

"Good morning, Keli! Still on vacation?"

I looked up to see my neighbor, Mrs. St. John, picking her way down the grassy path from her garden to mine, her floppy sun hat bobbing up and down with each step.

"Hello, Mrs. St. John. How are you today?"

"My arthritis is acting up, and my back is sore. And Mr. St. John is driving me batty. Other than that, I'm all right."

I smiled and stood up, then brushed the dirt off my knees. "Well, it's a lovely day, anyway."

"Yes, I suppose. Listen, the reason I came over here is to let you know there was someone hanging around your house earlier this morning."

"What?" I stiffened, my senses on alert.

"I was coming home from the store, pushing my cart up the sidewalk, when I saw him. He was standing on your stoop, kind of hesitating. At first I thought he had knocked on your door and was waiting for you to answer. Then he leaned over and appeared to be messing with your window."

I frowned and glanced over at my back door.

"I called out, 'Young man, what are you doing?' Then he took off running down the sidewalk and around the corner."

"What did he look like?" I asked, already anticipating the answer.

Mrs. St. John knitted her pale gray eyebrows, trying to picture him. "Kind of tall, wearing a blue baseball cap, jeans, a T-shirt. I mainly saw him from the back." She paused and cocked her head. "Who knows what he had in mind. It's a good thing I scared him away."

I shook my head. If not for my concern, I would be amused at the idea of Mrs. St. John scaring anyone—she was barely five feet tall and thin as a wisp. As it was, I was worried not only by someone possibly trying to break into my home, but also by Mrs. St. John's description of the prowler. It was amazing how many men I knew who seemed to meet those stats.

When Mrs. St. John left, I put away my garden tools, took my basket of veggies inside to the kitchen, and walked straight through the house to my front door. I looked all around, wishing vainly for a clue. I guessed footprints, cigarette butts, and hotel matchbooks appeared only for fictional detectives. *Darn.* I did note that my potted daisies needed watering, so I started to go back inside to get the watering can. Just then a delivery truck pulled up, so I waited to see who the package was for. It was my birthday, after all.

Much to my delight, it was a package from Moonstone Treasures. After signing for the delivery, I sat down on the front steps to open it. Carefully, I tore away the outer wrapping, then unfolded the glittery purple, green, and gold tissue paper within to find a beautiful colored-glass framed picture. It was a shimmering print depicting a lovely fairy with iridescent emerald wings twice the size of her delicate body. She sat curled on a tree branch set against a moonlit sky. A soft, mischievous smile played across her rosebud lips.

Beneath the picture was a caption in looping cursive lettering: *I am that merry wanderer of the night.*

Also in the package was a card from Mila. The

front of the card featured a circle of dancing women, while the printed message inside was a short poem about celebrating life. I smiled at this but was even more touched by the handwritten note on the side:

My Dear Keli,
    You have reached a very special milestone . . . and are at the threshold of a magical decade. (Ask me about the power of three sometime, if you'd like.) But, as every Gemini knows well, there are two sides to every coin. At this time in your life, embrace the wisdom of your maturity and the exuberance of your youth. Love your dreams and the trials along the way. Be serious and practical when you need to be, but have fun and laugh every day.
        Blessed be, my friend.
        Mila

P.S. The quote under the picture is Shakespeare ~ A Midsummer Night's Dream. He may have written about hags, but he wrote about fairies, too. It's all magic, don't you think?

I sat on the front stoop for a long time, lost in thought. I would head over to Mila's shop sometime soon to thank her for the lovely gift. But now something tugged at the corner of my mind. There was something I had to do, if I really wanted to help Eleanor. There was someone I had to see. And that someone, I realized, was the person I had been avoiding all along.

CHAPTER 18

Sometimes it was a plus that my family lived hundreds of miles away. It made it easier to fib about how perfectly peachy everything was in my life. After the first three birthday calls, the tall tale started to roll off my tongue with frightening ease. When my phone buzzed again as I walked down the sidewalk toward my car, I was all set to pour on the syrup yet again.

As it happened, I could be myself this time. It was Farrah.

"Hey, birthday chick! Welcome to the wonderful world of thirty. You're gonna love it here, I promise."

"Really?" I said, with the slightest little whine. "When does the wonderfulness kick in? From where I'm standing, the future's not so bright. In fact, I'd say it's flickering, at best."

Farrah laughed as if I were the most amusing thing. "Just you wait, girlfriend. Nothing but wonderfulness tonight. Don't forget. Be at the Loose at seven sharp. Fun-filled festivities await."

"I'll be there," I promised. And I had a feeling I was going to need all the fun I could get after the ringer I was about to put myself through. After starting up my car, I checked the address I'd jotted down, and headed over to Darlene's house.

It was high time, I realized, to make peace with the woman. I needed to find out what she knew and share with her what I had learned. We needed to work together.

About ten minutes later I pulled into a modest subdivision that abutted a local golf course. It wasn't quite the country club, but it was still nice. Unlike so many newer developments, the homes here weren't cookie cutter. I passed brick colonials, low-slung ranches, and shuttered split-levels. As I watched the house numbers, I saw that Darlene's home was a forest-green Craftsman bungalow. It would have been homey and welcoming if not for the police car parked out front, strobe light silently flashing.

Several other cars seemed to be at the house, as well, in the driveway and on the street. I parked across the street and walked over as Kirk bounded out the door and headed to one of the cars along the curb. Dressed in jeans and a plain light blue T-shirt, he looked even more youthful than when I had met him at the visitation. Spotting me, he twitched his mouth into a rueful smile and raised a palm in greeting.

"Never a dull moment," he said, getting into the car.

I watched him take off and raised my eyebrows as I caught a glimpse of his vanity plate: KNGLEAR.

I hesitated for a moment on the sidewalk. Maybe this wasn't the best time to pop in on Darlene. On the other hand, I was dying to know what the cops were doing there. It must not be too terrible if Kirk could joke about it.

Just then the front door opened again, and two unfamiliar police officers came outside.

"Hello," I said, walking over. "Is everything okay?"

The officers eyed me, and one of them pulled out a pocket-size spiral notepad. "There was a robbery here," he said. "Could I have your name and address, please?"

"Keli Milanni. Twelve-oh-eight East Springfield Lane."

"You just arrive?"

"Yes. That's my car there."

"Been here before?"

"No. It's my first time."

"What's your business here?"

That one threw me for a loop. "I'm, uh, here to see Darlene. I—I knew her mother, who passed away recently. I wanted to see how she's doing."

The officer wrote this down and seemed satisfied. He shut his notepad and nodded his head at me dismissively. But I couldn't resist trying to get information from him.

"So, what was stolen?"

"That's not for us to say, ma'am. Bye now."

I shrugged and walked up the steps to Darlene's front porch. I noted the porch swing, the cheerful hanging plants, and the natural jute welcome mat and thought Darlene was a woman after my own heart. Ringing the bell, I wondered if this was where

Wes had grown up. The house certainly seemed big enough to raise a family.

After a short wait, Sharon came to the door. She looked tired and worried.

"Hi, Sharon. I stopped by to see Darlene for a minute. Is . . . is she available?"

Sharon slowly shook her head and spoke softly. "Keli, dear, now is not really a good time. Darlene is resting. I'll tell her—"

"I was hoping to talk to Darlene about the Folio," I said quickly, before she could turn me away. "But I can see it's not a good time. The police told me there was a break-in here."

Sharon stepped outside onto the porch and pulled the door closed behind her. She sat heavily on the porch swing. "Can you believe it? First, the Shakespeare book, and now this."

"Was a lot taken?" I asked, sitting down in a wicker chair adjacent to the swing.

"Some jewelry and cash, for sure. It's hard to tell what else. The place was ransacked, absolutely ransacked. It's almost like they were looking for something specific. Drawers emptied, clothes and papers and books strewn *everywhere*. Oh, poor Darlene."

Sharon sighed and shook her head. I felt for her and the whole family, especially Darlene. The loss of money and valuables was bad enough, but to have someone go through your things and toss them around . . . I could only imagine how violated she must feel.

I decided to keep asking questions now that I was in full-on detective mode.

"When did it happen?"

"It must have happened this morning, while Darlene was at work. A neighbor came over to leave a box of berries on the back patio and noticed the back door standing open. He called Darlene right away."

"Is the door usually locked?"

"Yes. The lock had been forced. Wouldn't be too hard for someone to have snuck into their yard from the golf course out back. It's too bad the neighbor didn't come over sooner."

"I'm so sorry." I pursed my lips and fell silent, contemplating this new development. Was it connected with the theft of the Folio? Then I remembered the other question that had been gnawing at me for the past week. As much as I hated to, I had to bring it up.

"Sharon," I began delicately. "At Eleanor's visitation, you mentioned that you thought there should be an autopsy."

"Oh, there was one," she said, to my utter surprise.

"There was?"

"Yes, her doctor requested it—for medical reasons, not police ones. He wanted to find out if she had had a stroke or had gone into cardiac arrest. She was on various medications, and I guess he wanted to see if there was anything he could learn that might help future patients. Eleanor would have liked that."

"Oh," I said, still feeling a little stunned. "So, what did he learn?"

"Well, the bottom line is that Eleanor had blocked arteries, so it must have been a heart attack, after all."

Well, that's a relief. It was bad enough to be searching for a thief. I couldn't even fathom trying to track down a killer. I sighed, still feeling sad that Eleanor was gone.

"Would you like help cleaning up?" I asked. "I'd be happy to give you a hand."

"Oh, that's nice of you to offer. But we have enough helpers already. Neighbors keep stopping by, and Kirk will be coming back in a bit. And Wes and Rob should be here soon. Darlene is hoping they'll be able to help determine if anything else is missing."

"Okay. Well, I'll get going, then. But would you mind asking Darlene to give me a call whenever she feels up to it?" I jotted down my cell phone number on the back of my business card and handed it to Sharon. "Please tell her I'm sorry about all she's going through."

Sharon thanked me and went back inside. As I walked slowly back to my car, I kept an eye out for Wes or Rob to show up, and I thought about Darlene. I wondered if it was too much to hope that she would actually call me. Technically, it wasn't exactly ethical for an attorney to speak to an opposing party without going through her attorney. But I wasn't wearing my attorney hat today. For one thing, I was on leave from the law firm. Besides that, I didn't intend to talk to her about her lawsuit. I just wanted to talk to her about the missing Folio.

Maybe she had some ideas about who took it.

Or maybe, I couldn't help wondering . . . maybe someone else thought Darlene had it. Maybe that

was what they were looking for when they trashed
her place.

The question was, did they find it?

I decided to leave my car at home and walk to
the Loose for my birthday celebration. It was a
twenty-five-minute walk the long way, but only fifteen minutes if I cut through Fieldstone Park. It was
a nice evening, and I looked forward to seeing
some friendly faces. Farrah had told me she invited
our old friends from law school, as well as fellow
regulars we knew from the Loose. And she'd
promised me she had banned any and all talk even
remotely related to work. If anybody uttered a
single word about my office woes, they'd be ousted
from the party as quick as Farrah could toss a wink
at the bouncer. I smiled at the image.

My spirits lifted even higher when I entered the
club and saw my favorite local band setting up on
the stage. Spotting a gaily festooned area sectioned
off with balloons and streamers at the side of the
bar, I headed over to thank Farrah for arranging
both the band and the party—as well as for the
fact that there were no over-the-hill decorations
anywhere to be seen.

As I passed the bar, Jimi came over and handed
me a large fruity cocktail with a paper umbrella
stamped BIRTHDAY GIRL. "Drinks on the house
tonight," he said, kissing my cheek.

I lifted the glass in a toast of gratitude as he scurried back to the kitchen. Before the evening was
over, I planned to corner him and get the lowdown

on Wes. Glancing over at the closed office door, I wondered if I would see the elusive Rock Star tonight. Maybe Jimi had even mentioned my birthday to him. It was possible.

When I got to the reserved tables, I didn't see Farrah, but there were half a dozen other friends gathered around already. They all wished me happy birthday. Dawn placed a paper lei around my neck, and Katie held up her wallet.

"First round of birthday shots?" asked Katie.

I laughed. "No, no, please. Not just yet. The night's too young. Unlike me."

"Aw, you're still a baby," said Katie. "Don't let anyone tell you otherwise."

I smiled and shook my head. "Where's Farrah?"

"She was on the phone," said Dawn, pointing over to the booths along the wall.

I left the group and walked over to find Farrah sitting alone, staring into space. She looked uncharacteristically somber, a telltale line of worry shadowing her usually sparkling eyes. She looked up as I approached and immediately assumed a big smile.

"There's my groovy birthday chick! I see Dawn got you lei'd already."

I slid into the seat across from her and offered her a sip of my fruity cocktail. She waved it away. "It's all yours, baby. I've got a drink over there on the table somewhere."

"What's wrong, Farrah?"

"What are you talking about? Nothing's wrong. Everything's perfect."

I dipped my chin and gave her a "Gimme a break"

look. "Farrah. It's me. Who were you on the phone with?"

Farrah heaved a big sigh and rolled her eyes. "It was Jake. The big lug nut."

"What did he do?"

"He proposed."

"What!" My eyes popped, and I leaned over the table. "Are you kidding?"

"I wish I were. Can you believe it?"

"He proposed over the phone?"

"No. That was last night. He's been calling ever since I walked out. I told him I need some space, but he won't let up. Finally, I had to tell him to lay off tonight, so he won't keep interrupting the birthday party."

"Oh, honey. He proposed and you walked out?"

"Well, more or less."

I sat there quietly, waiting for Farrah to elaborate.

She tapped her fingernails on the table and looked around the room. Finally, she looked back at me. "Okay, so things were going good again, you know? We both agreed we wanted to be together. Only, his version of 'together' and mine are apparently two vastly different things."

I nodded at her sympathetically.

"I mean, I'm not ready to settle down. I'm only thirty! You understand. You and me, we're both happily single. We've got our careers, our homes, our oats."

"Our oats?"

She stood up and took my hand, then pulled me up with her. "Wild oats. Those ones that need to be sown?" She grinned and marched us back over to the party section. "What the heck does that expression mean, anyway? I've never understood it."

For the next few hours, I was toasted, feted, and generally spoiled. Really, it was much more than I felt I deserved. But I had a great time. We danced, we sang, we laughed. Some of the gang even brought presents. Farrah's gift was the most unique: a jumbo gold-rimmed magnifying glass.

"You're going to need help with the fine print now, given your advanced age and all," she said with a big wink.

I laughed and hugged her, then looked around the bar for the umpteenth time, hoping to catch a glimpse of Wes. No luck, but I did see Jimi talking to the bouncer at the door. I made my way over there before he could disappear again.

"Hi ya, Jimi," I said, linking my arm in his. I wasn't quite hammered, but I was definitely emboldened. "Where is Wes tonight? I know all about the cot in the back. No need to be all covert anymore."

"Sorry about that, Kel," said Jimi, looking down at me with appropriate contrition. "The cot's gone, anyway. Wes moved in with his parents."

My mouth fell open, and I was momentarily speechless. I wasn't sure which was worse, a grown man bunking in a bar or a grown man moving back in with his parents. I quickly snapped my mouth shut and twiddled a finger in my hair. "You don't say? When did he do that?"

"A couple days ago. Monday, I guess it was."

So he was already living there when the break-in happened this morning. I narrowed my eyes and faced Jimi squarely. "Jimi, what is the deal with your buddy Wes? He's a photographer, right? Is he, like, a starving artist or something? Why did he leave New York? Why doesn't he have a job?"

Jimi looked away and shifted uncomfortably. "Who says he doesn't have a job? He works. He bartends here sometimes."

I gripped Jimi's wrist and looked at him intently. "Why can't he afford his own place to live? Did he lose all his money gambling or something?"

Jimi looked at me in surprise, then pulled me to a quieter spot and lowered his voice. "Not Wes. Rob."

Now we were getting someplace. "Rob lost all his money?"

"Rob always needs money. It's gotten pretty bad in the past year or so. He went out to New York to see Wes, ask for a loan, I think. Wes had helped his brother before. But this time he wouldn't give him any money. So Rob stole it instead. He took Wes's wallet, took his debit card, and wiped out his bank account."

Stunned, I could only stare at Jimi.

"That's not all. Besides taking all the cash in Wes's wallet and emptying his bank account, Rob racked up huge bills on Wes's credit cards, too. Bought a bunch of merchandise, which he then sold for cash. Or that's what Wes thinks, anyway."

My brain was swimming. All the birthday drinks people had kept plying me with might have something to do with this, but more than that was my shock. Happy-go-lucky Rob had really done that to his brother? Eleanor's grandson Rob was capable of such a thing?

"And Wes," Jimi continued, "being who he is, refused to turn his brother in. I mean, he was pissed for sure. He had a huge argument with Rob, told him he needed help, really had it out. But he wouldn't call the police. Instead, he packed up and came back to Edindale—partly to start saving up money to pay off his debts and eventually move back to New York, and partly to keep an eye on Rob and convince him to get help."

So that was the big rift between Wes and Rob. Before I could think of any more questions, Jimi squeezed my arm and scooted off toward the kitchen. I noticed then that the band was packing up and the crowd was thinning. I was eager to find Farrah and share the new info I had on the Callahans. But she was occupied with Katie, apparently trying to cut her off and hold her up at the same time. *Yikes.*

I went to the washroom, still reeling from the news about Wes and Rob. When I came out, friends told me good-bye. Then Farrah came up and gave me a big hug.

"I hope you had a marvelous birthday, Keli-Beli. I called a cab for Katie. I'm going to ride with her and then go on home. You want to go with us?"

"Oh, no. I'm fine. It's such a short walk for me, and I could use the fresh air."

"Okay, girlfriend. Call me tomorrow!"

"I will! And thank you again for all this! I did have a marvelous birthday."

I gathered up my gifts, waved at Gary the bartender, and headed out into the night. It was nearly 1:00 a.m. and the streets were quiet as a ghost town. Frankly, I was surprised so many folks had stuck around so late, closing out the bar on a Wednesday night. Now there wasn't a soul in sight.

Everyone must be tucked safe and sound in their cozy little homes, I thought sleepily. *Which is where I ought to be.* For once I was grateful I didn't have to get up early for work in the morning. Yawning, I crossed the street to Fieldstone Park.

The paved walkways were well lit, so I didn't think twice about cutting through the park at this hour. I had done it before after late nights at the Loose. Granted, I was normally with a companion. As the seconds passed and my footsteps echoed in the silence, the shadows seemed to deepen around me. And I soon began to second-guess my cavalier attitude. Especially when my ears detected a second set of footsteps on the pavement behind me.

I picked up the pace, and the steps behind me did likewise. *Shit. You've got to be kidding me.* I couldn't tell how close the person was, but I guessed they were probably some distance back. But getting closer. And here I was, smack-dab in the middle of the park. Up ahead, I saw that the winding path was leading me under a thick canopy of trees.

This was not good.

My pulse quickened with my steps, and the bags I held shook from the bounce in my gait. Shifting my eyes to the left, I noticed the tennis courts next to an open grassy area. I could cut through there, I decided, and meet up with the sidewalk on the other side.

Still walking quickly and keeping an eye on the ground in front of me, I looked behind me. Sure enough, there was someone on the sidewalk about forty feet back. He was tall, well built, dressed in jeans and a T-shirt. And wearing a baseball cap.

Just like whoever had prowled around my front door that morning.

I sucked in my breath and walked faster, nearly breaking into a trot. I spared another glance over my shoulder and saw that the man had left the sidewalk, too. He was following me. And gaining on me.

Okay, sandals or not, I was done pussyfooting around here. I broke into a sprint and propelled myself forward with all my might. I was nearly to the path again, with lungs burning and an awful stitch piercing my side, when my pursuer called out to me.

"Keli! Wait up!"

Panting, I slowed to a stumbling jog and tried to place the voice. On the plus side, it hadn't sounded threatening. Even if it had, I was pretty much spent. Running at full tilt with a stomach full of alcohol was not working out so well. At this point, my best defense might be to hurl on the guy.

The sound of a passing car told me I had reached the edge of the park, so I slowed to a stop under a streetlamp. Fighting to calm my nerves, I turned around slowly and sized up the approaching figure.

"Jeez, Keli," he said, taking off his cap and wiping

his forehead. "You're hard to catch. I'm sorry if I freaked you out."

I squinted at him, then widened my eyes in recognition. "Jake?"

"I tried to get your attention, like, two miles back, but you were in your own world. And then you kept speeding up."

"Well, yeah! I didn't know who was following me. What do you expect, chasing a girl in a dark park?"

"I'm really sorry," he repeated, looking down. "I wanted to talk to you about Farrah."

"Walk with me," I said, heading out to the boulevard. "I need to keep moving to keep my stomach under control. I had a few too many tonight."

"Oh, right. Happy birthday." Jake walked alongside me, looking glum.

"Aw, it's over now, anyway. So . . . how are you, Jake?"

"Confused. I thought Farrah loved me. I thought we were in agreement about making a future together. I can't figure out what she wants."

We crossed the street together and neared my town house. I looked up at Jake and sighed. "You know, if there's one thing about Farrah, it's that she's honest. If she told you she needs space, then that's what she needs."

"Space for what? We were apart for three weeks. Then when we got back together. . . . She said she never wanted to be apart from me again. I don't get her."

"Jake, trust me. Farrah does love you. She's just a very independent person. I don't think you two had actually talked about marriage, did you? I think you caught her off guard. She needs time to think about things."

And I need to get to bed, I thought, pulling out my keys.

"I guess you're right," said Jake. "I'll give her some space, let her come to me when she's ready."

"Good. Now, go home and stop worrying." After sending Jake on his way, I went inside, locked the door behind me, and breathed a huge sigh of relief. What a night. The truth was, Jake was a really nice guy and would probably make a fabulous husband. I mean, I sort of understood Farrah's hesitance. Then again, I also sort of envied her opportunity.

The closest thing I had to a boyfriend right now was . . . not even close at all. I hadn't heard from Wes since our so-called date three days ago, and he had never showed up tonight.

Ugh. I kicked off my shoes and prepared to go flop into bed and sleep away all such boy troubles.

Until a rock came crashing through my front window, shattering all hope of a peaceful night's rest.

CHAPTER 19

It was always hard to get out of bed on an overcast morning. But after the night I had had, I expected to sleep in, anyway. When I woke up and pushed off the covers, I figured it must be at least 11:00 a.m. I squinted at my clock radio. It was nearly 1:00 p.m. *Oops.*

I padded to the bathroom, brushed my teeth, and turned on the shower. The fear and distress of the night before were starting to come back, and I wanted nothing more than to wash it all away. I groaned as I remembered the chaos that had followed the rock hurtling through my window. The noise from the breaking glass was so jarring, it had woken up my neighbors. Then everyone had seemed to arrive at once: Mr. and Mrs. St. John in their matching robes and Larabeth and Bryan, the couple who lived on the other side of my house, in their pajamas.

Luckily, Mrs. St. John had seen a car door slam

on a dark vehicle in front of my place. The car had
sped off, tires squealing, and had been gone before
she could notice any kind of detail.

Still, I'd been relieved that Mrs. St. John had
seen the vandal leave. At least then I had felt relatively safe from any further disturbances. I had
tried to tell my neighbors that it really wasn't necessary to call the police, as there was nothing
they could do. But they wouldn't listen to me. Mrs.
St. John kept telling me I was in shock and trying
to make me stay seated on the couch. Then she told
the others about the prowler she had scared off in
the morning, so I had to relent.

Farrah arrived right after the police did. In the
immediate aftermath, when everyone was talking at
once and my heart was still racing, I had called her
up for moral support. She had gotten home from
Katie's house and instantly said she would come
right over. She was both surprised and not surprised to find that Jake had come to talk to me.
When I told her about it, a look passed over her
face that was an odd mixture of affection and per-
turbation. I knew she would have a long talk with
him later. For now, she was more interested in the
rock the police were bagging up, and the letters
that were scratched into it.

Now I turned off the shower, toweled off, and
dressed in comfy shorts and a T-shirt. Then I went
out to the living room to take another look at my
damaged window. In the light of day, the whole in-
cident didn't seem quite as scary as it had the night

before. Still, I shuddered as I recalled finding the rock halfway across the room.

It was oblong, about three and a half inches long and two inches wide, with sharp edges. Whoever had thrown it had lobbed it hard, ensuring that it would break through the window. I shuddered to imagine what would have happened if it had hit me. I wondered if the perpetrator had thought about that or if they had even cared. One thing was for sure: They had a message for me, and they were going to make sure I got that message.

Before the police arrived, I had turned the rock over in my hands and had read the crudely scratched letters. *MYOB*. There was only one thing it could stand for.

Mind your own business.

Farrah had pulled me aside after the police left. "Do you realize what this means? Somebody is getting nervous. This means we're on the right track. The Shakespeare thief has to be somebody you've questioned. Or at least somebody who knows you've been asking questions. This is great!"

"I don't know if 'great' is quite the word I would use," I'd said, glancing at the jagged hole in my window. "I've just been told to back off. If the thief feels the need to threaten me . . ." I had trailed off, not wanting to finish the thought. Just what *was* the threat? What would this person do if I didn't back off?

"Do you want me to stay here tonight?" asked Farrah. "Better yet, why don't you come home with me?"

"No, that's okay. My neighbors are on alert now, and, anyway, I'm sure the creep won't come back tonight." I squeezed Farrah's arm and gave her a tired smile. "Besides, you need to go home and call Jake. Poor guy. Go easy on him, okay?"

Farrah rolled her eyes and sighed. "Right." Then she went to shuffle my neighbors back to their homes, while I got a broom to sweep up broken glass and soil from an overturned plant and found a board to cover the hole for the night.

After Farrah left, I burned a sprig of dried sage in a ceramic bowl on my coffee table. Then I walked around, sprinkling consecrated salt water on all my windows and doors, all the while murmuring a protection spell. This made me feel safer and allowed me to feel comfortable going to bed. Finally.

Now, in the early afternoon hours, which still felt like morning, I went into the kitchen to make myself some warm lemon water with a sprinkle of cayenne. It was just the thing I craved to cleanse my system. After that, I planned to make myself a great big brunch for one, but first I needed to call somebody about fixing the window.

While on the phone with a repair service, I walked over to remove the board and describe the damage. It was then that I noticed the envelope on the floor, next to the front door. Someone must have slid it underneath while I slept. The thought was alarming. Was it another warning?

As soon as I hung up the phone, I picked up the envelope and opened it warily. Then I breathed a sigh of relief. It was from my neighbor Larabeth.

There was a single sheet of paper folded over a postcard:

> *Keli,*
>   *In all the excitement last night, I forgot to tell*
> *you, this was mistakenly delivered to our mailbox.*
> *I didn't know it was your birthday yesterday!*
> *Happy belated b-day!*
>
>   *Larabeth*

I looked at the postcard and smiled, even as unexpected tears sprang to my eyes.

She was alive. She had remembered my birthday. And her timing was perfect.

Standing in my living room, I cradled the postcard in my palms like a priceless treasure as I read and reread the short lines. The front simply said *Birthday Greetings* over a picture of a candle-studded birthday cake. The back, however, was amazing. Like a voice from the beyond, Aunt Josephine's words spoke straight to my heart:

> *To my beautiful niece and kindred spirit, as*
> *lovely and strong on the inside as on the out.*
> *Carpe diem et sequere somnia tua.*

Aunt Josephine. Or Josie, as my mom sometimes called her. She would be sixty now. I always imagined her with waist-length hair, wearing a Bohemian skirt and Birkenstocks, still a hippie after all these years. Or maybe she was a gray-haired recluse, proud, eccentric, and set in her ways. But she would be kind and bighearted. Definitely bighearted.

* * *

It was about 5:30 in the evening when I picked up Farrah to set out for the Loose. Again. We were going to put our heads together, compare notes, analyze the mystery from all angles. I would grill Jimi some more if I could manage it. Plus there was my ever-present wish that I would bump into Wes again.

"Why don't you call the guy?" asked Farrah as we drove out of her parking lot.

"I don't know. I can't bring myself to do it. I feel kind of awkward about the whole thing." I sighed as I slowed to a stop at a red light. "I mean, I know I should. And maybe I will after . . ."

"After what?"

"Um." I lost my train of thought. Leaning forward, I peered through the windshield at a man leaving a check-cashing business in the next block. "Farrah, look at the guy across the street, the one getting in the black SUV."

"Whoa," said Farrah. "Bouncer, boxer, or hit man. What do you think?"

"He's the guy from the casino I told you about. Scarface."

"Oh! Right. No wonder Rob was running scared. Not to judge a book by its cover, but there's a thug if I ever saw one."

The SUV pulled away from the curb as the light changed and I entered the intersection.

"Follow him!" said Farrah.

"What? Really?"

"Yeah! Why not? We're supposed to be detectives, right? Maybe he'll lead us to a clue."

I could think of a few reasons why not. But I also believed things happened for a reason. This opportunity had to be a gift from the Goddess. Nodding at Farrah, I lowered my sunglasses, slid down in my seat, and pressed on the accelerator just in time to avoid being stopped at the next light.

We drove through town, trying to stay back far enough to avoid suspicion while still keeping the black vehicle in sight. Farrah bounced in the seat next to me, calling out instructions and location updates.

"Oh, change lanes. He's turning!" Then, "Speed up. He's losing us!" Then, a minute later, "Fall back. We're too close!"

I white-knuckled it, doing my best to keep up the chase while hoping to Goddess we wouldn't actually catch the dude. Originally, I had thought he might be going to the riverboat, but then he turned in the opposite direction. Pretty soon it became apparent that we were heading out of town, as we found ourselves on the same country road I had driven with Wes a few days earlier. Letting up on the gas, I allowed a greater distance between us and Scarface. After a few miles, he turned onto another hilly, winding road, and I followed, now more reluctantly.

"What do you think? How far should we go?" I said.

"Let's keep following for a few more minutes. This is so exciting!"

I glanced at Farrah and laughed. "You know, you're acting more and more like your namesake every day. Next thing you know, you'll be joining the police academy."

"Oh, please," said Farrah, waving off my comment. "As if . . . Oh, wait. He's slowing down!"

I hit the brakes, holding back while the SUV made a right turn off the country road. Alongside us, I could see a whitewashed rail fence lining the road and a bucolic pasture on the other side. As we came to the point where the SUV had left the road, we looked up at the arched Western-style gateway marking the entrance to a private tree-lined lane. Elegant lettering on the arch named the place Dogwood Ranch.

"I don't think we should follow him in," I said.

"No. It would be too obvious. Just keep going and then find a place to pull over."

Less than a mile farther down the road, we spotted a tractor path in a wheat field. I pulled over and turned off the car. "Now what?"

"Let's walk back and follow that lane. There were a lot of trees. We should be able to stay more or less hidden."

"It's the *less* part I'm worried about," I murmured as I got out of the car to join Farrah on the edge of the road.

We trekked along, trying not to scratch up our bare legs too badly on the weeds and brambles. When we arrived at the private lane, we crossed under the black steel archway and slunk behind the tall oaks lining the driveway. At least, I felt like we were slinking. As we picked our way cautiously farther onto this private property, I kept imagining what I would say if we were caught.

"Check out the spread," Farrah whispered beside me.

I peeked through the trees to see an expansive, beautifully landscaped front yard with manicured shrubbery and a dozen deep-green dogwood trees. In the center of it all stood a large brick colonial, complete with imposing white pillars. An ornate hanging sign on a tall oak post declared the owner of the estate: Harrison.

As in Edgar Harrison: investor, landowner, prominent citizen of Edindale. And important client to Olsen, Sykes, and Rafferty.

Farrah and I looked at one another; then Farrah snapped her fingers. "Of course! Edgar Harrison owns the casino. There's the connection."

"He does? I didn't know that."

"Yeah, it was in the news years ago, before you moved here. There was some opposition to the riverboat, as there always is with gambling. But Harrison pulled strings or greased palms or whatever, and the city approved his plans."

"So Scarface must work for him, then." I looked back at the house as the front door opened. "Oh, speak of the devil. Back up. Here he comes!"

From behind the trees, we watched as the thuggish figure jogged down the front steps and circled toward the rear of the house. Creeping forward, we saw a mammoth four-car garage at the end of the driveway and farther back a stable attached to a horse corral and a grazing area. Scarface headed toward the stable.

I was about to suggest to Farrah that we retreat while we had a chance when I heard the sound of

tires crunching on the gravel lane behind us. Just
then the front door of the house opened again, and
a middle-aged woman came outside to greet the approaching car. Without a second to lose, Farrah
and I darted around the corner of the garage.

"Ooh. Close call," said Farrah, exhaling.

"No kidding."

Cautiously, I peered around the edge of the
garage and observed a young family of four pour
out of both sides of the car, which had parked
behind the black SUV. The youngest child yelled,
"Grandma!" and ran into the open arms of the
woman from the house. Then two more cars rum-
bled up the driveway.

"Oh, man," I breathed. "This doesn't look good."

From out of the second car emerged a young
couple carrying a bocce ball set, which they proceeded to set up in the front yard. The third car
held another family, this one bearing bags of food.
A kid from that car ran back toward the stables,
shouting, "Can I see the horses?"

"This is *really* not good," I repeated, nervously
tapping my knuckles on my mouth.

As we crouched behind the garage, feeling like
trapped animals, the smell of lighter fluid and wood
smoke drifted from the direction of the backyard.
"Guess they're having a barbecue," said Farrah.
"Maybe we could act like we were invited?"

I shook my head. "The party's not big enough
to pull that off. I think they'd notice we're not
members of their family."

"What about Scarface? We could say we work for
the casino, too."

"I don't think so, Farrah. They would know we're lying. We have to find a way to get out of here."

I looked around for a possible escape, cringing as I heard another vehicle come up the lane. Clearly, we couldn't go back the way we came. For one thing, there were too many gaps between the oak trees, and behind the line of trees was an open field with nowhere to hide. An even bigger challenge would be coming out from behind the garage without being seen.

However, looking in the other direction, behind the garage, I noticed that the open field abutted a thicket of woods. And the woods appeared to fan out into a forest for who knew how many miles. To get to the woods, we would have to climb over a barbed-wire fence and escape the notice of anyone who happened to be behind the stable. Glancing that way, I could see a brown horse grazing along the edge of the corral. Children's laughter filled the air, followed by a shrill whistle. The horse looked up and trotted toward the sound.

"We've got to get to the woods," I whispered, my heart thumping a rapid cadence in my chest. "Fast."

Farrah nodded. "You know that will take us away from your car, right?"

"Doesn't matter. We'll find a way back. We'll exit the woods someplace else, far away from here."

We backed away from the garage, and the farther we strayed from its shelter, the more anxious I became. When we reached the barbed-wire fence, a rusty, mean-looking obstacle, we hesitated, trying to figure out how we would get over the thing without suffering great bodily harm. Finally, after some tricky stepping, holding, and squeezing, we were halfway over the fence. And then my shorts caught on a barb.

"Ouch!" Farrah made it to the other side, but not without a long scratch on the side of her leg. "Ooh, that stings!" Ignoring the trickle of blood on her leg, Farrah tried to help me free my shorts from the sharp barb. Suddenly, we both jumped at the sound of a deep, resonant bark of a big, big dog.

CHAPTER 20

I jerked my head toward the corral and saw the brown horse again, this time with a rider on its back. The horseman, dressed in designer denim and plaid, was a silver-haired man whom I'd met once or twice before, and whose picture often graced the pages of the *Edindale Gazette*. It was the gentleman of the gentleman's ranch, the master of his domain, the wheeler-dealer powerhouse that was Edgar Harrison. And he stared right at me. As I stood there, caught on the barbed-wire fence in an awkward straddle, part of me prayed he wouldn't recognize me as one of the lawyers at Olsen, Sykes, and Rafferty. The other part realized I had even bigger problems right now.

Edgar yelled something I couldn't understand, and then another man walked around the stable, the barking dog at his heels. It was Scarface, looking none too happy to find us guilty-looking interlopers. Striding over quickly, he opened the gate of the corral and let out the zealous watchdog—which turned out to be a Doberman pinscher. *Perfect.*

I didn't know if I was more scared of Scarface or the Doberman, but I ripped my shorts from the fence and took off headlong for the woods in a heartbeat, Farrah right beside me. We were both experienced runners, but I didn't think we had ever pounded the ground like this before. Flying over the earth, our legs and arms pumping, we reached the woods in seconds and kept going. Hurdling over fallen limbs and twisty roots, slapped by insects and branches, but never looking back, we drove ourselves deeper and deeper into the forest.

At first, we followed a well-worn bridle path, then a dry gully, until finally we found ourselves with no trail to follow at all. When we reached a small clearing with no obvious path out, we stopped running and instead walked in circles as we gathered our bearings. The only sound to be heard was our own panting and wheezing.

After a minute, we looked at one another, taking in the scratches, the flushed skin, the leaves in our hair—and burst out laughing. Farrah doubled over, then winced at a pain but kept laughing. I drew my fingers through my shredded shorts, giggling at the absurdity of it all, and hobbled over to sit on a fallen tree trunk.

"Oh, God," Farrah gasped through her laughter. "Were they even chasing us?"

I shook my head and tried to pull myself together. "I don't know. Maybe at first?"

"Where are we?" asked Farrah, looking around again as her giggles subsided. "Got a GPS app on your phone?"

I pulled the phone out of my mini–sling purse and frowned. "No signal out here."

"Figures." Farrah reached out to touch the mossy back of a nearby tree. "What's that saying? Moss grows toward what direction?"

"I think the sun is more reliable," I said, looking up at the sky. "So . . . setting sun in the west. We parked west of the ranch. So let's walk that way for a while and then cut south." I pointed with my straightened arm toward the lowering sun and realized we had maybe an hour of daylight left at most.

"We better get a move on," Farrah said, evidently having the same thought.

I pushed myself to my feet, and together we picked our way through the brambles and under brush in a more or less westerly direction. As my body cooled down, the air on my damp skin started to make me feel chilly, and I shivered in spite of myself.

"I once thought trail running sounded kind of fun," Farrah remarked, stepping over a large, snaky root. "Not anymore."

I grunted in agreement. "You'd have to like a certain element of risk, for sure. I prefer to play it much safer."

"This coming from a woman who trailed a goon and trespassed onto private property." Farrah laughed.

"Hey," I protested. "Not my idea. I'm going to have to stop listening to you."

"Sure," drawled Farrah. "Just remember, this whole caper started with you."

"Humph."

After a moment's silence, Farrah spoke in a more serious tone. "So you think Scarface threw the rock at your window? He seems menacing enough."

"Doesn't really make sense. What would he have to warn me about?"

"Good point. Okay, let's think about this. We can be fairly certain our buddy Rob has a gambling problem, right? Scarface guy seems to want something with Rob, while Rob wants nothing to do with him."

"I bet Rob owes him money," I said. "Scarface is probably a loan shark or something."

"Rob probably has a pretty good throwing arm, being a baseball player and all," Farrah ventured.

I sighed. "I thought of that. And it would seem he had a compelling motive for taking the Folio."

"He's not the only one, though. I didn't get a chance to tell you what I learned about Kirk."

"Something interesting?" I paused while Farrah picked up a broken branch and broke off the twigs to fashion a walking stick. We had finally found a genuine dirt path, which made for easier hiking and gave me hope that we might actually be getting someplace.

"Mm-hmm. He not only went off to New York to be a Shakespearean actor, but he also tried to bring Shakespeare back home. After bumming around in the Big Apple, never quite making it to Broadway, I guess, he moved to Indianapolis and started up a Shakespeare theater company with another guy. They struggled for a time, then had a big falling-out. Evidently, Kirk shut the guy out and tried to make a go of it himself. Well, the partner wound up suing Kirk for breach of contract, among other things. And Kirk lost. I found a record of the court decision."

"Pays to have a legal research expert on your side," I quipped. "So, bummer for Kirk. How much did he owe?"

"Eighty thousand dollars."

"Yikes. That's not a little."

"And that's not all. Around the same time, his wife divorced him. Then the theater went under, leaving Kirk with a boatload of debt."

"When did all this happen?"

"Three years ago. He's been doing odd jobs ever since, trying to get acting jobs here and there. He moved from Indy to a small town right on the border of Illinois and Indiana, so he's not too far from Edindale. Just an hour's drive or so."

I thought about this as we walked on, but I was soon distracted by a symphony of tree frogs, which had started up all at once. Farrah and I chuckled at this, but I glanced nervously at the sky. The sun was sinking ever closer to the horizon, and we had no idea how much farther we had to go. And although I didn't want to mention it, my throat was exceedingly dry and my stomach growled.

"I heard that," said Farrah. "I'm starving, too. Oh! What's that up ahead? A bench?"

We raced for the simple wooden bench and plopped down side by side. We were both cheered by this sign of civilization. I figured we must be in the Forest Preserve. With any luck, we should at least happen upon a trail map or a guidepost or maybe even a real hiker.

"Ready to go on?" I asked.

"Yeah," said Farrah, getting up with a groan.

We continued down the path, moving slower than ever. There didn't seem to be any part of me that didn't ache. To keep my mind off my body—and the darkening trees around us—I brought up the mystery again.

"So Kirk needs money. Rob needs money. Lots of people need money, if you think about it."

"True. Wes needs money, too, since his brother wiped out his savings and maxed out his credit cards," said Farrah, giving me a sidelong glance.

I didn't say anything, just kept plodding along in the dusk.

"Speaking of Wes," Farrah continued, "there was something else I learned from Jimi that night I found out Wes was sleeping in the back room at the Loose. Jimi told me Wes and Rob used to be really close. Rob would look up to Wes, while Wes looked after Rob. Rob would get into trouble, and Wes would bail him out."

"Okay. So what are you saying?"

"All I'm saying is that maybe, possibly, Wes found a way to bail out his brother again. Either that or he could be protecting him. I'm just saying we can't rule him out."

"Mmm." I wasn't ready to concede Farrah's point, though I knew she was right.

We walked along in silence, listening to the night sounds and shuffling our feet in the dust. I was grateful that at least it wasn't raining. In fact, the moon above cast a soft glow bright enough for us to see the path ahead.

Still, I felt so weary. I felt like we had been in the woods for hours and hours. Now, surrounded by an oppressive darkness beyond the moonlight, I feared I might be bordering on delirium. For sure, I was starting to feel faint from hunger and exertion. I was also becoming a little freaked about where we were going to end up spending the night. With all these thoughts swirling, my heart began racing until I could almost feel the vibration of it in the earth beneath my feet.

"Do you hear that?" Farrah whispered.

I started at the sound of her voice and looked at her in surprise. She appeared a little freaked herself.

"Is that drumbeats?"

I furrowed my eyebrows and listened. Sure enough, the air carried a steady rhythmic pounding, which was not coming from my chest. We took a few more steps forward and found ourselves at a fork in the trail. I turned in the direction of the drumming, and Farrah followed close behind.

"What is that? A powwow?" she asked. "Is there an Indian reservation near here?"

I shook my head. "I don't—"

"I see something!" Farrah hissed, grabbing my arm.

Following her gaze, I saw it, too. Up ahead we could see firelight flickering behind a wall of trees and hear the rise and fall of spirited voices. All at once, I knew what it was.

"Oh, my God," said Farrah, sounding panicky. "How many are there?"

"Shh. Calm down." I spoke softly, trying to soothe Farrah. Moving closer, we crouched behind a fallen tree to witness the solstice celebration.

It was just as Mila's friends had told me. At least twenty women, men, and children were gathered around the sacred bonfire, dancing, chanting, and drumming. The revelers looked to be having a good time, laughing and passing jugs of cider and ale. Some of the women wore rings of flowers in their hair and floaty cotton dresses, giving them the appearance of woodland nymphs, while the men represented the Horned God or the Oak King with antlers or chaplets of oak leaves on their heads. A few dancers tossed herbs into the flames as they circled the fire, causing it to crackle merrily.

As we watched the scene, I could feel my earlier fear and worry dissolve away. The once foreboding darkness was now a mysterious and comforting blend of light and dark, the shadows soothing and warm like a mother's embrace. It was Midsummer Eve, a time for gratitude and celebration. I smiled, suddenly feeling close to my aunt Josephine, who, I was certain, had once lived somewhere out here in these woods.

Then I spotted Mila, smiling and radiant, with a chain of daisies on her head. She twirled gracefully with the other dancers. I almost stood up to go join her.

"I am freaking out!" whispered Farrah. "I can't

even believe this. We've stumbled upon some kind of cult, some kind of sacrificial ritual."

I felt my heart sink as I turned toward my friend. "Get a grip, Farrah. This looks peaceful to me."

"How do you know?" demanded Farrah, her eyes wide, "I have never seen anything like this before."

"It's some kind of festival, I'm sure of it. Look, they've got flowers in their hair. Today's the first day of summer. That must be it. Nothing to worry about."

Farrah shook her head doubtfully, the disgust apparent in her expression. "It's weird, whatever it is."

I was at a loss, caught between two worlds and too tired to think of a response. That was when my cell phone rang.

I jumped and backed farther away from the bonfire, though no one could have heard the ring above all the party noise. With Farrah watching expectantly, I took my phone from my purse and answered.

"Hello?"

"Hello, Counselor! T.C. Satterly here. Satterly's Rare Books. Your office gave me your personal number after I insisted I needed to speak with you. I hope this is a convenient time."

"Um." I glanced at Farrah and shrugged. "Sure."

"Listen, I had a *very* interesting message on my answering machine today. Male voice, sort of muffled like. Said he's having a silent auction, and if I'm interested in rare Shakespearean works, I'm to tweet the words 'Got a penchant for seventeen c reserve #ytfnrq.' Said that he will contact me if he sees that tweet. Strange, I know. Still, I wrote it down. Got it right here."

"Wow. You're kidding."

"I kid you not. And that's not all. Word on the street is that a *certain* broker is going to be at LitCon this Saturday. This *certain* broker is well known in the book world to have, let's say, *questionable* scruples, if you know what I mean. Rumor has it that he might be meeting with a prospect to discuss a *certain* acquisition. It's all very hush-hush. But I do know that this broker wouldn't normally come to LitCon unless he believed he might get something lucrative out of it."

"So, you think this guy got the same kind of message? And he posted some obscure code tweet?"

"Now, I don't know about all that. All I'm saying is, if you're still on this case, you *must* be at LitCon on Saturday."

"Okay. All right. So who is the broker? What's his name?"

"Now, remember, you didn't hear it from me. I'm not one to cast aspersions on other dealers. But look out for a fellow by the name of Stenislaw. Got me? *Stenislaw*."

"Stenislaw," I repeated.

"Very good. Well, bye now."

"Wait! Mr. Satterly?"

I looked at my phone, saw the call had ended, and slipped it back in my purse. Farrah stared at me, eyebrows knit and hands on her hips.

"What was that all about? And why didn't you ask

him for help? He could have called the police or a forest ranger or something."

I rubbed my eyes and yawned. "Not necessary. I think I know where we are. Ever hear of Briar Creek Cabins?"

Leaving the joyful sun celebration behind, I led Farrah out of the forest. After we reached the main cabin and coaxed the sleepy manager to drive us the eight miles back to my car, I drove Farrah home. Then I took myself home, where I went straight to bed and slept a long, dreamless sleep.

CHAPTER 21

I woke to the sound of the phone jangling beside my bed. Without opening my eyes, I fumbled for the receiver and brought it to my ear

"Hello?"

"Hello. May I speak with Miss Milanni, please?"

"Speaking."

"Oh, I didn't recognize your voice. This is Wendell Knotts. I'm calling about the Mostriak Folio, which we discussed earlier this week."

Now I was awake. I opened my eyes, tossed away the sheets, and swung my feet to the floor. "Did you find the original appraiser?"

"Indeed I did. I tracked down the appraisal company in New York, explained who I was and what I was looking for. And they, most obligingly, agreed to search their archives. In fact, I received a call from them this morning. They found their copy of the original certificate and will fax it to me this afternoon."

"That's wonderful."

"Interestingly, when I spoke with them this morning, they told me that someone else had called them about this very document yesterday."

"Oh?"

"Yes. Apparently, it was a man claiming to be a member of the Mostriak family."

That *was* interesting. "So what did the appraiser say to him?"

"Why, they said they would fax it to him, like they did for me. There are no protections for a document like that. The certificate without the Folio is little more than a piece of paper, albeit with modest historical value for a small number of people."

Except that it would have considerably more value to whoever possessed the Folio.

"Do you think you could ask the appraiser for the fax number the person provided?"

"Certainly. I'll be calling them, anyway, when I'm ready to receive the fax myself."

"Thank you. I really appreciate your help."

"Not at all, I'm happy to help. Now, I have a proposition for you. Would you come to LitCon tomorrow morning? I'll meet you there to give you the faxed document, as well as the information I learn from the appraiser. And you might find the convention enjoyable. Besides that, we could use more attendees. I've seen an unfortunate decline in the numbers year after year."

"I'll be there," I promised.

I now had two reasons to attend the Literary Convention. Maybe I would even catch some of the Shakespeare in the Park performance while I was at it.

Later that day, as I headed out for a jog, I received a third compelling reason to go to the fair. I had a phone call from Wes, my own private hot and cold rock star.

"Hey, Keli. I've been meaning to call you. How have you been?"

Just peachy, I thought. *I always love spending five days of radio silence following a date with a guy I like.* "I've been great. How about you?"

"Well, less than stellar, to tell the truth." Wes heaved an audible sigh. "My family's going through some stuff. I've actually moved in with my folks for a little while. You know, so I can help my mom out until my dad returns, try to give her some peace of mind."

Right. And get off the cot in the bar. But he did have a point about helping Darlene. "How *is* your mom? I've been thinking about her lately."

"She's doing better." Wes paused, and I began to wonder why he had actually called. "So, listen, uh, I had a nice time last Sunday. But since we didn't get to have a proper picnic, I was wondering if you'd want to try again tomorrow. My uncle Kirk is performing in the play at the Renaissance Faire. Want to meet up and have a picnic on the lawn at the park?"

I couldn't help smiling. I *absolutely* wanted to have a picnic in the park with Wes. "Well, there's something I have to do in the morning, but I should be able to meet you there. What time?"

"There are three performances. Ten a.m., one, and four. Can you meet up for the one o'clock? I'll bring the food. All vegan, I promise."

"Sure. Sounds great."

"Terrific. I'll find a spot front and center, but call me if you can't find me."

"Absolutely."

After the call, I took off for my run, all aflutter again over Wes. I took my usual route, through Fieldstone Park and over to the rail trail. At the two-mile point, I turned around and ran back the way I had come. Only this time, as I approached the spot where the trail passed behind the Woodbine Village housing development, I slowed my run to a walk. Without quite knowing why, I stopped to look toward Rob's apartment.

A narrow strip of trees and brush separated the trail from the parking lot in front of the apartment complex. Peering through the trees, I located Rob's sad little stoop with the neglected lawn chair. Then I started when I recognized the car parked in front of the apartment building, next to Rob's own dusty sedan. It was a black SUV, and I was almost certain it belonged to Scarface.

Then my eyes slid to the car on the other side of the SUV. This car was also familiar. It was Wes's car.

As I stood there wondering, Rob's front door opened and Wes himself came out. He walked, eyes on the ground, toward his car.

My heart clenched at the worried expression on his handsome face. I longed to go over there to comfort him and be his friend.

But what I still didn't know was if this was a man with deep concern for a brother in trouble or if Wes himself was the one in too deep.

Either way, I intended to find out.

* * *

After a quick shower and a bite to eat, I threw on a long T-shirt and a pair of black cropped leggings, wrapped my hair in a silk scarf, and dug out my old mirrored aviators. It was the closest thing to a disguise I could come up with. To top it off, I applied a thick coat of uncharacteristically bright salmon-pink lipstick I had once bought by mistake. Then I hopped into my little silver-blue car and headed toward the River Queen Casino.

On the way, however, I felt my resolve seep right out of the bottom of my wedge-clad feet. When I reached the street leading to the casino, I kept right on going. Why hadn't I called Farrah? I didn't want to skulk around the riverboat by myself.

Feeling a little silly and a lot frustrated, I drove around town with no particular destination in mind until I found myself nearing the check-cashing facility where Farrah and I had started our crazy car chase the day before. Not that I expected to see Scarface again, but there was something odd about how he seemed to keep popping up. I couldn't help wondering what he was up to—and what it might have to do with Rob and Wes.

And then, like a mad case of déjà vu, I did see him again.

I had to blink twice and lift the shades from my eyes to be sure. The imposing figure coming out of the check-cashing facility was definitely Scarface. I was still half a block away, so I hit the brakes and proceeded slowly, watching as he climbed into his SUV and sped away.

Without pausing to formulate a plan, I maneuvered my car into the curbside parking space he had vacated, slipped out of my car, and marched right up to the Miller Avenue Cash Mart.

The place was empty except for the large woman perched on a stool behind one of three small transaction windows. She looked at me expectantly, her broad features and double chin visible through the clear security barrier. I took a deep breath and crossed my fingers.

"Hi, there. Maybe you can help me. Uh, I think I just missed . . ." I trailed off, gesturing toward the door and tracing a line on my face in the spot of Scarface's scar.

"Mr. Derello?"

I let out my breath and nodded vigorously. "Yes. Mr. Derello. From the River Queen? Uh, he said that I should stop by here if I ever have need of . . . of the services that—"

"Honey, you don't have to be nervous."

"I don't?" Wiping my palms on my pant legs, I managed a tentative smile.

"Now, just relax. Fill out this form here, and we'll take care of you." I watched as she slid a sheet of paper through the opening at the bottom of the window. "You can fill it out right here, or you can go sit down at that little table over there."

I looked at the paper, which appeared to be a loan application. The top third contained blank spaces asking for my vitals—everything from my name, address, and birthday to my bank account number and Social Security number. The rest of the page, and all of the back, was a blur of fine print.

"Hmm. I think I'll just take this home and—"

Before I knew what was happening, the woman reached through the opening and snatched the application out of my grasp. "Didn't Mr. Derello tell you how this works?" she said sharply. "You fill this out here, and you'll get your money right away. No wait. No questions asked. Isn't that what you want?"

I opened my mouth to respond but was too startled to speak when a door to a back room suddenly swung open. An armed security guard walked toward me, narrowed his eyes, then stationed himself against a wall, where he surveyed the empty room. I swallowed hard.

"You know," I said hoarsely, "I do want all that. I think. It's just that I don't have all this info on me. So, I'll come back later."

Without waiting for a reaction, I fled the room, letting the door slam shut behind me. I didn't dare look back until I was safely in my car. And well down the road.

CHAPTER 22

The University Ballroom had been transformed into a book lover's paradise. Across the wide floor, lines of display tables represented every genre imaginable. At one end of the room, a local independent bookstore sponsored a book-signing table featuring a different author every hour. And at the other end of the room, rows of folding chairs faced a podium, at which various speakers were scheduled to appear. It was there that I found Wendell Knotts, looking very much the part of an English professor in his tweeds and brown oxfords. His cane was propped on a briefcase at his feet.

As I approached the front of the room, grateful I had opted for a pretty summer dress instead of shorts or leggings today, Wendell spotted me and waved me over with a pleased smile. He patted the chair next to him, then nodded toward the podium. So I sat down and directed my attention to the speaker, an earnest middle-aged man with humorously unruly hair. I suppressed a grin as I politely tuned in to his talk.

According to the large poster taped to the front of the podium, the topic was Edgar Allan Poe. After a couple of minutes, I gathered that the focus was Poe's three stories featuring the original deductive-reasoning, crime-solving sleuth C. Auguste Dupin. A detective. How appropriate.

Letting my gaze wander around the convention, I wondered if the notorious Stenislaw was here someplace. More to the point, was the book thief here? From what I could tell, the crowd seemed to consist mainly of librarian and professor types, with a smattering of college students out for extra credit, plus the odd lord, lady, knight, or wench who had wandered in from the Renaissance Faire. So far, I hadn't seen anyone I recognized.

I turned back to the speaker, who announced that he would now read Poe's third Dupin story, "The Purloined Letter." The whole thing.

Seeing that Wendell was engrossed, I crossed my legs and settled back in my seat. It took a mighty effort to resist pulling out my cell phone. Soon, however, I found myself drawn into the short story, too, and I remembered reading it in college. It really was a clever little tale, with the twist at the end being that the stolen letter was hidden in plain sight all along.

As the speaker read the final words, and as I recalled knowing the ending already, I had a sudden flashback to my interrupted vision the other day. In the midst of the finding spell, I had seen Eleanor's garden. Then I had seen shelves upon shelves of books.

In my mind's eye, I saw those shelves again. Even

as the speaker ended his reading and we all clapped,
I thought about the hall of books and realized it
could be a library. Wouldn't it be something if the
Folio was hidden in plain sight like the purloined
letter?

"The simplest puzzles are sometimes the most
vexing, aren't they?"

I turned to find Wendell regarding me with interest. I smiled. "The problem is, you don't know
they're simple at the time. It's not until you have
the solution that the puzzle appears simple."

"True, true." Wendell nodded, tenting his fingers under his chin.

I shifted in my seat. "I was surprised I didn't find
you at the Shakespeare table," I said, inclining my
head to the floor displays.

"Oh, been there, done that, as the young people
say." Wendell grinned cheekily, and I had to chuckle.
Then he leaned over to retrieve a manila envelope
from the briefcase on the floor. He lifted the flap
and slid out a paper, which he handed to me. "Your
certificate, my dear."

Signed and sealed by the New York appraisal
company, the certificate attested to the authenticity
of the First Folio acquired by Alexander Mostriak
at auction in 1898 and later bequeathed to his
nephew Frank Mostriak. I stared at the document,
which included a detailed physical description of
the Mostriak copy. Once again I felt the weight of
the loss.

Thanking Wendell, I replaced the certificate in
the envelope and slipped it in my tote. "So were you
able to find out who else asked for a copy of this?"

"Not a name but a number." Wendell took out a slip of paper from his inside jacket pocket. "It's an Edindale number, but that's all I know."

I raised one eyebrow. "A number, huh? Well, let's see whose number it is." I whipped out my phone, opened the search screen, and typed "reverse lookup."

Wendell handed me the paper. "Is there anything those little gadgets can't do?" he murmured over my shoulder as I typed in the number.

"Hmm. Apparently so." I sighed and looked at Wendell with a shrug. "Nothing's coming up. Must be a prepaid cell phone or something."

"Prepaid?" Wendell looked perplexed.

I smiled at him, dropped the slip of paper in my tote with the envelope, and stood up. He stood up with me.

"No worries. I'll keep trying. Professor, thank you again. I'm not sure how, but I am hopeful the Folio will be recovered. And this might help yet." I patted the tote, which was hanging from my shoulder. "By the way, do you know a book dealer by the name of Stenislaw?"

Wendell scowled. "We've met once or twice. He's out of St. Louis. Doesn't come here often."

"I get the feeling you're happy about that."

"Well now, I try not to take stock in rumors. But Mr. Stenislaw is not the most reputable dealer around. Why do you ask?"

"I had a tip to watch out for him."

"Good advice. I haven't seen him today. If I do, I'll let you know. Good luck, Miss Milanni, and enjoy your day."

Wendell headed over to talk to the Poe expert, while I wandered among the book displays. The crowd actually seemed to be growing, and I realized the first Shakespeare play outside must have finished. I maneuvered around tables, trying to make my way to the rare-books section I had spotted off to the side, and was actually jostled near the popular fiction table. Apparently, there was a flash sale under way on a steamy new best seller. I rolled my eyes.

"Sex sells, don't you know? Always has, always will."

I turned to see a familiar redhead wearing a wry smirk.

"Professor Eisenberry. How are you?"

"Call me Max. I'm harried and hurried at the moment, but otherwise okay. I've got to work the Shakespeare table here in between performances outside."

I walked with her over to the Shakespeare table. Draped in a long burgundy cloth and backed by large cloth-covered display boards, the table exhibited a dazzling array of Shakespeare collections.

"I'm going to the next performance," I said, picking up a glossy copy of *A Midsummer Night's Dream* and placing it back down.

"You'll love it," she said. "Did you ever reach out to Professor Knotts?"

"I did, yes. And I just saw him again a few minutes ago. I can't thank you enough for putting me in touch with him."

"My pleasure. He's a sweet man and still sharp as a tack. I still call him for advice now and then."

"Say, do you know T.C. Satterly?"

"Sure I do. Just passed him outside, carrying a

turkey leg in one hand and a pint of mead in the other."

I laughed and cast my eyes to the ceiling. "Guess I won't find him at the rare-books table, then."

"He was there first thing this morning. He'll probably find his way back in later on."

"How about Stenislaw? Book dealer from St. Louis?"

Professor Eisenberry slowly shook her head. "Can't say I've heard of him."

After leaving Professor Eisenberry, I made it over to the rare-books table, only to find a university student who knew all about the antique books on display but nothing about book dealers from St. Louis. I was gazing around the room again, not sure what to do next, when I felt a buzzing from my tote. It was a text from Farrah.

Are you at the fair yet?

I replied, Yep, @ LitCon.

Seconds later, Farrah wrote, Meet me at the archery contest. I have something for you.

I was glad to have a reason for leaving the convention. I wasn't learning anything here. Slipping my phone back in my tote, I walked along the edge of the room toward the exit. Then I glanced back in my tote, where something unusual caught my eye. Next to the envelope from Wendell was a postcard, which I didn't remember picking up.

Standing by the door, I pulled out the postcard and frowned. The image on the front was a ghastly-looking skeleton dripping blood on a black backdrop. According to the crimson caption, the picture was a depiction of one of Poe's more macabre stories, "The Masque of the Red Death."

I flipped the postcard over and found something equally sinister. Scrawled across the back in thick black marker were four capital letters: *MYOB*.

I swirled around, scanning the ballroom. LitCon was the picture of innocence. Strolling book lovers went about their business, browsing the tables, lining up for author autographs, discussing the latest *New York Times* book review.

Narrowing my eyes, I marched over to the Poe table. But then I thought better of it. Whoever had slipped the postcard in my tote could have done so anytime over the past hour. It would be impossible to identify the person now. Besides, Farrah was waiting for me.

So I left the building and headed out into the bright sunshine. I followed the paved walkway through campus and soon found myself entering the imaginary world of Ye Olde Edindale Village Marketplace.

With vendor booths lining both sides of the wide center aisle, face-painting stations, ball-toss games, and the smell of beer and carnival food permeating the air, this could have been any other Saturday festival—except that at least half the fairgoers were dressed in medievalesque garb. Ranging from the authentic to the fantastical, the costumes alone provided ample entertainment as I strolled through the fair. I grinned as I imagined this was what the back lot of a movie studio might look like, with mingling cast members from the likes of *Xena: Warrior Princess*, *Pirates of the Caribbean*, and *The Lord of the Rings* right alongside women in brightly colored dirndls, men in kilts, and unknown individuals in full-body devil costumes.

In fact, several of the participants wore masks. I passed fairies in feathered Mardi Gras masks, pirates in black cloth half masks, and even one of the Shakespeare actors wearing a fully enclosed donkey head. This last individual I recognized as Bottom from *A Midsummer Night's Dream*. To the amusement of a few spectators, he appeared to be antagonizing a jester by snatching his juggling pins.

Maneuvering past a trio of minstrels, I cut across the quad to an adjacent parking lot that had been cordoned off for jousting demonstrations, pony rides, and an archery contest. I found Farrah retrieving her arrows from one of three targets in front of a wall of hay bales. She replaced her bow and joined me on the sidelines.

"You missed my stunning performance," she said.

"How'd you do?"

Farrah laughed. "Well, Katniss I ain't. But at least I hit the target."

We walked over to a picnic table on the edge of the green, near the kids' tent. Not far away, some of the Shakespeare players were putting on a little skit. I spotted the donkey-headed Bottom again, this time the brunt of the other characters' antics. They appeared to kick him from behind, causing him to engage in all sorts of amusing pratfalls.

I turned back to Farrah. "No costume for you?"

"Well, I would have, but my corset's at the cleaners."

"Ah. Of course."

"Actually," said Farrah, reaching into her roomy cross-body purse, "we would have fit right in wearing our Old West costumes." She handed me a manila envelope much like the one Wendell had given me. I opened it to find an eight-by-ten photo of Farrah and me in all our sepia-toned glory.

"Aw, you made me a copy? It's not bad, really." I studied the photo, recalling how Wes had come up to me shortly after it was taken.

"Not bad? Look at us hotties. We're awesome. In fact, the photographer that night asked me if he could use our picture on his Web site."

I looked at Farrah and raised my eyebrows.

"I told him it would cost him," she went on. "Ten thousand dollars each for all rights or else a percent of all sales as long as the image remains on the site. I told him I'd draw up a contract if he was interested."

I whistled, then laughed, as I looked at the photo again. It was cute. I knew where I'd hang it as soon as I could find a good frame. Then I squinted and held the photo up in front of me.

"I wish I had my new magnifying glass on me," I said.

"Why? What do you see?"

"There's a reflection in the mirror behind us. It looks like a person standing off to the side."

"Let me see." Farrah came around to look over my shoulder.

Shifting the picture out of the glare of the sun, I

caught my breath. "I think it's Scarface. Look." I handed the photo to Farrah, who sat down next to me on the bench.

"Oh, my God. You're right. He was watching us. How creepy is that?"

"You don't know the half of it," I muttered.

"What do you mean?"

I told Farrah about seeing Scarface's car at Rob's apartment and then later seeing the man himself leave the check-cashing place again. Swallowing my embarrassment, I also told her about my little charade in the facility.

"You nut," she said, lightly pushing my shoulder. "You should have called me. But good work, though. So this Mr. Derello really is some kind of loan shark?"

"Sure looks like it to me. I plan on calling the Attorney General's office first thing on Monday so they can look into it."

"I'd wait a little while, chica. If they start investigating now, this Derello guy is going to put two and two together. They have cameras at those check-cashing places, you know."

"Ugh. You're right." I slumped on the bench and blew a wisp of hair out of my eyes. "The last thing I want is that hulk coming after me. Which reminds me. Someone dropped a little love note in my bag while I was over at LitCon." I took out the Edgar Allan Poe postcard and showed it to Farrah.

"Not very romantic," remarked Farrah, setting down the Old West photo and taking the postcard. Then she turned it over. "What the . . . ?"

"Rock thrower was right beside me, and I didn't even know it."

Farrah met my eyes. "Are you okay? Are you freaking out?"

"No. I'm fine. Surprisingly, I'm not really freaked at all. I'm pissed that this person is so close yet is apparently getting away scot-free."

"Not yet they're not," said Farrah. She tapped the postcard on the table and squinted in the sun. "So what do we do next?"

I stared across the lawn, vaguely aware that Robin Hood and Friar Tuck were moving toward our table. "I'm not sure, Farrah, but I've been thinking about the fact that we do have a limited number of suspects. What if—"

"Oh, shit! It's almost one o'clock." Farrah glanced up from her phone and hopped out of her seat. "I'm sorry, Kel, but I'm supposed to meet Jake by the entrance."

"Ooh, I've got to go, too." I grabbed the creepy postcard from the table and tossed it in my tote. Then I carefully slipped our souvenir photo back in its envelope and slipped it in my bag, as well.

Farrah squeezed my arm before we parted ways. "Let's meet up and discuss this later. If the thief is about to sell the Folio, we're running out of time."

I knew she was right, except for one thing. It wasn't *we* who were running out of time. It was *I* who was running out of time. My job was the one on the line.

The lawn in front of the stage was filling up quickly. I spared a glance at my phone as I hurried through the crowd. It was five minutes until 1:00 p.m. *Yikes*. I had to find Wes.

Well, maybe the play will start late, I thought when I noticed a couple of the entertainers I had seen before trying to steer people toward the stage. Suddenly, I found myself face-to-face with the donkey character. We were each trying to get through a narrow opening in the crowd and now found ourselves blocking one another's progress. As a result, I found myself dancing with an ass. *Terrific*.

Of course, Bottom had to make a big show of it. It was almost as if he was blocking my way on purpose, like a goalie before the net. It was actually pretty disconcerting, facing the giant donkey head and not knowing who was really inside. For a minute, we engaged in an embarrassing little two-step as I tried to avoid being stepped on by his brown- and white-leather wing tips. *Fancy shoes for a donkey man*. Finally, with an exaggerated flourish, he allowed me to pass.

"Thanks," I muttered as I squeezed by. Now, where was Wes?

As I approached the stage, looking left and right, I spotted a pair of women seated on a large blanket and sharing wine, cheese, and fruit. I wondered if they were reliving their childhood picnics with Eleanor and Frank. They looked up as I passed by, so I called a cheery hello. Sharon waved at me, raising her glass in greeting. Darlene looked away.

Finally, I caught sight of Wes right where he had said he would be, front and center. Looking scrumptious in gray jeans and a crisp white Henley shirt, he stood, leaning casually back on the stage, as he scanned the crowd. He smiled when he saw me.

"I'm so sorry," I said, a little breathless. "I wanted to get here earlier."

"You're right on time," he said, taking my hand and leading me to a checkered blanket about ten feet in front of the stage. "But I have to admit, this would have made for a sad little scene if you hadn't shown."

I sat down next to him and admired the spread. In the center of the blanket was a two-inch-high wooden tray table that contained two glasses of white wine, two cloth napkins, and two dinner plates filled with triangle sandwiches, carrot sticks, bell pepper strips, and cherry tomatoes. In the center of the little table was a tea candle, which Wes now lit.

"Oh, this looks delicious. Wow, Wes. I am really impressed." I knew I was gushing, but I couldn't help it.

"Well, I had a little help from the vegan bakery. After those sandwiches the other day, I knew I had to go back. That place rocks."

You rock, I thought. I smiled at him as I took a sip of my wine.

"And there's more food in the basket. Oh, here's a hummus dip for the veggies. And we have chocolate-covered strawberries for dessert."

"Mmm," I murmured, taking a bite of my sandwich and another sip of wine. "Good. I'm starving."

Wes grinned and lifted his glass. "To second chances—again. Seems to be a pattern with us, huh?"

I clinked my glass to his and nodded. "I'm a big

believer in second chances," I said. "Takes some of the pressure off the first chance."

"I like that," said Wes. "You look fantastic, by the way. I should have told you that before."

"So do you," I said. "I have to tell you, I was kind of relieved to find you not wearing a puffy shirt and breeches. Or a codpiece."

Wes tossed his head back and laughed.

Just then the curtains parted and the play began. Wes shifted around closer to me, and we spent the next forty-five minutes munching on our food and enjoying the show. At the intermission, Wes got out the strawberries and poured more wine.

"Your uncle is really good," I said.

"Yeah, he's a pro," Wes agreed. "We can go see him for a minute after the show. I think he would appreciate knowing how much we liked his performance."

"I'd like that."

For a minute, we were quiet. I wanted to bring up the Folio, but I didn't know how. I wanted to tell Wes what I had learned from T.C. Satterly and Wendell Knotts. I even longed to show him the mysterious postcard and tell him about the rock being thrown at my window. But I couldn't. Not as long as he and his family were implicated in this whole thing.

"Hey," Wes said, "Jimi told me it was your birthday the other day. I don't know why he told me after the fact. Otherwise I would have tried to stop by the club."

"Oh, yeah. It was fun. My friend Farrah went all out. It would have been nice to see you there. But, you know, this is pretty special, too." I indicated the picnic and chose another strawberry.

The intermission ended, and we watched the second half of the play shoulder to shoulder. Although it was a bright sunny afternoon, the scene on the stage was an enchanted woodland in the middle of the night. When Wes reached over and slipped his hand into mine, I felt like we were sitting under the stars. I felt like I was dreaming. Or else maybe I was under the fairy's spell, like the characters in the play.

When the actors took their final bow, we untwined our fingers to applaud. Then the curtain closed, and the audience started dispersing. While Wes folded the blanket, I put our dishes in the basket and wondered what we would do after seeing Kirk backstage. I wasn't ready for the date to end yet.

Idly, I scanned the faces in the crowd, expecting we might see Darlene and Sharon heading backstage, as well. Instead, I saw someone I never would have expected to see at the Renaissance Faire: my boss, Beverly Olsen. I swallowed, preparing myself to be calm and casual, as she drew nearer. Then I saw who she was chatting with. Lord, help me. It was Edgar Harrison.

They hadn't seen me yet, but it was only a matter of seconds. Unfortunately, they seemed to be approaching the stage, as well. I had to get out of there. Edgar was sure to recognize me as the trespasser who had snagged herself on the barbed-wire fence behind his house and then had bolted like a maniac into the forest.

"Um, Wes, I just remembered something I have to do," I said quickly. "I'm sorry, but I have to leave now. Please tell your uncle how much I enjoyed the show. And the picnic was wonderful. Good-bye."

Leaving Wes with a bewildered expression and no chance to ask questions, I darted into the thickest part of the crowd, heading away from the stage. Without looking back, I zigzagged my way to the other side of the quad, eager to leave the festival and get myself home. I felt like such a heel for leaving Wes like that, but what could I do? Maybe I'd explain myself someday, and we could have a good laugh. Assuming he would see me again.

With the exit in sight, I slowed my steps. I jumped when I felt a tap on my shoulder.

"Ms. Milanni?"

Slowly, I turned to find Darlene standing before me, her face a mask of sadness and worry. Sharon stood at her side like a guard. Or maybe just close family.

"Do you have minute? Could we talk?"

"Of course," I said, finally finding my voice. "How about here?" I pointed to a bench under some trees, and Darlene nodded her head. Sharon stood quietly nearby, letting Darlene take the lead.

"I want to apologize," said Darlene. "I know you advised Mom to secure the book. And I know you've been trying to help. I never should have let my attorney send that letter. I never intended to make you pay for the loss."

Darlene looked down at her hands, clasped tightly in her lap, and pressed her lips together. Her brow was furrowed so tightly, I imagined she must have one hell of a headache. I wanted to tell her to take a breath and let it all out.

Instead, I took a breath and tried to exude enough calmness for both of us. I reached out and touched the back of her hand. "It's okay. I'm sorry too."

Darlene looked up. "It's just that . . . Well, it's not so much the loss of the Folio itself. It's that . . . I'm afraid . . ." Her voice faded to a whisper, and I noticed that her hands trembled. Finally, it dawned on me what she was really worried about. I decided to make it easier on her.

"Darlene," I said softly, "I know about Rob."

Darlene's eyes flashed, and for a moment I was afraid she was going to go all Mama Bear on me. Then her expression crumpled, and she put her hands over her face. Sharon came over and handed her a tissue.

"What do you know?" Darlene whispered, wiping her eyes.

"I know Rob has a gambling problem. And I know he took money from Wes." I thought back to the day Farrah and I had found Rob at Eleanor's house, and I remembered the open drawers upstairs. Rob had probably been searching for money or valuables when we showed up at the door.

Darlene didn't say anything, so I went on. "Do you think he's the one who stole your jewelry the other day? Do you think he staged a break-in?"

Darlene sighed and nodded. "I think so, yes. But we haven't confronted him about it. And I don't have proof."

I had to ask the next question. "Darlene, do you think Rob took the Shakespeare Folio?"

She set her jaw. "No. No, I really don't think so. Otherwise, why steal from me and Bill? If he had the Folio, he wouldn't still need money."

There was a flaw in Darlene's logic, but I didn't point it out. I could tell Darlene already knew. If Rob had the Folio, he probably hadn't sold it yet. So he very well might feel the need to steal again to cover debts that couldn't wait. Especially debts collected by a thug with a nasty scar across his face.

"I just wish Rob would talk to me. His father and I have tried to convince him to get help, but he won't listen to us. I'm so afraid he's going to end up in prison." Darlene's voice hitched, and her eyes filled with tears again. I had to do something.

With my mind racing, an idea started to take shape. Maybe if Rob were confronted with the evidence against him and presented with an opportunity to confess, he would do the right thing. Maybe if he were in a safe place, surrounded by family, it would be like an intervention. Maybe he would come clean and return the Folio, and all would be well. In fact, it might be just the thing to bring this case to a close.

CHAPTER 23

On Monday morning, I went for an early run to clear my head and calm my nerves. The weather forecasters had predicted a heat wave, and as it happened, they were right. Not ten minutes into my run and already I was drenched in sweat. I cut it short after twenty minutes and headed home, passing under every sprinkler I encountered along the way.

After a cool shower and a cold drink, I sat down in my breakfast nook to review the plan for this evening. I was still amazed at how quickly it was all coming together. As soon as I returned home from the Renaissance Faire on Saturday, I'd called Farrah to tell her my idea: We were going to stage a reading of Eleanor's will. Even though it was usually not necessary to gather all the beneficiaries for a reading, I figured everyone would want to come and find out what they had inherited. Plus, as soon as Darlene had made up her mind to trust me, she was fully on board.

Once we had everyone gathered together in one

place, I would bring up the Folio and act like we already knew who had taken it. As I'd explained to Darlene, we did have an eyewitness. So it was entirely plausible that we might know who did it. No one else had to know that Brandi had no clue who she had seen leaving Eleanor's house the night of the visitation.

Saturday night I had called Beverly to get permission to use the office. First, though, I had asked Darlene to call Beverly, and she had readily agreed. Darlene had told the truth when she informed Beverly that she was ditching her other lawyer and retaining our firm to administer her mother's will. Then all I had had to do was tell Beverly that Darlene had requested a reading without delay. Beverly couldn't object to that. At Olsen, Sykes, and Rafferty, we always accommodated our clients' wishes.

"Do you need Julie to assist?" Beverly had asked.

"No, that shouldn't be necessary. But I will need Pammy and Jeremy. They witnessed the will." Since Eleanor had died so soon after executing her will, I knew it was a wise precaution to have the witnesses present at the reading. It wasn't uncommon for wills to be challenged under such circumstances. However, I had other reasons for wanting Jeremy there. He and Rob had gambled side by side on the riverboat. Jeremy might know something. At least, Rob might be led to *think* Jeremy knew something.

"I'll call Pammy and Jeremy," Beverly had said. "And I'll ask Crenshaw to attend, as well. This estate case has been fraught with abnormalities. I think it could prove helpful to have Crenshaw on hand.

He's been looking after your cases while you've been away."

"Okay. Thanks." I couldn't argue with Beverly. Crenshaw wasn't my favorite person, but it was highly likely that things would be tense tonight. I could probably use all the support I could get.

Farrah would be my primary support, though. We had spent all afternoon yesterday on my back deck, preparing for this evening. She would be my pro bono assistant, which, I would tell the other attorneys, was the client's wish. Farrah and I would tag team during the "big reveal," as we were calling it. She would carefully note everyone's reactions while I talked, and vice versa. And if the game called for any good cop–bad cop action, she would play the bad cop, letting me protect my relationship with the family—to the extent that I still had any such relationship.

I glanced at my kitchen clock. Ten a.m. I had to do something to keep busy. Seven o'clock was a long way off. I decided to go see Mila.

Before leaving the house, I wanted to switch to a smaller purse. I went to grab my wallet and keys out of the tote I'd used on Saturday. I hadn't gone anywhere yesterday, so the tote was still where I had left it hanging on a doorknob. When I opened it, I saw immediately that something was wrong. Something was missing.

I looked all around on the floor to see if it had fallen out. Then I took the tote over to my bed and dumped out the contents: wallet, keys on a wishing stone keychain, makeup case, date book, peppermint gum, creepy postcard, and manila envelope. One manila envelope.

What had happened to the other one?

I opened the remaining envelope and slid out the certificate of authenticity for the Mostriak First Folio. Which meant that someone had stolen the Old West photo of Farrah and me.

Soothing harp music and a subtle cinnamon scent greeted me when I entered Mila's shop. Mila was behind the counter, finishing a phone call. Her eyes lit up when she saw me.

"Happy Solstice, my dear! I've been singing 'Here Comes the Sun' all weekend, and Mother Nature heard my call. Isn't it glorious?"

Pulling a tissue from my purse to dab my forehead, I said, "It's good and hot, all right. Are you sure you want to take credit for this?"

Mila laughed and poured me a glass of water. "Oh, I'm kidding, of course. Sort of."

"Mila, I stopped in to thank you for the gorgeous present you sent. You didn't have to do that. You already gave me the love charm, remember?"

"Oh, that is a gorgeous picture, isn't it? When I saw it, I knew it was meant for you."

"Well, thank you," I said, leaning in to give her a hug.

"You're very welcome. So how is the love charm working, anyway?"

"Hmm. Good question." I laughed at Mila's eager expression and patted my purse. "I think it's too early to tell, but I do carry it with me everywhere. I'll keep you posted."

As I turned my head, something shiny glinted on the floor in front of me. Looking closer, I saw that it was a small silver key. I picked it up and handed it to Mila.

"Oh, there it is," she said. "I was looking for this earlier. It's the key to the jewelry case. I must have dropped it."

My eyes must have glazed over for a second, because Mila waved her hand in front of my face. "What is it? What were you thinking just now?"

"Oh, sorry. It's nothing. Something about the way you talked about a lost key reminded me of a dream I had the other night. I had forgotten all about it."

"Ahh," said Mila. "Pay attention then. I'm sure it's a sign. We can learn a lot from our dreams if we care to."

"Don't tell me. 'We are such stuff as dreams are made on'?"

Mila cocked her head. "Maybe. Is that Shakespeare?"

"I think so. He's been popping up a lot lately."

"Interesting. Would you like me to read your cards? Dream interpretation and the tarot are very similar. If the gods are trying to tell you something, we're sure to find a clue."

"You know, that's not a bad idea. A clue is exactly what I need right now."

"Excellent," said Mila, clapping her hands together. She grabbed a small dry-erase board from under the counter and scrawled "Be back at one o'clock." Then she hung the sign on the front door, turned the lock, and beckoned me to follow her through the purple curtain into the back room.

The private room was bigger than I expected. One side contained file cabinets, boxes, and metal storage shelves, but these were mostly obscured by two Japanese folding screens. The other side was decorated much like the shop, with soft oriental rugs, scented candles, and Buddhist-inspired tapestries. A gold-fringed violet cloth covered a round table, which was encircled by three cushioned armchairs. Mila led me to the chairs and took a seat on the far side of the table.

As I got comfortable, I watched Mila turn to open a drawer in the painted bureau next to the table. She removed a small box, slid out a deck of tarot cards, and fanned them faceup in the center of the table.

"This deck is called the Wizards Tarot. It has a fun theme, but it's based on the classic Rider-Waite Tarot. Would you like to look it over? It's one of my favorites, but I have several other decks, as well."

"This one is fine," I said, admiring the lush, colorful images.

Mila gathered the deck, tapped on the top, raised it to her lips, and blew, releasing any residual energy from past readings. Then she began to shuffle the cards.

"Tell me about your dream. You said you had lost something? I take it the finding spell I gave you hasn't worked yet."

"Not yet, but I feel I'm getting closer. In fact,

besides the missing object, I'm also looking for a person. A thief."

It occurred to me that I should use this opportunity to find out if I was on the right track. I was nervous about making accusations at the reading of the will—especially considering I'd be accusing members of Eleanor's family. It would be nice to have some reassurance that I wasn't completely off target.

"So, you'd like to focus on the thief?"

I nodded. "Yeah. I'm trying to smoke him out, and I think he's onto me. I've received a couple of warnings to back off." I told her briefly about the rock, the postcard, and the prowler at my house.

Mila furrowed her brow. "This sounds serious, Keli. Maybe we should do a protection spell first."

I didn't protest as she stood up to gather a few items from the bureau, including a black candle, a smooth obsidian stone, a crow's feather, and an ebony goblet, which she filled with water from a nearby pitcher. She placed the items on the table, one at each compass point, then proceeded to walk around the table, sprinkling salt on the floor and murmuring an incantation as she went.

After casting the circle, Mila opened a small vial of sage oil and wet the tip of her finger with the oil. Then she touched her finger to each of the elemental objects on the table. Next, she dabbed some oil on me: on my shoulders, the back of my neck, and my forehead. Finally, she lit the candle, sat down, and reached for my hands.

"Close your eyes, Keli, and take a deep breath."

I did as she asked.

"I want you to visualize a soft golden-white light surrounding you like an aura. Now see the white light growing brighter. The light radiates around you and moves with you, repelling all negative energy. Imagine yourself completely shielded by this powerful, magical light. You are in its protection."

After a moment of silence, Mila told me to repeat these words after her:

> *Within this sphere of sacred light,*
> *No threat may pierce nor foe may bite.*
>
> *To keep all danger far at bay,*
> *I call the Goddess Hecate.*
>
> *With Darkness banish, fire defend,*
> *Cross her path, and she will rend.*
>
> *I am safe and I am free,*
> *As I will, so mote it be!*

Mila clapped her hands to seal the spell, then gave me a minute to absorb and ground the crackling energy around us. I took a few calming breaths, while she began shuffling the tarot cards again.

"Feeling all right?" she asked.

"I do. I feel . . . more confident."

"Good. You should repeat the words of the spell in your mind at least six times a day. And before you leave, I'll give you an amulet for extra protection. Now then, it's time to think about what you want to ask the tarot."

As I watched Mila deftly handle the cards, I was reminded of the River Queen Casino. Was Rob's gambling problem really at the root of the mystery? Or was I shaking the wrong apple tree?

"I need guidance," I said. "As kids say, I need to know if I'm hot or cold."

"Okay. Got it. This calls for a simple three-card spread representing past, present, and future. The first card will show you where you've come from, what you bring to this moment. It will tell you whether you're on the right path. The second card will illuminate the present situation, highlighting where you are in the journey and whether you really are nearing the end. The third card will predict the outcome based on the path you've chosen."

Mila set the cards in front of me.

"Place your left hand on top of the deck and silently ask your question. Then cut the deck into three piles, while keeping your question in mind. When it's time, I'll turn over the first card and read it before revealing the next one, and so on. This will ensure that each card gets its due without the distraction of the other cards."

I did as Mila asked, eager to see what the cards would reveal. I was familiar with tarot, having used it for spells and divination in the craft. But I was no expert. I trusted Mila to interpret any messages the cards would have for me.

She took the three piles I had created and stacked them on top of one another. Then slowly, like opening the first page of a sacred book, she turned over the first card and placed it on the table, facing me.

It was the High Priestess, which in this version of
the tarot took on the guise of a Professor of Divination, a beautiful goddess-like woman sitting at a
small table next to an open window. She was reading cards by the light of a full moon and a flickering
white candle.

"Are you sure this is my past and not my present?"

Mila smiled. "This shows what you've brought
with you from the past into this present moment.
The High Priestess is you. As you can see, she's associated with the moon and psychic energies. You
have the same gift of insight. This is a message to
listen to your dreams and trust your intuition—
which, apparently, you've been doing."

"That makes sense," I said, studying the imagery
on the card.

"Oh, and see the pomegranate design on the
curtain? The High Priestess is also associated with
Persephone, who ate a pomegranate seed in the
underworld. Another link to your recent past, no?"

"That's right." I laughed, remembering the finding spell Mila had given me. "Well, this is reassuring."

"Okay," said Mila. "Let's look at your present." She
turned over the next card in the stack and placed it
to the right of the first card. It was the Eight of Cups.
Mila pointed at the card as she described the illus-
tration. "In the foreground, you can see eight cups
stacked somewhat precariously. It would appear
there's one missing from the arrangement."

"Well, this is obvious, right? Something's definitely missing. That's why we're here."

"Beyond the cups," Mila continued, "is a boy

walking away from them. He's carrying a walking stick, as if he's going to be gone for a while. For some people, this card represents change or leaving something behind."

"Leaving something behind? Like my job?" I asked, feeling a twinge of alarm.

"Remember your question," Mila said soothingly. "Something is missing, and you're looking for it. The retreating figure could be setting off to look for the missing object."

"Oh," I said, relieved.

"As this is the eight card—which is toward the end of the cards numbered one through ten—I would say you're nearing the end of your search. We also see an autumn landscape, which is another indication of a cycle nearing completion."

"Good to know," I said, though the thought made my stomach jumpy.

"One more thing," said Mila. "The suit of Cups is associated with our emotions and feelings, as well as love and relationships. Perhaps you're turning your back on something in that realm? Or something is missing from your life as you conduct this search?"

"Humph," I snorted. "Let's move on."

Mila laughed. "Very well. Let's see what the future has in store."

My heart started to thud a little faster as I watched Mila slowly turn over the third card. I frowned when I saw what it was.

"Interesting," said Mila.

"I'm not sure *interesting* is the word I'd use. This card doesn't look so good."

"I just meant it's interesting that it's another Cups card."

It was the Five of Cups, and it depicted a sad-looking girl wrapped in a cloak, gazing forlornly at some toppled cups that were spilling their contents into a stream or river.

"This is a card of loss and disappointment, isn't it?" I asked, biting my lip. "Does this mean I won't be successful in my search? Or that I won't like what I find?"

"Now, now," said Mila. "Don't get ahead of yourself. Take a closer look. There are five cups, but only three are knocked over. Two are still standing. That means all is not lost."

Small comfort, I thought. But I let her continue.

"And remember what the cups represent. I would say you are emotionally invested in this search. Perhaps some of your emotions have yet to spill over."

"But you said cups also represent relationships," I countered. "So this could mean I'm going to lose a relationship?"

"It could," Mila responded gently. "There could be some regret. But the flowing river indicates that life will go on. You'll move on. Whatever happens."

After the comfortably temperate atmosphere of Moonstone Treasures, the blazing heat outside felt like a punch in the gut. I walked a few blocks under the noonday sun, brooding over my unpleasant future, before deciding I needed to drop in some-place to cool off. I wasn't too far from the Cozy Café. But when I neared the restaurant, I had a sudden notion to visit the library around the corner instead.

The Edindale Public Library was housed in a solid three-story limestone structure built around the turn of the century. It was a peaceful, old-fashioned Carnegie library with a sizable collection. As I ascended the stone steps and entered through heavy double doors, I thought to myself that I really should come more often. The hushed coolness inside was especially welcome on a day like today.

Without quite knowing what I was looking for, I headed to the fiction area and scanned author names. Nothing jumped out at me.

As I wandered through the quiet stacks, I once again recalled my vision of books. What was the Goddess, or the High Priestess, trying to tell me? I walked to the English literature section, found two whole rows of Shakespeare, and stared at the books, as if they would speak to me. After a minute, I did hear something— the squeaky wheel of a book cart on the other side of the floor. I peeked my head around the shelves and stared, experiencing the strange sensation that I was having another psychic vision. Why did the library worker look like Wes?

I jumped back behind the shelves, ducked down, and peeked through an empty space between books. By Goddess, it was Wes! He stopped the cart, placed a book on a shelf, then moved the cart up another row.

I was torn. Should I step out and say hello? Or sneak down the back staircase before he reached my row? It was so odd, seeing him restock books here, out of the blue. Then my phone buzzed inside my purse, making the decision for me.

Once in the stairwell on my way down, I answered my phone. "Hey, Farrah," I said quietly. "What's up?"

"Please don't hate me."

"What?"

"Please, please, please don't kill me. Don't defriend me. I'll make it up to you somehow, I promise."

"What's going on? What are you talking about?" By this time, I had reached the first floor and had exited the library. I crossed over to the shady side of the street, trying to ignore the sinking sensation in the pit of my stomach.

"I can't be there tonight. This guy at work broke his leg and can't present at this bar association conference in Chicago . . . tonight. The boss asked me to go in his place."

"Oh, man."

"I'm on my way up there now. I am *so*, so sorry. You know I'd never do this to you if I could help it."

"I know," I said.

I knew Farrah had no choice. I wasn't mad at her. However, now I was more nervous than ever. Without my partner in detection, I was going to be the lone woman in the spotlight. How was I ever going to pull it off?

CHAPTER 24

The conference room was full, and all eyes were on me. Outside the plate-glass windows, the trees along the boulevard appeared as dark shadows against the evening sky. Conversation stopped when I took a seat at the head of the table. It was Beverly's usual spot, but I hardly felt like the Queen Mother. More like the royal jester maybe, about to make a fool of myself.

Keep it together, Milanni. Stick to the plan, and you'll be fine.

I cleared my throat and turned to Pammy, who sat on my left. "Pammy, would you mind passing around these copies of the will?"

Then I turned to Darlene on my right. "Is everyone here who's coming?"

She nodded and pressed her lips together, appearing as tense as I felt.

I looked around the table at all the expectant faces. Sharon smiled at me encouragingly, while her husband looked slightly bored. Wes, who sat next to Kirk in the farthest chair from Rob, winked at me when he met my eye. If he harbored any annoyance about me rushing off from our date on Saturday, he didn't show it.

We'll see how long that lasts, I thought unhappily.

Directly across from me, at the other end of the table, Crenshaw, wearing a trim brown suit, sat upright, drumming his fingers on the tabletop. I looked at the empty chair next to Pammy and then glanced at the clock. It was 7:15 p.m., and Jeremy still hadn't arrived.

"Okay, well, I guess we'll go ahead and get started. You all should have a copy of the will before you, if you'd like to follow along. Oh, and I'll be making arrangements to see that all of the beneficiaries who couldn't be here tonight receive a copy, as well. So no need to worry about that." I nodded toward Kirk, whose youngest daughter was back in California and whose eldest daughter was home with her baby.

I cleared my throat again. "When Eleanor was in my office a few short weeks ago, she certainly didn't expect we would be reading her last wishes so soon. But, of course, she knew we would be reading them at some point. And I want to tell you that it was very clear to me how much she loved each and every one of you." I paused, glanced at Eleanor's children and grandchildren, and for once felt I was doing right by my late client.

"While there won't be any surprises tonight about how she divided the bulk of her estate—equal percentages to each of her children—she did leave special bequests, special gifts, to all of her relatives. Now, as you may or may not know, reading the will aloud like this is merely a formality. However, Darlene, as executor, felt that it would be consistent with her mother's wishes to gather together and read the list of gifts for all to hear. And I agree."

I took a sip of water from the glass in front of me, then proceeded to read Eleanor's will. I was on the second page when Jeremy slipped in, a sheepish grin on his face. He ducked his head and waved apologetically at everyone in the room, though I noticed he didn't look directly at Rob. If I wasn't mistaken, Rob seemed slightly surprised to see Jeremy but kept his mouth shut.

Jeremy clapped Crenshaw's shoulder as he walked by and winked at Pammy when he took his seat. "Sorry," he whispered loudly. "Please, continue."

I disregarded Jeremy, doing my best to keep a neutral face. As I read each gift Eleanor had selected for her family members, there was some quiet murmuring, a few laughs, and some tears and sniffles. After about twenty minutes, I was finished with the reading.

Now it was time for the real show.

With my heart thudding beneath my navy blue silk blouse, I took a deep breath. I so wanted to scrap the whole plan at this point. But Darlene looked at me anxiously, her cheeks flushed and her hands clasped tightly in front of her. I needed to do this, and I needed to do it before people started to leave. Oh, how I wished Farrah were with me!

Stacking the papers on the table in front of me, I cleared my throat yet again and launched into my rehearsed opening.

"Ladies and gentlemen, we have one more matter

to discuss this evening, which I think will be of great interest to everyone here. As you know, when Eleanor prepared her will, she anticipated that her estate would be significantly larger than it had been previously. This was, of course, due to the discovery in her attic of a rare collection of Shakespeare's plays, known as the First Folio."

That got everyone's attention. Crenshaw, not knowing about this item on the agenda, squinted his eyes but remained silent. Pammy and Jeremy also looked at me with interest.

"As you probably also know, this edition of the First Folio rightfully belonged to Eleanor, because she inherited the entirety of her husband's estate upon Frank's death four years ago. And Frank's claim to the rare book is documented by a certificate of authenticity—a copy of which I have right here."

I held up the certificate and tried to note everyone's reaction. There wasn't much to see. Kirk leaned forward; Wes raised an eyebrow. Crenshaw jutted out his chin. *Darn it.* Without Farrah, this was going to be even harder than I'd thought. Still, I pressed onward.

"The Folio, unfortunately, is missing at the moment. It was taken from Eleanor's home on the evening of the memorial service. However, I believe it might be returned. As a matter of fact, I'm hoping that the person who took it will voluntarily return it. Tonight. For, you see, that person is sitting here with us in this room at this very moment."

There was a sharp intake of breath. Shifting chairs creaked on both sides of the table. Other than that, it was much quieter than I'd expected. I quickly swept the room with my eyes, looking for any signs of guilt. Everyone looked at me, waiting for me to go on.

Stalling for time, I took a sip of water. Okay, that bought me exactly one and a half seconds. *Ugh*.

"That's right, ladies and gentlemen. The person who took the Folio is sitting here at this table. I know this because the person who took it was seen leaving Eleanor's house that night, carrying a duffel bag. There was an eyewitness. And I spoke to that eyewitness. But the eyewitness has not gone to the police, and neither have I. Yet."

A soft moan escaped Darlene's lips, and Sharon patted her arm. Rob stared at me impassively, while Wes furrowed his brow. I could almost hear him wondering why I had never mentioned any of this to him before.

"As I said, I am hoping that the person will come clean. He's not really a criminal. I think he saw an opportunity. And in a high-stress, misguided moment, he took that opportunity without thinking it through."

Silence.

"But now he has a chance to make it right. A chance for amnesty. Return the Folio now, and all will be forgiven."

More silence.

Damn it. I was going to have to go forward with the accusations one by one, just like in the movies. Crenshaw's eyebrows were drawn so close together, they were practically touching. As I sat there, looking across the table at him, I suddenly had the wild idea that I would start with him.

"All right, then. I told you the culprit is in this room. As a matter of fact, it *could* have been any one of a number of people, right? Take Crenshaw, for example."

Now those eyebrows were sky high. Pammy gasped, and Jeremy leaned back in his seat with crossed arms, looking nothing more than amused, while all heads swiveled toward Crenshaw.

Now that I had begun, there was no turning back. My words tumbled forth. "Yes, Crenshaw. You love Shakespeare, don't you? You're a real Shakespeare buff, a devotee. You quote him. You emulate him. Why, you knew all about the First Folio, as you demonstrated to our office that morning when I told you about Eleanor's find. You also knew that the Folio would have very likely been left unguarded at Eleanor's house the night of the visitation. You even asked me about it that day at the office. Remember?"

"But—but that doesn't prove that I took it!" Crenshaw sputtered.

"Keli, really," said Pammy beside me. "How can you suggest such a thing?"

Ignoring Pammy, I responded to Crenshaw. "No, that's true. It doesn't. In fact, our whole law office knew about the Folio. But there was only a handful who knew about the visitation and the rare opportunity it would provide, including Pammy and Jeremy."

Pammy's hand flew to her heart, while Jeremy

rocked back in his chair, looking less amused, traces of his earlier joviality frozen across his forehead.

"But, Keli," Pammy breathed. "Why in the world would any of us do such a thing? We're not thieves."

"Why? The Folio is worth a fortune, Pammy. Money like that can be a powerful motivator. Especially to someone who has a special need for money." I looked from Pammy to Jeremy and then back to Crenshaw. I could see the vein throbbing in Crenshaw's temple from clear across the table. I quickly looked away.

"In any event, besides Crenshaw, there's someone else here tonight with a special fondness for Shakespeare." I turned to Kirk, whose eyes widened in disbelief.

Speaking as gently as possible, while still trying to maintain the appearance that I knew what the hell I was talking about, I made my case. "Kirk, your love of Shakespeare is part of a special connection you had with your father, isn't it? In fact, you were against selling the Folio after your mother found it. You wanted to keep it in the family. And then you had your chance. While everyone else was at the visitation, you stepped out for a little while. I saw you come back. You could easily have popped over to your mother's house, slipped in and out, and come back without anyone being the wiser."

Kirk scoffed. "Is this a joke? You can't be serious. You think I left my own mother's visitation to steal from her?"

"Actually, you weren't the only one who left the visitation." I shifted my attention to Wes, who was seated to the right of Kirk. In his eyes, I saw a flicker of shocked comprehension, which quickly turned steely. I swallowed the lump in my throat and forced myself to continue.

"Wes, you and your brother left the visitation early and didn't come back. You knew exactly where the Folio was. You knew how to get into your grandmother's house. And you had a particular need for a large amount of cash."

My voice had dropped to one shade above a whisper, but it still resounded in my ears, as if it were bouncing off the walls. I had intended to mention how Wes was so interested in hearing what Brandi was going to say to the police that day we followed them throughout the neighborhood. But I couldn't bring myself to do it.

Now it was Rob's turn. He stared at the table in front of him and didn't look up when I spoke. "Rob, everything I said about Wes goes for you, too. You had the means, the motive, and the opportunity. But perhaps your motive was even greater. Perhaps you needed money more desperately than your brother. With all the gambling debts you've accrued, and with pressure building—" I stopped. I looked around the room at a sea of unfriendly faces staring at me, waiting for my next move. And I felt myself shrinking in as I realized I didn't have one.

The silence in the air lingered. And lingered.

No one was confessing.

Finally, with a scrape of his chair, Rob pushed back from the table. "This is bogus," he said, right before he walked out the door.

Jeremy stood up next, clucking his tongue and

shaking his head like it was all such a damn shame. He patted my arm, then followed Rob out the door.

I looked at Pammy, who appeared to be rooted to her seat, in shock. She gazed at me as if I had sprouted horns. Then I saw Crenshaw stand up and pull his phone from his jacket pocket. With a rigid jaw, he shot me a glare, then turned his head and started dialing his phone as he walked out the door and down the hall. I could guess who he was calling. I might as well kiss my job good-bye.

Seeing Wes head for the door shook me from my mortified paralysis. I hurried over to him and placed a hand on his arm. I promptly dropped it when I saw the hurt look he gave me.

"Nice game," he said gruffly. "But I think I'll pass." And then he was gone, too.

I stood there by the door, feeling lower than low as people shuffled by. When Darlene came up to me, I braced myself for her anger. But when I saw her face, I perceived only worry and confusion.

"So who did it, then? Are you going to call the police now?"

Taking a breath, I shook my head. "Not yet," I murmured.

Looking into Darlene's eyes, I could see a strong resemblance to her mother. Then I had a sudden flash of Eleanor in her home, finding the book. Once again I recalled my vision, and a wave of certainty washed over me. Relying on my intuition, I straightened my spine and spoke quietly and urgently to Darlene.

"Would it be okay if I took a look around your

mom's house? Tonight? I promise I won't mess anything up. And I'll explain everything later."

With a trust that might have been borne of exhaustion, Darlene opened her purse and retrieved the key to Eleanor's house. She handed it to me without question. I thanked her—and thanked the Goddess—then slipped out of the room. A crack of light was visible at the bottom of Crenshaw's closed office door. He could lock up. I was outta there.

CHAPTER 25

It was dark when I arrived at Eleanor's house. By the glow of the streetlamp, I managed to unlock her front door and let myself in. I felt along the wall and flicked on the foyer light. As an afterthought, I turned around and slid the dead bolt in place. I felt a little nervous, being alone in the quiet, empty house. I wished Farrah were with me. Yet I also felt a strange calling to do this on my own.

Treading lightly, I went upstairs, walked down the hall, and opened the door to the large linen closet I had peeked in the last time I was there. I looked up. There, just within reach, was the rope that opened the attic hatch. With a strong yank, I pulled the hatch open and stepped back as the pull-down stairs unfolded before me.

Looking up into the dark expanse, I hesitated. Then I laughed under my breath. "Okay. I may be brave, but I'm not that brave." I wasn't about to creep into the dusty, possibly spider-filled attic of a deceased woman without at least arming myself with a flashlight. Leaving the steps extended, I trotted down to the kitchen to check the drawers and cabinets.

Good ole Eleanor. The first drawer I tried held a slender red plastic flashlight, and it even had working batteries. Now I was ready. I was turning to head back upstairs when the blinking of fireflies in the garden captured my attention. Peering out the kitchen window, I watched with curiosity as the yellow flickering formed a winking path through the grass toward the toolshed.

This was a sign. I knew it. Without a second thought, I unlocked the back door and followed the way shown by the sporadic glowing lights.

The garden was fragrant in the dark, humid air. Cicadas and tree frogs competed for the title of most vocal nighttime critter. Strangely, I wasn't a bit afraid, even though the surrounding foliage screened the yard from neighbors on all sides.

When I reached the windowless toolshed, I pulled open the old wooden door and shined the flashlight inside. From the doorway, I trained the beam all around, searching for whatever it was I was supposed to see. There was a lawn mower, a rake, a hoe. An antique bicycle, a cobweb-covered hula hoop. Buckets of old paint, an extension ladder.

A ladder. One of those lightweight aluminum extension ladders. Easy enough for one person to carry to the side of a house, slide open to full length, prop under a window and climb right in. It would be a brazen move, but entirely possible.

I nodded to myself as I remembered the piece

of dried mud on the floor in Eleanor's bedroom, beneath the open window. So the spare key under the rock wasn't used, after all. Score one for the family . . . but I still didn't know who had used the ladder. I closed the shed door and returned to the house. The attic was still waiting.

Flashlight in hand, I carefully climbed the attic stairs and poked my head inside. It was hot and airless and smelled like old wood. As soon as I got my bearings, I went straight over to the window to let in some air. Then I located the light switch and turned on two overhead bulbs. Unfortunately, their dim illumination failed to reach the shadowy corners, so I kept the flashlight on as I took inventory.

Boxes and bins, cabinets and cases lined the walls. There was Christmas paraphernalia, of course, and other seasonal decorations. There were bins labeled DARLENE and KIRK, which seemed to hold childhood keepsakes. There were old toys, old books, old furniture, and even a box of Shakespeare memorabilia, which included playbills and ticket stubs from the 1950s through the 1970s. These last items made me think of Kirk—which caused me to cringe with embarrassment as I recalled the earlier disastrous meeting.

Then I spotted two trunks side by side. One appeared to be an army footlocker; the other a steamer trunk. I opened the army trunk first. Inside were woolly olive drab blankets, pressed World War II uniforms, a box of photos, and a big Folio-shaped hole, from where the book had been extracted like

a tooth. I set the flashlight down and ran my hands
carefully through and under the contents of the
trunk. No clues here.

Next, I lifted the lid of the other trunk. This one
contained photo albums, scrapbooks, and assorted
keepsakes. There were also several bundles of letters. Kneeling before the trunk, I hesitated for a
moment. Then I took a centering breath and closed
my eyes. In a faint whisper, I murmured, "Guide
me, Persephone. Reveal for me the missing thing
unveiled before my eyes."

I opened my eyes, let my hand hover over the
contents of the trunk, then selected a large bundle
of letters. Sitting down cross-legged, I carefully removed the twine that held them together. Then I
paused, feeling a twinge of guilt at what I was about
to do—these were personal letters, after all. But this
was for Eleanor, to solve the mystery for her. I felt
sure she wouldn't mind. I slid a folded piece of stationery out of the first envelope and perused the
faded writing.

Dear Ellie,

*Happy New Year! How was your holiday? Mine
was okay, except for the bad news about the farm.
As you have probably guessed by now, I'm not
coming back to the university. You'll have to carry
on without me. We had some fun times, but now
you're the last musketeer. Promise me you'll write. . . .
I still want to know everything!*

> *Friends always,*
> *Sadie*

Okay. This didn't tell me much. I moved on to the next letter.

Dear Ellie,
*   The apple trees are blossoming and the seeds are*
sprouting in our fields . . . and on the neighboring
farms. And that's not all that's blooming next door.
Ever since you came to visit, Frankie Mostriak will
not stop talking about you!

I smiled as I read. So, this was how Eleanor and Frank met. I skimmed through the next few letters and learned all about Frank and Eleanor's courtship, marriage, and first baby, all through the secondhand comments of Eleanor's friend Sadie. Along the way, I also learned about Sadie's life on the farm and her eventual marriage and child rearing. Now and then, she mentioned the Mostriak family, as well as another farming family in the community, the McPeppers.

Now, that was a familiar name. It took me a second, but then I remembered Sharon's story about a dispute over the Folio between Frank and Little Bo McPepper. I went back to the letters, keeping an eye out for the name. It popped up now and then, but not in any really significant way.

When I realized I was nearing the end of the stack of letters, I furrowed my brow. Sadie had been a faithful correspondent, writing at least a couple times a year for decades. But why was I reading this now? Was this all a waste of time? My intuition told me to keep going, and when I opened the next envelope, my senses began to tingle.

Dear Ellie,

Well, the corn is not quite knee-high, but it's getting there. We had a nice Fourth of July celebration last weekend, country style. The McPeppers brought in a big stash of fireworks from Indiana, as they always do. Bo Jr. was there this year, all puffed up with the news that his only grandson was accepted into law school. Little Bo always was a character. . . .

I stopped and looked up, staring into the dusty darkness before me. *Eureka!* Connections snapped into place in my mind. Based on the date of the letter, McPepper's grandson would probably be close to my age now. A lawyer . . . who might believe he had a claim to the Folio based on his grandfather's assertion he had won it in a bet.

Lost in thought, I folded the letter and replaced it in the envelope.

And then a floorboard creaked behind me.

Please let it be the wind. Please let it be the wind. This was an old house. Creaks and groans were perfectly normal. As I bundled the letters together and retied the twine, I tried to convince myself that the noise behind me was nothing. At the same time, I cast around for anything that could be used as a weapon. I couldn't see a single thing.

Slowly, I pushed myself to my feet and replaced the letters in the trunk.

Creak.

The sound was unmistakable this time. With my

heart jumping, I twirled around, clutching the little flashlight in my palm. There was a man standing in the attic, blocking my way to the hatch.

I screamed. He stepped under the light. It was Wes.

"Oh, thank God." Exhaling heavily, I sat down on the army footlocker. Wes walked over to me with narrowed eyes.

"What? You're not afraid of me? After all, if I stole the book, who knows what else I might do?"

"I know it wasn't you, Wes."

"Oh? What makes you so sure?"

What indeed? I looked at Wes as he stared at me, his dark eyes penetrating and . . . wary. His face was unshaven, like the first time I laid eyes on him; his hair disheveled, as if he had been running his hand through it repeatedly. He reminded me of a wild animal that was trying to decide whether to run, hide, or pounce.

"What are you doing here, anyway?" I asked.

"Looking for you. My mom said you were coming here. But you didn't answer my question. How do you know it wasn't me?"

"Well, I just—"

"You were investigating us the whole time, weren't you? Rob, and me and our whole family. All this time, you were just trying to get information. You and your flirting—it was all a ruse."

"What? No, Wes. That's not true."

He shook his head. "It was all a trick. You played me."

My eyes widened in dismay, and I inhaled sharply. Then I started coughing, choking on the dry air and the attic dust.

"Are you okay?" Just like that, Wes dropped his accusatory stance and looked concerned.

I nodded my head as I turned away and continued to cough into both of my hands.

"We should get out of here," Wes said, tentatively touching my shoulder.

"Yeah," I wheezed. As my coughs subsided, I wiped away the tears that had leaked from my eyes. "Wes, I want to—"

"Let's get you some water first," Wes interrupted. "You go first. I'll get the lights."

It was just as well. I wasn't sure what I was going to say. Why should Wes trust me when there was some truth to what he said? If I were in his position I probably wouldn't trust me.

In the kitchen, Wes took a glass from a cabinet and filled it from the dispenser on the refrigerator door. Gazing out the window, I saw a single firefly blink once in the shadowy garden.

"Want to sit on the patio?" I asked.

"Sure," said Wes, handing me the drink.

I took a grateful sip, then followed Wes outside. We sat side by side in lawn chairs, looking up at the stars. The waning moon, slightly smaller than a half circle, perched above the treetops like a curved beacon. We heard a rustling on the other side of the fence and then the yowl of an alley cat. After that it was quiet.

I sighed and looked at Wes. A little voice inside told me to open my heart and be honest.

"Wes?"

"Yeah?"

"I'm sorry."

He met my eyes, his expression inscrutable. I plunged ahead.

"You're right that I've been investigating your family. I think you know I was trying to find out what happened to the Folio. I felt I owed it to your grandmother, as well as to your mom and everyone else So I had to be thorough. I couldn't rule anyone out."

Wes looked away, running his fingers through his hair, and remained silent.

"But I hope you'll believe me when I say I was never dishonest with you. I never played you. You and I met before all this happened, and my . . . interest in you has been genuine."

A flicker of a smile crossed his lips. He looked down at his hands and slowly nodded his head. "Yeah," he said. "I believe you."

"You do?" My spirits soared as I let out the breath I didn't know I'd been holding.

Wes looked up at me and grinned briefly. "It has always felt genuine to me. I'm sorry about the scene upstairs. The truth is, I've suspected Rob all along. I've been trying to get through to him before this whole thing escalates. I mean, that was a nice try tonight, but I could have told you it wouldn't work. Though, to be honest, I'm out of ideas myself." Wes heaved a sigh and pushed back his hair again.

I sat up straight. "Oh, but, Wes, I don't think Rob did it, after all."

"What?"

"No, listen. I have this theory. Let me run it by you."

I told Wes about the open window and the ladder

in the shed—minus the part about being guided by fireflies. And I told him about the letter I'd found and about how Sharon had told me about the events leading up to the fire that had supposedly destroyed the Folio.

Wes looked thoughtful as he listened. "Interesting," he murmured.

I sat back, feeling a little less excited now that I had articulated my idea. It sounded pretty flimsy. "The only problem is, I don't have any proof. And I don't know what to do next."

Wes tapped his fingers on his knees. "Hmm. Seems to me the only way might be to catch the guy in some kind of trap. Like a sting, you know?"

I smiled, so happy to be on the same side as Wes again. Impulsively, I reached over and took his hand and gave it a little squeeze. "I'll tell you one thing. I'm not gonna give up."

He looked at me, then leaned over and brushed my lips with his. "You know," he said softly, "you really don't have to do this. But thank you."

"You're welcome," I said, right before kissing him back.

CHAPTER 26

Today was the day. I felt it in my bones. After a late night spent talking—and *finally* getting to know Wes better—Tuesday morning came a little too early. But as I lay under the sheets, stretching and yawning, my mind began to whirl. And soon I became overcome with the strong sense that this was an important day. Call it divine inspiration, or call it earthly intuition—either way, I knew. If I was going to find the First Folio, it had to be today.

After rolling out of bed, I hurried into the bathroom to splash water on my face. Then I quickly drew the shades and gathered some candles and jars of dried herbs, roots, and powders. Arranging the candles in a circle on my bedroom floor, I invoked the four elements. Then, forcing myself to slow down, I sprinkled the roots, powders, and herbs in concentric rings, forming a spiral that ended with me in the center. With a nod to the Weird Sisters, I chanted an improvised spell as I went:

Round about the circle go.
In the herbal magics throw
Leaf of basil, sprig of thyme.
Give me courage with this rhyme.

Frond of rue and oil of pine,
Centered purpose, clear of mind.
Root of ginger, breath of air,
Victr'y comes to those who dare.

Reaching the center, I stood still and muttered the final words, a small smile tugging at the corners of my mouth:

Double, double, guard from trouble,
Fire burn, and magic bubble.

With a deep breath, I lowered my eyelids and pressed my palms together. For the next few minutes, I visualized myself as a powerful sorceress. I was confident and self-assured. I was wise and brave, as heroic as any knight on a quest. And I was supported—lifted up—by a whole pantheon of powerful, magical goddesses, who would show me the way.

Finally, I opened my eyes and raised my arms, performing a partial sun salutation. Feeling fortified and encouraged, I released the vision. Quietly, I closed the circle and cleared the floor. Then I took a shower, got dressed, and went into the kitchen to make breakfast.

Just your average, ordinary Tuesday morning.

At around 9:00 a.m., Farrah called, back from

her conference and eager for a play-by-play of the "big reveal." I told her that the true reveal had yet to happen, but something was brewing. I promised to fill her in very soon. There was something I had to do first.

With my cells still vibrating from the ritual, I hauled my bicycle out of the garage and rode through town to the university. After locking my bike in the rack near the law school, I walked inside the familiar three-story glass-and-steel building and headed for the law library, which made up the entirety of the school's east wing.

As I entered the library, I flashed my attorney ID card to the security guard, who gave me a bored nod. Strolling into the cool interior, I surveyed the first floor. Behind the circulation desk, a single librarian tapped at a computer. Since intersession hadn't started yet, I figured the library would be used primarily by local attorneys rather than students. But this morning, the library seemed to be largely empty of any patrons. That was fine by me.

Bypassing the casebooks and reference shelves, I made my way to the basement. Here and there, study cubicles were nestled between sections of foreign periodicals, superseded materials, and historical treatises. As the quietest area in the library, it made an ideal study spot. In theory. When I'd tried studying here during law school, I had found the deathly quiet disconcerting. I'd been too creeped out to concentrate.

Now, as I wandered deeper and deeper into the cavernous stacks, I felt goose bumps rise on my arms. And not because of the quiet. It was because I recognized the lines of bookshelves from my vision.

As I walked, I read the alphabetical labels on the end of each row. *Hmm. F* for "Folio"? *S* for "Shakespeare"? *W* for "William"? *No.* The Folio wouldn't be shelved like any other book. If it was here, it might be in plain sight . . . but it would still be hidden.

I continued down a side aisle, then stopped. Way in the back, against the far wall, tucked in a corner behind a study desk, was a column of shelves holding oversize Old English tomes in faded gray and brown. When I reached the shelves, I ran my fingertips lightly over a couple of dusty spines and caught a faint whiff of history and mildew. Looking up, I saw that the shelves reached to the ceiling. Nearly. In between the top of the uppermost shelf and the ceiling was a dark space of indeterminate size.

Grabbing a nearby stepladder, I climbed up, stretched to my tiptoes, craned my neck, and peered over the top of the shelf. Something was there. A book, lying flat on its cover, spine to the wall. My heartbeat quickened as I reached out and slid the book forward to the edge of the shelf. Without taking it down, I gingerly touched the pages with my thumb and then carefully rotated the book and turned it over so that I could read the cover. My breath caught in my throat.

Mr. William Shakespeares Comedies, Histories, & Tragedies. Published according to the True Originall Copies.

The First Folio.

I could hardly believe it. I found it! After all this time, I actually found Eleanor's book.

The only problem was, I couldn't rescue it. In order to catch the thief, I was going to have to leave the book in place.

Damn.

After glancing over my shoulder to make sure I was still alone, I turned the book back over and reluctantly pushed it toward the rear wall, then rotated it to its original position. With wobbly legs, I climbed down and moved the stepladder back to where I had found it. Looking back up at the top shelf, I bit my lip.

Trust the Goddess.

Now wasn't the time to retrieve the book. Now was the time to follow Wes's suggestion. It was time to set up a sting.

Before unlocking my bike, I texted Farrah and asked her to meet me at T.C. Satterly's shop. On the way, I formulated a plan. It might be a long shot . . . but, then again, I had magic on my side.

"So?" said Farrah as I rode up to where she was leaning against her car in front of Satterly's Rare Books. "I take it there wasn't a shoot-out last night. How about a confession? Do we have the culprit?"

"Better. We have the book."

"Get out! You found the book? Where is it?"

"It's still where the thief hid it."

"What? Oh, I get it." said Farrah, following me as I locked my bike to a street pole and entered the bookshop. "A mousetrap? The book is the cheese, and we're gonna catch ourselves a mouse?"

"That's the idea."

"Detective Milanni! Always a pleasure!" T.C. squeezed himself around the counter to greet me, then shook my hand with both of his plump mitts. Today he wore a white T-shirt featuring a print of Shakespeare's visage above the words *Will Power*.

Perfect, I thought, smiling broadly.

"T.C., this is my friend Farrah. She's been helping me track down the Folio."

"Wonderful, wonderful. So tell me, did you see *Stenislaw*?" He said the name in an exaggerated whisper, looking left and right as he did so. I had to chuckle.

"Um, no. Somehow I missed him. But it doesn't matter. He doesn't have the Folio, anyway. At least, not yet."

"Oh?" T.C. raised his bushy brows. "Then you know where it is?"

"I do. But it may not be there for long, so we'll have to act fast. Do you still have that message about the Twitter post?"

T.C.'s eyes lit up. "Yes, yes. It's right here." He reached for a spiral notepad behind the counter.

"Okay, so here's the deal. I'd like you to post the message and wait for a call. When he calls you, tell him you have a cash buyer, but he's leaving the country tonight. So the exchange has to take place today."

T.C. rubbed his hands together. "You betcha. I can do this. Oh, boy."

Farrah, appearing impressed and a little bit

astonished, looked from T.C. to me. "Well done, Scooby Gang. And then what? Do we rig up a giant fishnet?"

"Ha-ha," I said. "Actually, I was hoping you could call Jake's friend, the police officer. Think he could wire me with a little recording device?"

"Oh, yeah," said Farrah. "I'm sure he could. But are *you* sure about this? This sounds a little danger-ous. We are talking about a rock-wielding, creepy note–leaving criminal here."

"I'm sure," I said.

Wasn't I?

Sure or not, five hours later I was back in the law school library basement, this time hidden inside a dark storeroom. I stood close to the door, which was open a crack, and waited for my cell phone to buzz. It would be Farrah's signal to me that someone— anyone—was entering the stacks. Although I had a pretty good idea, I wasn't 100 percent certain who had stolen the Folio. Or if he was working alone.

The first time my phone buzzed, it almost slid out of my slick palm. With heart thudding, I spied out the storeroom door. Footsteps sounded on the parquet floor, growing louder as the person ap-proached. I held my breath. Finally, a young woman came into view. I watched as she entered a row of casebooks and soon emerged with a book. Then she left.

I sighed. Goddess, how long was I going to have to stay in this storeroom? I had unlocked my phone and had started typing a text to Farrah, to let her know the first person was leaving, when the phone buzzed again, causing me to jump. Jeesh. I closed my eyes, touched the amulet Mila had given me, and said a brief prayer to the goddesses Diana for courage and Hecate for protection. Then I peeked through the crack again.

Once again, I heard footsteps, this time approaching more rapidly. It sounded like the person was moving toward the rear section, but he or she was outside my field of vision. Slowly, I pushed open the door another inch. And then another, until I saw a man dragging a step stool to the back wall.

Taking a deep breath, I opened the door farther and slipped out. Quick as a ghost, I darted behind the bookshelves adjacent to the back wall and peered through the gaps between books. As I watched, the guy climbed onto the step stool, grabbed the Folio, and stuffed it into a navy blue duffel bag. Although his back was to me, I recognized him right away— and remembered seeing that duffel bag before, too, under his desk. When he climbed down and turned to leave, I stepped out into the aisle right in front of him, blocking his path.

"Hi, Jeremy."

At first he looked startled and confused. Then he feigned delight. "Keli! What a pleasure. Are you . . . doing research?"

"Actually, I've already found what I was looking for."

Jeremy cocked his head inquisitively and continued with the false pleasantries. "Oh? Well, that's good. Me too. Want to walk out together?" He looked beyond me, clearly eyeing the exit.

"You can give it up, Jeremy. I know what you're doing. I know what you did."

"What are you talking about? I didn't do anything. But I have to go now. I have an appointment with a client."

He walked forward, as if to pass me, but I didn't budge.

"No," I said, holding out my hand. "That doesn't belong to you. I know you have the Shakespeare Folio, Jeremy. You took it from Eleanor's home, and you've been contacting book dealers, looking for a buyer. It's time to come clean. Just do the right thing and turn it over."

Like a dark cloud passing before the sun, Jeremy's fake smile transformed into a menacing sneer.

"Maybe it does belong to me. Ever think of that?"

"Come on, Jeremy. If you're talking about a gambling prize that may or may not have been won in an illegal poker game sixty-odd years ago, you know that can't be a legitimate claim."

He shrugged his shoulders. "Ever hear of history repeating itself?"

"Are you talking about Rob? I *knew* you knew him."

"Yeah, I know Rob. I've known him for years. I even met his grandmother once, when Rob needed help moving something out of her shed. Robby's a regular at the casinos around here."

"So Rob told you about the Folio?"

"He bragged about it. But what he didn't know was that I already knew about it."

"Do you mean—"

"Enough of the chitchat, boss. Get out of my way."

"I'm not moving, Jeremy."

"Oh, I think you will."

"Jeremy—"

"You'll let me pass, and you'll pretend this whole conversation never took place."

"You're dreaming." *The gall of this guy!*

Jeremy narrowed his eyes. "You want your little vacation from work to turn into permanent unemployment? You really want to be fired?"

"What? You can't fire me." What was he talking about?

"Ever hear of sexual harassment? Beverly would never tolerate it. And neither will the Attorney Disciplinary Commission."

My mouth dropped open. Jeremy took another step closer. "You can't deny it, can you? You've been coming on to me ever since I started at the firm. Touching me, insinuating things."

Now he hovered over me, his breath warm on my face.

"You want me," he jeered. "Everyone knows it. It's so obvious. When I tell Beverly that you've been demanding special favors from me, you'll be out on the streets faster than you can say 'quid pro quo.'"

My stomach clenched; I was so taken aback. Maybe I had broken some ethical rules in my interactions with Jeremy, but I had never demanded anything of him. I had never initiated anything— he was the one who had always started things.

Still, if anyone *had* seen us together, I supposed they might have gotten the wrong idea.

I felt light-headed and confused. Jeremy moved

to pass me again, and the heavy duffel bag bumped my leg. I backed up—and suddenly laughed.

"Who would believe you, Jeremy? You're a liar and a thief."

Before I knew what was happening, Jeremy reached out and shoved me. I staggered for a moment but managed to grab a bookshelf to keep from falling over. Then I turned to watch as Jeremy ran down the center aisle. He made it to the elevator as the door opened and a tall police officer stepped out with one hand on his holster.

"It's in the bag!" I called out.

Literally.

CHAPTER 27

My first day back at the office was a fairly typical Wednesday. I had messages to return, appointments to schedule, mail to review. What was surprising, though, was the fact that all my case files were stacked neatly on my desk, beneath detailed notes on any actions taken and the current status. Notes written in Crenshaw's slanted hand-writing. *Interesting.*

When I met with Beverly later that morning, she repeated what she had said before about Crenshaw looking after my cases for me while I was away.

"A lot can happen in two weeks," she said.

"Tell me about it."

We sat in Beverly's lounge, in two wingback chairs near the window. Sunlight streamed in, making speckled shadows across the table between us. Beverly had welcomed me back and had congratu-lated me on solving the case. However, she hadn't apologized for my forced vacation. I guessed it was the price I had to pay for causing any kind of threat to the firm in the first place.

Even though it *so* clearly wasn't my fault.

"So, have you heard from Jeremy?" I asked.

She shook her head. "He's being held pending arraignment, which should be later today or tomorrow. The state's attorney told me Jeremy has decided to defend himself."

"Ooh. That doesn't sound like a very good idea."

Beverly raised one eyebrow. "I think we now know that Jeremy's judgment is seriously lacking in a lot of areas."

"Yeah. I feel sorry for his girlfriend. Although, she's probably better off without him." I didn't mean to sound so cold, but I was still pissed at Jeremy for what he did. Not only did he cause a lot of heartache for a lot of people, but he was also now causing a hardship for the office. In fact, it occurred to me that the lost relationship predicted by my tarot reading was probably the loss of Jeremy as my coworker and friend.

"Well, I truly feel sad for both of them," said Beverly. "I don't see Jeremy getting out of this without forfeiting his law license and serving jail time—which, of course, he should."

"Right. Of course. He has to pay the consequences." I thought back to my conversation with Darlene the night before. She was so relieved to have the Folio back, and even more relieved the thief wasn't one of her sons or her brother, that she had almost declined to press charges. I didn't know which of her family members had convinced her otherwise, but I had to agree with them. I certainly intended to press charges for the vandalism Jeremy had done to my front window. He wouldn't admit to it, but I was hoping the police would find some evidence that linked him to the crime.

Shortly after taking Jeremy to the jailhouse, the police had received an anonymous tip that Jeremy was involved in an illegal money-lending racket. I had a strong hunch it was Rob who had made that call to the police. Wes had told me his brother felt guilty about informing Jeremy that the Folio was at his grandmother's house. Apparently, Rob had said he would do whatever he could to make things right. Wes was hopeful Rob would turn his life around now and get the help he needed to kick his gambling addiction.

Because of Rob's tip, the police had been able to obtain a warrant to search Jeremy's apartment. Besides finding a list of rare-books dealers and a list of names under the label "RQ Regulars," they'd uncovered another disturbing item. It was a picture of me, printed from the Internet, with a big *X* across my face. The letters *MYOB* were written across the top.

I shuddered to think how Jeremy had planned to deliver that charming little message. The creep.

On the bright side, I'd learned it wasn't Jeremy who had been prowling around my home the morning of my birthday. Farrah had told me that Jake had confessed to lurking on my doorstep, but that he wasn't trying to break in. He was trying to see if Farrah was inside after she failed to return his calls following his proposal. Mrs. St. John might have exaggerated her tale just a little bit.

Beverly checked her phone and sighed. "Kris and Randall are reaching out to all of Jeremy's clients. And we'll have an all-staff meeting tomorrow to discuss messaging and next steps." Beverly paused, gazing out the window. "Interestingly, I already had a visit from Edgar Harrison last night."

"Oh?"

"Apparently, Jeremy had been moonlighting as an agent for a company that does security and collections work for River Queen Casino. Edgar assured me that Jeremy had no direct ties to Edgar, the casino, or any other Harrison enterprise. He'll be counting on our firm to ensure his name never appears in connection with Jeremy or his crime."

I nodded, even as I thought to myself how challenging this might be. I didn't tell Beverly I already knew about Jeremy's side business. According to Wes, Rob had also admitted that Jeremy pushed Rob into taking out a "bad loan." He said Jeremy had spent a lot of time at the casino, getting friendly with the regular customers and leading them to Mr. Derello's "loan shop."

Well, I would let the police conduct their investigation, come what may. If Jeremy had been working for Scarface instead of directly for Harrison, Harrison should have nothing to worry about. He would just have to find another security company. That was all.

Beverly stood up, her cue that our meeting was over. "The next couple weeks are going to be difficult for our little workplace family," she said. "But we'll get through it."

After leaving Beverly's lounge, I headed down

the hall toward my office. As I passed the open door to the reception area, I overheard Julie say something about the master key. I froze.

Oops.

I had forgotten to return the key that night I searched Jeremy's office. Hovering out of sight, I listened to Julie, who seemed to be talking to Pammy and Crenshaw.

"The police officers will be here with a search warrant in an hour. If I can't find that key, we're going to have to bust the door to Jeremy's office. Beverly is *not* gonna like that."

"That's not even the biggest concern," Pammy said. "If the key is missing, we have a potential security breach to address. You know, it really should be kept in a locked drawer."

I winced and took a step forward. Crenshaw saw me. But then he turned to Julie and Pammy and held both palms forward.

"Ladies, not to worry. I have the key. I borrowed it when I locked myself out the other day. I simply forgot to return it. I believe I left it at home. I—I'll pop home and get it before the officers arrive."

Raising my eyebrows, I silently backed away and hurried to my office.

Wow.

First, Crenshaw takes care of my work for two weeks, and then he covers for me so I don't have to admit to sneaking around the office at night. What in the world was going on?

Ohhh.

I sat down at my desk, slapping my forehead as I

did so. As the light dawned, I felt my face grow hot, even in the privacy of my own office.

Crenshaw liked me. He *like* liked me. Crenshaw's love sonnet was about me.

I found it hard to believe, yet I knew it must be true.

After grabbing my purse, I dug out the master key and set it on my desk. Then I pulled out a piece of stationery and wrote the only thing I could say:

> *Crenshaw,*
>   *Thank you.*
>   *Keli*

I placed the key in the center of the paper and folded it in half.

After making sure the coast was clear, I dashed over to Crenshaw's office and left the note on top of his cleared desk, where he would be sure to see it. Then, out of the corner of my eye, I noticed an open briefcase propped on a nearby chair. A manila envelope was sticking out of the case.

An envelope much like the one that contained the Old West photo of Farrah and me and that had disappeared from my tote.

Then I spotted the shoes on the floor, next to the chair. They were shiny brown-and-white wing tips like the ones worn by the donkey-headed actor at the Renaissance Faire.

Slowly, I reached over toward the envelope. Then I hesitated.

Did I really want to know?

I dashed back out of the office.

* * *

I checked my hair in the mirror, checked the time again, checked my pulse. I still had ten minutes until Wes was due to pick me up, and all I could do was pace the living room. We were going to dinner and a movie, nothing fancy. Just a simple, old-fashioned date. I smiled, thinking that Eleanor would approve.

Wes and I had spoken on the phone several times in the past week, and each time he had opened up to me more and more. So much so that I was now seriously considering opening up to him, too, about being Wiccan. If we were to have any kind of lasting relationship, I wanted it to be based on honesty. I had a good feeling about our future, and if I'd learned anything this midsummer, it was to trust my inner feelings.

I imagined Eleanor would also approve of the family's decision about the Folio. As I circled my living room again, I paused at the mantel and reread the thank-you note Darlene had sent me. Honoring Kirk's wish, as well as Eleanor's, they had all decided to hold on to the Folio for one year. Each of the two kids would keep it for six months— safely and securely, under lock and key, of course. And they would make it freely accessible to all the family during each person's turn. After the year was over, they would sell the First Folio at auction, giving T.C. Satterly the right of first refusal.

My eyes shifted from the thank-you card to the beautiful framed fairy picture from Mila, then to the birthday cards I had propped on the mantel shelf, and then finally rested on the postcard from Aunt Josephine. I picked up the postcard and studied it once again. I furrowed my brow. Aside from the Latin phrases, which were quirky and inspirational, her choice of wording was a little bit peculiar. "To my beautiful niece and kindred spirit, as lovely and strong on the inside as on the out."

I had never met my aunt Josephine. She had never seen me, as far as I knew. So why would she call me beautiful? And how would she know I was "as lovely and strong on the inside as on the out"?

For that matter, what did she mean by "kindred spirit"?

Okay, maybe I was overthinking this. Or maybe, possibly, my appetite had now been whetted for mystery solving. Maybe I would see mysteries everywhere now.

I smiled at this thought as I glanced again at the fairy picture, sparkling in a sunbeam. That would be okay. After all, life *was* a mystery.

Keli Milanni will return in . . .

BELL, BOOK AND CANDLEMAS
A WICCAN WHEEL MYSTERY

A Kensington mass-market and e-book
on sale January 2017!

Grab These Cozy Mysteries
from
Kensington Books

Forget Me Knot Mary Marks	978-0-7582-9205-6	$7.99US/$8.99CAN
Death of a Chocoholic Lee Hollis	978-0-7582-9449-4	$7.99US/$8.99CAN
Green Living Can Be Deadly Staci McLaughlin	978-0-7582-7502-8	$7.99US/$8.99CAN
Death of an Irish Diva Mollie Cox Bryan	978-0-7582-6633-0	$7.99US/$8.99CAN
Board Stiff Annelise Ryan	978-0-7582-7276-8	$7.99US/$8.99CAN
A Biscuit, A Casket Liz Mugavero	978-0-7582-8480-8	$7.99US/$8.99CAN
Boiled Over Barbara Ross	978-0-7582-8687-1	$7.99US/$8.99CAN
Scene of the Climb Kate Dyer-Seeley	978-0-7582-9531-6	$7.99US/$8.99CAN
Deadly Decor Karen Rose Smith	978-0-7582-8486-0	$7.99US/$8.99CAN
To Kill a Matzo Ball Delia Rosen	978-0-7582-8201-9	$7.99US/$8.99CAN

Available Wherever Books Are Sold!

All available as e-books, too!

Visit our website at **www.kensingtonbooks.com**

Follow P.I. Savannah Reid
with
G.A. McKevett